# BREAKAWAY

Other titles from Coteau Books
in the *Jessie Mac* series by Maureen Ulrich

*Power Plays*
*Face Off*

# BREAKAWAY

**Maureen Ulrich**

COTEAU
BOOKS

www.coteaubooks.com

Edited by Alison Acheson
Typeset by Susan Buck
Cover photograph by Tracy (Kerestesh) Portraits
Printed and bound in Canada at Friesens

**Library and Archives Canada Cataloguing in Publication**

Ulrich, Maureen, 1958–
        Breakaway / Maureen Ulrich.

ISBN 978-1-55050-512-2

        I. Title.

PS8641.L75B74 2012          jC813'.6          C2012-903811-3

Issued also in electronic formats.

**Library of Congress Control Number:** 2012936050

2517 Victoria Avenue
Regina, Saskatchewan
Canada    S4P 0T2
www.coteaubooks.com

*Available in Canada from:*
Publishers Group Canada
9050 Shaughnessy Street
Vancouver, British Columbia
Canada   V6P 6E5

*Available in the US from:*
Orca Book Publishers
www.orcabook.com
1-800-210-5277

10   9   8   7   6   5   4   3   2   1

Coteau Books gratefully acknowledges the financial support of its publishing program by: the Saskatchewan Arts Board, the Canada Council for the Arts, the Government of Canada through the Canada Book Fund and the City of Regina Arts Commission.

*For Mom and Dad, Herman and Marlene*

# chapter one

It's my first time at a professional football game, and my first time wearing a watermelon. I've got a skullcap underneath, but juice keeps slithering down my back.

"How do I look?" I ask Kathy Parker.

She turns away from the mirror where she's been applying a green S to each cheek and stares at me, one blonde eyebrow cocked. "You look like that little Martian from Bugs Bunny. What's his name again?"

"I don't know who you mean," I say.

"McIntyre, you're pathetic. Didn't you ever watch cartoons as a kid?" She tightens the elastic on each blonde pigtail, dyed bright green, before jamming on her own watermelon.

I don't answer. After three years of playing hockey with Kathy, I know the majority of her questions are rhetorical.

Teneil and Miranda are waiting for us outside the bathroom, sucking on their fountain pops. From the smug looks on their faces, I know they conned somebody into buying them alcoholic drinks, and they've dumped them in their cups. Teneil's wearing a green crop top and skanky shorts. Miranda's got on a Roughrider halter and green beads in her jet-black cornbraids. Way too much chocolate skin showing on her.

Teneil beckons to us impatiently. "Hurry up!"

We don't need to ask the attendant at the top of the stairs for directions since we're using the Parkers' season tickets.

I look up into the stands. It's a scorching Sunday afternoon, the hottest day yet in August. Our seats are in the nineteenth row under the roof, but there's scarcely a breath of wind, and the humidity is killer. I fan my program and try not to think about the moist, sticky patches between my shoulder blades, the lack of oxygen in this stifling air, and the watermelon compressing my head into an egg shape.

"It's so *hot*. What if I pass out on the way up?" I ask Kathy.

She smacks me on the head. "That's what the melon's for!"

I concentrate on every step until we finally reach Row Nineteen. The Parkers' seats are in the middle of the section. Some guys wearing green body paint stand up to let us by.

"You ladies thirsty?" one of them asks.

Miranda and Teneil stop to flirt, but Kathy and I keep going. When we get to our seats, I sit down and take it all in – the prairie vista of browns and blue, Regina's red brick skyline, and Mosaic Stadium's patchwork quilt of greens. Someone taps me on the shoulder, and I turn around. A short, bald man who looks like he's trying to digest a watermelon is beaming at me.

Bud Prentice, my coach from SaskFirst.

"Hey, Bud!" I stand up and give him a hug. Not a big hug because I'm too sweaty. "Kathy never said you had season tickets here."

"I don't. I bought these off a friend." He gives Kathy a hug too. "Where's your fella?"

"Sitting down there with his homeys." Kathy gestures to a lower section.

"The Queen of the Penalty Box and the Referee." Bud shakes his head and laughs. "So ironic."

Kathy gives him a patient smile. "Yeah, you're the first one to point that out."

"You got a fella, Jessie?" Bud asks.

"Nope."

"Evan's a fella," Kathy says.

"Not my fella," I say. "Who are you here with, Bud?"

Bud turns his belly, so we can see the little boy absorbed in the video game he's playing. "This is my grandson Zack," Bud says. "Say hello, Zack."

"Hello Zack." The little guy grins at us.

"You're cute," Kathy says.

Teneil and Miranda squeeze past Kathy and me, balancing their cokes and now...cans of Pilsner.

"Made some friends?" I ask.

Teneil narrows her eyes at me. "What are you? The Fun Police?"

Bud raises a fuzzy grey eyebrow.

Miranda looks at Bud and puts both her drinks under her seat. "Hi, Bud." If her dark skin could show it, she'd be blushing.

Teneil, on the other hand, tips back the Pilsner. She's never made SaskFirst, and Bud's never coached her, so I guess she doesn't care what he thinks.

Embarrassed, I make the introductions.

"I remember you," Teneil says to Bud. "You cut me last year at Zones, but I didn't care. I play Club Volleyball."

I don't have to look at Kathy to know she's rolling her eyes.

A tight smile tugs at the corners of Bud's mouth. "Glad to hear it. Girls who play sports are more likely to finish school and stay out of trouble." He removes his ball cap and mops his damp forehead with a handkerchief. "What was it you girls called yourselves in SaskFirst?"

"The Onerfuls," Kathy says.

We all start reminiscing about the week we spent in Humboldt two years ago during the Winter Games.

But not Teneil. I can tell from her body language she's ticked.

**4**

Zack tugs at Bud's sleeve. "Grandpa, I'm hungry."

Bud rubs his round belly. "What're we having now?"

"Fries," the boy says.

Bud introduces him to Miranda and Teneil.

"Hey, Zack." Miranda holds her hand out for a high-five. Zack rears back and smacks it.

"Zack's from your neck of the woods," Bud explains. "My daughter and son-in-law live in North Portal now."

"Grandpa!" Zack says impatiently. "Fries!"

Bud sighs and sits down heavily. "The walk's too much for me. Would one of you girls mind?"

Miranda holds out a hand. "Wanna come with us, little man? We'll score you some fries."

Without another word, Zack climbs over the back of the seat and leads Miranda down the row. Teneil starts to take her beer with her, but I snipe it out of her hand.

"I'll hold it until you get back," I say.

Teneil shoots me a dirty look.

"So tell me about Triple A," Bud says after they're gone.

"The league voted at their annual meeting to let us in," Kathy explains.

Bud whistles. "Nine midget girls' teams next year. I didn't think the league would expand beyond eight."

"Most teams wanted more games, so now there'll be thirty-two in the schedule, instead of twenty-eight," I say.

"How'll you afford ice time?" asks Bud.

"An oilfield supply company is donating it." Kathy spreads her hands. "We're going to be the Estevan McGillicky Oilers."

Bud whistles. "Very appropriate, since Estevan is Boomtown. Lots of oil money down there."

"Dad says southeast Saskatchewan is the only place in the world untouched by the recession," I point out.

Kathy snorts. "There you go, McIntyre. Trying to sound all grown up."

"It's true," I say, sitting down.

"Big money usually means big problems," Bud says.

"Tell me about it." I try to waft some air under my tank top. "We go to a great high school, but there're too many kids doing drugs."

"I hope you girls are careful," Bud says.

"We're seventeen, Bud," Kathy says.

Bud laughs. "Of course."

"I'll tell you what else big money does." Kathy hovers over me, blocking what little breeze there is. "It builds a kickass rink. Did you hear about it?"

Bud nods while we tell him about Spectra Place, the brand new facility where the Estevan Bruins and our hockey team will be playing.

"Think you'll have a decent team?" Bud asks.

Kathy steps down hard on my toes. A warning. The look

she's giving me is loaded.

"Depends on who comes to our camp next weekend," I say.

"And Sue's coaching?" he persists. "How's she going to manage that and her engineering job?"

"She says she can't do it full time. Marty can't help her either because he's a vice-principal now. Minor Hockey's trying to find us a head coach."

"Still?"

The word hangs in the air.

And then the dreaded question.

"You girls have any plans for after graduation?"

"I don't have a clue," Kathy says.

"What about you, Jessie?" Bud asks.

"I wish I knew."

Kathy's cellphone plinks, and she stares at the screen. "It's Brett," she says. "Jessie, you sure you don't want to hang out with us tonight?"

"I don't have fake ID, remember?"

She turns away and starts texting.

"Are you going to try for a hockey scholarship?" Bud asks.

I look into his pale blue eyes. "Kathy and I are going to the U of S camp on Labour Day weekend. Do you think we have a shot at playing there next year?"

"Course you do. I could see that the first year you played Midget."

Thirty thousand fans boo as the Edmonton team is introduced, then rise collectively and roar as the Riders take the field.

"Talk to you later!" I shout at Bud.

Kathy and I get caught up in the pregame festivities and the opening kickoff. Miranda, Teneil and Zack come back with the fries. I give Teneil her beer when she asks for it, but Miranda never touches hers again. Kathy provides a running commentary about what's going on at field level. Good thing she knows football because I don't. By the end of the first quarter, the Riders are leading by a touchdown, and we are dancing, cheering and chanting with the rest of the fans.

"I have to take a leak," Kathy says. "Come with me!"

After we use the washroom, we try to wash off the watermelon juice in the communal sink. The green Kool-Aid in Kathy's hair starts leaking down her neck.

"You're bleeding green," I say, wringing out the collar of my jersey.

Kathy laughs and squeezes the excess moisture out of her pigtails. "I'm also hungry," she says. "Want a hot dog?"

"Sue says we're supposed to be in training," I argue. "There's no nutritional value in a wiener."

"Live a little, McIntyre," Kathy says.

I push the bathroom door open. "You think Sue will stick around if Minor Hockey finds us a head coach?"

"Sue loves us," Kathy replies.

"Maybe she loves *you*," I reply. "I never know where I stand with her."

Even after two years of coaching, Sue Hannah seems to have her guard up. Not like Bud.

"You just stand there and think about how far playing it safe gets you while I go load up a hot dog with Rider mix," Kathy says.

"I'm wearing a watermelon," I reply. "For me, that's living on the edge."

Kathy snickers and heads towards the concession while I contemplate tossing my melon in the garbage. Then again, what will my hair look like without it?

"Now that's what I call dedication," a voice says behind me.

I turn around. The speaker is a tall, dark-haired girl wearing a green cowboy hat and a short white skirt. Something about her laugh is familiar, but I can't place her.

"You actually like wearing that?" she asks.

I try to fake it. "What are you up to nowadays?"

She seems to enjoy my discomfort. "You have no idea who I am."

"No," I admit. "Give me a hint."

Her grin broadens, and a diamond sparkles in one of her teeth. "You still play hockey?"

"Yes." Something clicks, and I look for the rose tattoo on her ankle. "Brittni Wade."

"You honestly didn't recognize me?" Brittni asks.

"Your hair's a different colour. And you're thinner."

"Thanks." She adjusts the brim of her cowboy hat.

"Didn't you go to hairdressing school?" I ask.

Brittni opens the purse slung over her shoulder and removes a business card. "I'm at a salon on Rochdale. Come see me next time you're in town. I've always wanted to do something with this." She lifts a crunchy strand of my hair.

I change the subject. "What's Cory up to?"

"Cory's a slut. I haven't seen her since she slept with my ex."

A tall guy holding two beer cans comes up behind Brittni and touches one to her bare shoulder.

She starts. "Hey!"

"Hey yourself," he says.

"Jessie, this is Jamie, my fiancé."

My eyes dart from the rock on Brittni's left hand to the guy. His broken nose and reddish hair look familiar too.

"Hi, Jamie," I say.

"I'd shake your hand, but as you can see..." Jamie gestures with the two beer cans.

"So when's the big day?"

"Night," Brittni corrects me. "We're getting married on New Year's Eve."

"Can you believe it?" Jamie scowls. "I'll miss watching Canada in the World Juniors, and so will my buds. I'll never hear the end of it."

Brittni's face darkens, but for me, a light flips on.

"You played in Humboldt with Mark Taylor," I say.

He nods while taking a sip of beer.

"So what do you do now?" I ask.

He wipes his mouth. "Plumber's apprentice."

"I used to play hockey with Jessie," Brittni interrupts. "Back in Estevan. Good times. Right, Jessie?"

"Right." Apparently she's forgotten about calling me an f'ing do-gooder.

"That dyke still coaching?"

I pretend not to hear her question. "So Mark's playing with Calgary again?" I ask Jamie.

He salutes me with a beer can, then drains it and belches loudly. "Go Hitmen." He offers me the other can.

"I don't drink beer," I say quickly.

"Jessie doesn't drink at *all*," Brittni explains. "At least she doesn't any more. Isn't that right, Jessie?"

I hate it when people know your dirt.

"Look me up on Mainpage." Brittni hands me her business card. "Remember what I said about your hair."

As they walk away, I think about Jamie's metamorphosis from hockey player to plumber. When did he give up the Dream?

For guys, it's the NHL. For girls, it's the National Team.

If you want them badly enough, your dreams will all come true, adults are always telling us. Very few of us don't succumb to *that* myth. Sometimes wanting isn't enough.

Like Mark and me. I want him back something fierce, but I'm not any closer to that dream than I was two years ago.

When I was going out with him, he said he wouldn't play hockey after high school. He said he wanted to be an engineer – not an ex-hockey player with bad knees and an identity crisis.

That was *before* he broke up with me, started dating Holly, and moved to Humboldt to play with the Broncos. From there he stepped up to the Calgary Hitmen. Apparently the dream caught hold of him too.

And then Mark's dad was diagnosed with stomach cancer. Poor Mark. What good are your dreams when you're worried about losing one of your parents?

Kathy approaches, balancing a coke and two hot dogs. "You wouldn't believe the lineup. Help me out, will ya?"

I take one of the hot dogs off her hands. "Parker, you should lay off the pop."

"And you should get off my case."

I follow her out of the concourse. At the top of the exit, we wait in the stairwell for a stoppage in play. I tell Kathy about seeing Brittni Wade, and Kathy nearly chokes on a mouthful of her drink. I pound her back.

"Brittni was *nice* to you?" she coughs. "Good thing I wasn't around. She called me an f'ing puckhog, remember?"

"I remember."

I fill her in on Brittni and Jamie's career paths and wedding plans.

"Never mind that," Kathy says impatiently. "What else did you and *Bud* talk about?"

This question is definitely *not* rhetorical.

"Not much."

"Jessie, the SHA can make or break us if we need to get releases for players from other teams. You didn't tell him about Whitney's dad recruiting the Weyburn girls, did you?"

"I didn't say anything," I assure her. "Let's go up to our seats already. I'm missing part of my first football game."

She winces at me, then turns and heads up the stairs.

Speaking of firsts. If we don't find a head coach soon, our midget season will be over before we have our first practice.

Maybe moving up to AAA wasn't worth the risk.

# chapter *two*

**J**essie, will you give Courtney a ride to the pool?" Mom calls from upstairs.

I'm in the basement, packing my hockey equipment for tryouts. I've had everything laid out for weeks.

"Sure!" I stuff a roll of sock tape in my helmet. "But I'm leaving right away!"

Mom comes down the stairs. "Do you have time to pick up Pam?"

"As long as she's ready when I get there."

"Thanks, Jessie," Mom says, heading back up.

As I finish wrapping my skates inside my old black and gold Xtreme socks, I ignore the butterflies tickling my stomach, and the nagging concern about where we'll get a new head coach. I try to focus on something else...like team colours. I hear we're going to wear black and orange.

"I'm taking my equipment out right now!" I heave my

bag onto my shoulder and pick up the stick I just finished retaping.

When I got my steering papers, Mom bought Sunny, my green Sunfire, from one of my old teammates. At first Dad wasn't thrilled to have me driving, but once I started chauffeuring Courtney to figure skating, picking up groceries and getting myself to school and hockey practice, he saw the light.

Courtney's already in Sunny. My little sister has shot up this summer, making her nearly as tall as I am, even though she's only going into Grade Six.

"You called Pam?" I ask.

Courtney nods and tucks her long, blonde hair behind her ears. She stares out the side window as we head west down Valley Street and turn right on Souris Avenue. I plug in my iPod and we sing along to Justin Bieber. Mom took us to see his concert in Saskatoon last year, and even though I said I wouldn't like it, I found myself in the mosh pit, screaming along with Courtney and the rest of the tweenies.

"I'm going to Regina next Saturday to buy back-to-school clothes," I tell her as we pull into Pam's driveway. "Want to come along?"

"Can Pam come too?" she asks.

"Sure."

Courtney gets out, so Pam can climb in the back. Pam's had a growth spurt too, though she's not nearly as tall as Courtney.

She has long dark hair and an upturned, freckled nose.

"Thanks for picking me up, Jessie," Pam says.

On the way to the Leisure Centre, Pam and Courtney chatter about figure skating, which is how they met. When the topic shifts to school, Courtney slips into silence. Pam goes to a different elementary school, and she's excited about going back because she's got lots of friends in her grade.

Lucky Pam.

Courtney's classmates fluctuate between ignoring and tormenting her, and now that the junior high has closed, she has three more years of catfights to look forward to.

"Pam, are you playing volleyball this year?" I ask.

"For sure," Pam says. "What about you, Court?"

Courtney rolls and unrolls the towel in her lap. "None of the Grade Six girls like it, so there won't be enough to make a team." Her voice wavers. "It'll be like that every year until I get to the Comp, and by then, I won't be good enough to make an Elecs team."

"Maybe it'll turn out okay," I assure her.

"Yeah, wait and see," Pam says.

I park near the main entrance to the Leisure Centre.

"I'll pick you up in two hours," I tell the girls as we get out of the car. "Don't make me come looking for you."

"Just text me when you want to go," Pam says. "We'll be ready."

"Wish I had a phone," Courtney says.

Inside the building, they turn right and walk towards the pool while I stare at the entrance to Spectra Place. The butterflies I've been trying to ignore are beating like crazy. It was great to start out last year with Sue and Marty as coaches. We hardly cared that Sue has no sense of ha-ha. We knew what to expect from them, and we had a great season. But Sue *won't* coach a AAA team by herself.

"If I could give up my day job and coach full-time, I'd do it," Sue told us last June, "but coaching AAA won't pay my bills."

Then there's the matter of having enough talent to field a decent team. We'd be competitive if we still had Tara and Shauna. Shauna's playing AAA in Notre Dame, and Tara's doing the same at Balmoral in Winnipeg. Jodi Palmer's not well enough to play AAA, so it'll be Senior Ladies for her. The thought makes me feel suddenly old.

Regina and Saskatoon don't have tryouts for two weeks, but Weyburn and Swift Current are holding their camps *this* weekend. If Mr. Johnstone's recruits from Weyburn don't show up, we're screwed.

Inside the lobby Mrs. Johnstone is parked at a table, texting. Her laptop sits next to a stack of registration forms.

"Hi, Mrs. Johnstone." I dump my equipment beside the table.

She finishes the message on her phone before looking up. "Hello, Jessie. All set for the weekend?" As usual her makeup is flawless. I wonder if her eyeliner is tattooed on.

"You bet."

"You're in Dressing Room 2." She reaches into a box beside her and pulls out a plain white practice jersey with an orange Number 13 on the back.

That's my lucky number, the number I've been wearing for three years.

"Here's your schedule for the weekend." She hands me a piece of paper.

"How many girls are registered?" I stuff the jersey and schedule into a side pocket on my bag.

"Twenty-eight." Her cellphone chirps.

My butterflies are at it again as I shoulder my bag and walk downstairs to Dressing Room 2. There's no sign on the door yet, just a piece of paper with a large two scrawled in felt marker.

But two isn't the number occupying my thoughts. It's twenty-eight.

How many of them play defence, my little voice wonders.

I open the dressing-room door.

"My boyfriend gave me a Tim Horton's gift card for my birthday," Randi Hildebrand is saying.

"What's so bad about that? You love those iced cappuccinos," Teneil observes.

"Yeah, but the card had already been used. It had $15.38 left on it. He was regifting." Randi examines the end of a long auburn braid.

"Randi, you've only been going out with him for two weeks. Cut him some slack," Kathy says.

"You're lucky you got anything," says Carla Bisson. "I got squat from my old man."

"Jessie got jewelry from Evan for her birthday," Kathy says, "and she says he's *not* her boyfriend."

I dump my equipment on the floor and kick off my flip-flops.

"You ever wear those earrings?" Kathy asks.

I unzip my bag and start unpacking my stuff.

"Pretty expensive," Kathy persists. "Real emeralds, right?"

I ignore her until the girls turn their attention to something else. There're some new girls sitting in the corner, and I move over to introduce myself. I know what it feels like to be a newcomer. Two of them are from Radville.

The third one is a lanky girl with broad shoulders and long brown hair. "Amy Fox," she says.

I know that name.

Along with her size, Amy Fox has ridiculous skill. She was the goalie for the Wawota Midget boys' team for two provincial championships. She's never come out for female SaskFirst, but here she is, large as life, with her pads stacked in the corner.

And a pop can in her hand. She spits some dark juice into it.

"Um, that's not allowed," I tell her.

She narrows her brown eyes at me.

"I'm just giving you a heads-up," I say. "Sue won't like it."

Amy removes the tobacco plug from her lip and deposits it in the can.

"Hey, Parker, who're the players coming from Weyburn?" Carla calls out.

Kathy lists their names.

"And Whitney's dad is sure they're coming?" Carla asks.

"Apparently they weren't happy with the Gold Wings," Kathy says.

"The last thing we need is players jockeying for a better deal," Carla replies. "We need girls who are committed."

"You're a fine one to talk about commitment." Kathy's tone is sharp. "When Steve left, you dumped us to play with the boys in Oxbow. Sue's the only reason *you're* here."

Carla glares at Kathy, but thankfully she doesn't snipe back.

Besides being Queen of the Penalty Box and our team captain for the last two years, Kathy was born without tact. Consequently, our dressing room can be a gong show.

"Jodi says she's trying out," Randi announces.

"Jodi's *not* coming back!" Kathy sounds disgusted. "There's no *way* Dr. Bilkhu's clearing her to play."

"Fine. Don't believe me then," Randi says.

Jodi? Here? The news is both exciting and disturbing.

The door opens, and Whitney Johnstone storms in. She's tall, with long black hair and darkly tanned limbs. Her dark brown eyes – with the eyelashes we'd kill for – are thoroughly pissed. She drops her equipment on the floor and kicks it twice.

"Rough day?" Teneil asks.

Whitney flops on the opposite bench. "They're not coming," she says.

"Who's not coming?"

"The Weyburn girls." She stares at the floor.

"Will they come tomorrow?" Teneil asks.

"Don't you get it? They're not coming *at all.*" Whitney bites off each word. "Easton told my dad she wasn't comfortable committing to a team with an 'ambiguous coaching situation.' She's been talking to Saskatoon, and they already told her she's made the team. Bloor's going to Notre Dame and Mackenzie's staying in Weyburn."

"Did Easton and Bloor get releases?" Carla asks.

"Dad says Weyburn's going to con*test* them, same as if they tried coming here," Whitney says.

"What do you mean – con*test?*" Teneil asks.

"If a team contests a release, the player has to sit out the first five games of the season and the team she's going to has to pay a fine," Carla explains. *"Plus* she has to miss any games those two teams play during the season and playoffs. The coach has to serve a suspension to start the season as well."

"But we were counting on them!" Kathy sounds pissed.

"Maybe they heard we jump ship at the drop of a hat." Carla's tone challenges Kathy. "Run back to our *boys'* teams."

"If the shoe fits," Kathy says.

"Whitney, your dad *promised* he would get us two goal scorers and another left-handed defenceman," Randi says. "Now what?"

"Never mind what he said." Whitney picks at her gel nails. "It's over."

"What's over?" Teneil asks.

"Our *season!* We're done. Before we even got started." Whitney wrenches off one of her sneakers and throws it across the dressing room.

Kathy picks up the sneaker and wings it right back, nearly hitting Whitney in the head.

"Hey!" Whitney exclaims.

"Thanks for the vote of confidence," I say. "I didn't think we were *that* bad. We won the league and provincials last year."

"Our league was weak. The better teams, like Swift Current, had moved up to AAA. That's the reason we won," says Whitney. "The *only* reason. We are going to suck."

"Nice to know where we stand with you," I say.

"What *I* think doesn't matter," Whitney says. "If we're not one of the top four teams in the league, we don't get an invite to the Mac's Tournament in Calgary. And the Mac's is where the scouts are."

"I've heard there'll be more scouts at the Notre Dame tournament," Carla says.

The talk of scouts and what players are playing where and who's got a scholarship to which university goes on and on. My butterflies turn into snakes.

I make a point of being the first one out of the dressing room. I turn the corner and stop at the entrance to the ice surface, admiring the corporate boxes suspended above the stands and the big Bruin symbol at the other end.

It's the Big Time. A brand new arena. A brand new team.

I hope we'll be all right, even without the Weyburn girls.

Whitney's dad is leaning against the boards, wearing a black wind suit with orange trim, and talking on his cell-phone. Hopefully he's trying to score us another left-handed defenceman.

Mr. Johnstone's got personality to burn. That's why he's been successful in lobbying the AAA League and the SHA and recruiting sponsors. Corporate sponsorships will keep our costs down. On some AAA teams, parents have to ante up to $5,000 for their daughters to play.

Still, I have a tough time liking Mr. Johnstone. He says all the right stuff, but I suspect the only thing he cares about is promoting Whitney's hockey career.

The Dream.

Behind me, I hear skate blades on rubber.

Kathy.

"It's gonna be a long season." She sighs.

I try to lighten her mood. "Things can happen. We don't play a league game until the first week of October."

She stares at me like I'm stupid. "Jessie, we need *talent*. No offence – but we've got plugs on our roster."

"Parker, you're talking about our friends."

"I know," she says, "but it doesn't change the facts."

I fasten one of the straps attaching my cage to my helmet. "Are we going on the ice or what?"

"I'm afraid I'll kill Whitney's dad," she says. "Hanging us out to dry like that. Making us think we have a chance to form a decent team."

"It's not his fault. He can't control what players do," I say.

Carla comes around the corner, her helmet tucked under her arm. She freezes when she sees Kathy, and her features harden.

"Can't you gals smoke the peace pipe?" I ask. "This is a lousy way to start tryouts."

"Parker has to go first," Carla says.

"Oh all right," Kathy says. "Sorry about saying you're not committed. My mouth runs away with me sometimes."

"Yeah, it does," Carla says, "but no harm done."

I let out the breath I've been holding.

"Just look at this rink." Kathy steps closer to the glass. "Is this going to be an awesome place to take a shit kicking or what?"

"These stands will be packed with red-blooded Canadian boys," Carla says. "All coming to watch your skinny white asses."

Mr. Johnstone puts his phone away and skates towards us. He's actually an okay skater. He played some junior hockey back in the day.

"Here he comes," I say.

"It drives me crazy the way he uses our names all the time," Kathy says.

"Hold me back. Please." Carla opens the latch and swings the gate open just as Mr. Johnstone comes to a stop, spraying ice chips.

He gives us a charming smile. "Jessie. Kathy. Carla. Have I mentioned I never would've considered a bid for a AAA team without you three on the roster?"

"Every damn day, Mr. Johnstone," Kathy says.

He looks at her uncertainly then focuses on me. "Ready

to strut your stuff, Jessie?"

"Sure am, Mr. Johnstone."

"I hear you struck out getting Jessie a new D partner," Carla says.

He looks even more uncomfortable. "Things don't always go according to plan, Carla. But I'm confident we've got a super crop of rookies."

"We don't need rookies," Kathy interrupts. "We need size and speed and experience."

"I got you the best goaltender in this part of the province," he says. "That should help a lot. Now if you'll excuse me, I've got things to do."

He skates away.

"That man's got an ass that just doesn't quit," Carla says.

"He *is* an ass," Kathy says.

"I'm warming up," I say, stepping onto the ice. Carla and Kathy follow me.

Sue and Marty appear in the players' box, along with two Estevan Bruins. The boys are holding clipboards and taking instructions from Sue. I gather they're going to be evaluating us from the stands. If that's not enough, another Bruin is setting up a video camera at the concourse level.

"The tape never lies!" Carla calls to me.

The other girls trickle onto the ice, and Kathy leads us in our stretches and for the rest of the warm-up.

When Sue blows her whistle, we move towards the players' box and take a knee around her. Sue's in her early thirties and is tall with short blonde hair. I don't know when she finds time to work out, but she can easily out bench press anybody on the team, including Carla.

I try to concentrate on Sue's words, but it's hard when everything she says makes me think of something else.

Right now she's saying, "Your registration fee entitles you to two skill sessions and two controlled scrimmages this weekend. Saturday morning there'll be fitness testing, followed by a tour of the high school for those of you who could be billeting in Estevan. We'll make the first cuts after the scrimmage tomorrow afternoon. Final cuts will occur after the last scrimmage on Sunday. It's our intention to retain seventeen players. Ideally, we want ten forwards, five defence, and two goaltenders..."

That means eleven girls are not making the team. Once cuts are made, will the fifth defenceman only get to play if one of the other four gets hurt or benched?

"...practices will begin on the Tuesday following the Labour Day weekend. You'll be on the ice three times a week and have a dryland session every Wednesday. Attendance will be mandatory unless prior arrangements are made with your coach..."

I'll have to hit the gym or the road *every* day until then, I think. If I make the team, she'll expect me to show up in shape after Labour Day.

"...wondering about who will be the head coach. Minor Hockey is confident they'll find the best possible candidate in the next few weeks. What you need to do is concentrate on having a good tryout and showing us..."

What if they don't find a qualified candidate? What if one of the dads has to take over? What if Mr. Johnstone ends up on the bench?

"...drills will be far more difficult than the ones you may be accustomed to. They will challenge you both mentally and physically..."

Some of the ones we did on the Rage last year were hard enough. Like that triangular offensive cycling/defensive support drill. Every time we did it, it felt like the first time.

Soon enough, we find out Sue isn't kidding about the difficulty of the drills. She starts off with power skating, working on inside and outside edge holds. Testing linear, lateral and transitional speeds. It's clear she's concentrating on assessing our individual skills and ferreting out our weaknesses.

Finally she tells a Bruin to toss out the pucks.

Teneil and some of the other girls struggle with the puck handling and passing exercises. They can skate well, but they don't have soft hands.

Hands are something Sue can't teach.

Some dads have drifted in to watch us. I've heard them over the years, murmuring amongst themselves during those long breaks between tournament games, or in the lobby after a tough loss. They all respect Sue, but they have their own ideas about coaching just the same.

"If only she'd shorten the bench more often," they say. "She tries too hard to be fair."

But this year, Sue won't be taking any prisoners. Her whole approach has changed.

"Really looking forward to fitness testing tomorrow," Randi gasps, lining up behind me.

"Me too."

I'm watching Amy at the other end of the ice where Mr. Johnstone and the Bruins' starting netminder are working with her. Right now they're passing to each another, then shooting on Amy, forcing her to shift rapidly from side to side. As big as she is, she's smooth and confident in her movements, and she never takes her eyes off the puck.

Carla gives me a little push from behind.

I'm up.

# *chapter*
## *three*

**W**hen our skills session ends, the other "team" is lined up along the Plexiglas, watching us. They're wearing black jerseys with orange numbers.

Amber Kowalski is blocking my path as I step off the ice. She's staring over my shoulder, like Bambi in the headlights.

"Hey." I give Amber a little poke. "How about making some room?"

Amber steps back, and her big blue eyes shift to my face. She's terrified.

"You'll be okay," I tell her.

"I've never tried out for *anything*," she says.

Miranda's standing behind Amber, with much the same expression. She's likely heard about Amy Fox. Her dream of being our starting goaltender is going up in smoke.

As I walk by, I make eye contact with each girl in a black jersey. There's Jennifer McQueen, my D partner from two years ago who, like me, has given up school sports so she can focus on hockey. Larissa Bilkhu was a solid centreman for us last year, all the while juggling her commitment to senior girls' basketball. Crystal Jordan shelved her pads a few years ago when we had too many goalies.

I tap knuckles with all of them and turn towards the hallway. A door opens, and another player steps out, nearly running into me. I'd know that Reebok helmet anywhere.

Jodi Palmer.

"Fancy meeting you here," she says. "How'd your session go?"

"Okay." I move aside so the girls behind me can get past. Jodi nods and smiles at each of them.

"You never told me you were trying out," I say when the last one has gone by.

"I've been praying about it," she says.

How am I supposed to respond to that? Jesus is wrong? You're not supposed to be playing AAA because your brain will be mush if you get another concussion?

"Good luck," I tell her.

"Thanks." She continues down the hallway.

Last fall Jodi wanted to play with us, but she was still battling weak knees, headaches, and nausea. Skating backwards was impossible.

Since Christmas, she's been steadily improving. She

started skating with a senior ladies' team and competed in
track and field at school.

The thing about Jodi is: she doesn't know how to hold
back. If she makes our team, she'll go hard into the corners.
Forecheck aggressively. Drive to the net.

It's too dangerous.

In the dressing room, some girls are discussing the Bruins
who helped with our ice session. I wonder if it's just a ploy to
cover what they're really thinking...

If I don't make this team, where in the hell am I going to
play?

"Did your dad know Jodi was coming out?" I ask
Whitney.

"He talked her into it," she says.

"You're kidding me, right?"

"Sounds like you don't want Jodi on the team," Whitney
speculates. "Are you afraid she'll be the defensive star you
wish *you* were?"

"Take a hike," Kathy says. "You know Jessie's not like
that."

"*You* take a hike," Whitney says. "This is Jodi's decision.
You should quit bashing her for wanting to come back."

"And you should quit pushing our buttons," Kathy says.

"Whitney, you weren't around when Jodi had her accident," I say, "so you don't know how risky this is."

"She looked fine at hockey school this summer," Whitney says. "I think you guys are exaggerating how bad her head injury is."

"Spoken like someone who is suffering from her own head injury," Kathy says.

I jump in before Kathy starts shooting her mouth off again. "Look, Whitney, everybody appreciates what your dad's done to help us go AAA..."

"Enough of your phony team building shit," Whitney interrupts. "You're going to be gone next year. You don't give a rat's ass about what happens after you graduate."

"Whitney's right," Randi says. "There aren't enough younger girls coming up to make a team. That's why *I* voted to go AAA."

My phone starts vibrating on the bench. I pick it up and see the message from Pam.

Ready, it says.

I start pulling on my shorts and T-shirt.

"Aren't you showering?" Kathy asks.

"I'll shower at home." I hurl the last of my equipment in my bag.

"Way to go, Johnstone," Kathy says.

"Screw you, Parker," Whitney says.

I heft my bag onto my shoulder. "I suggest we *all* go home and take a shower. We're setting a poor example for the new girls."

"You got that right," Amy Fox says.

It's the first time she's addressed us.

I continue. "Let's each focus on having a good camp. We can't control who's here – or who's not. Let's concentrate on the things we *can* control."

I leave the rink without so much as a glance at the ice surface. I don't want to know how it's going out there for Jodi or Amber or my other teammates.

There's nothing I can do to help any of them.

Saturday morning is hell.

We go to the curling rink – where there's no ice – to start our fitness testing. I come out okay on weight, height, and the vertical jump, and I think...this isn't so hard.

Then Sue brings out the whistles and stopwatches.

The beep test is awful, but it's not the worst. The RHIET or Repeated High Intensity Endurance Test is criminal. Pylons are set forty metres apart. We have thirty seconds to run from one pylon and back to the start line. The time we don't use is time to rest.

It's only six times, I think. That's three minutes. How bad can it be?

I soon find out.

Agonized lungs screaming for air. Muscles on fire. Guts

aching. I want to curl up and die.

Then we head over to the fitness centre for bench press. I haven't done much of this before because Sue always told us we were too young to weight train. At the end of this station, I learn my one-rep max is eighty pounds. Decent. But Carla out-presses all of us with ninety-five.

I go home, eat and have a nap before driving back to the rink for the controlled scrimmage. Mom comes along to watch.

On the ice, I take my own advice. Control the things I can control. Move my feet. Get to the puck first. Find some chemistry with a new defenceman. I shut Jodi down each time she comes to my side, frustrating the hell out of her.

Focus.

**F**irst cuts.

Amber is the last one out of the dressing room, bag on her shoulder, sticks in hand, head so low I can't see her big blue eyes.

Marty is right behind her.

From the wet patches on Amber's cheeks, I know he's already told her she's off the team. He puts his arm around her and guides her towards the exit.

She gives me a shaky smile before she disappears from view.

# *chapter four*

**W**hat time's Evan leaving for Calgary tomorrow?" I ask Breanne, Evan's little sister. We're sitting at the Gedaks' kitchen counter colouring, while I wait for Evan to finish getting ready for the Saturday night church service.

"Early," Breanne says.

"You going along?" I ask.

She shakes her blonde pigtails. "Just Mom. She says he'll need help buying stuff for his apartment." She shows me some pictures she's already drawn and coloured. "These are for him to put on his fridge."

"Good for you, Short Stuff." I get an empty feeling when I look at the picture she drew of Evan in his Dinos uniform. "He must be pretty excited about making the squad this year, huh?"

Breanne nods, blonde pigtails jiggling.

Evan red-shirted last year with the University of Calgary

basketball team, which means he practiced with the Dinos but didn't play any games. This year he'll try to crack the starting lineup as a point guard.

If anybody can do *that,* Evan can.

He's single-minded in anything he pursues. His overall average was 93.4 percent last year even though he was taking three labs and practicing nearly every day. The only thing he's failed at getting is...

Me.

"Ready to go?" Evan asks from the doorway.

His voice startles me, and I swing around on the high stool to look at him. He grew another inch over the summer, adding to a cumulative total of 6'5". His dark hair is cut very short, which makes his broad forehead more prominent.

"Sure." I reach for my purse and keys.

"Can I come too?" Breanne asks.

"We'll be out past your bedtime," Evan says.

"But it's summer," Breanne says.

"She's right," I inform Evan. "I don't mind her tagging along. If you don't."

Breanne is an A+ chaperone. Her lively chatter keeps our conversation from getting serious.

"Please," she begs.

Evan picks her up and hangs her by the ankles until she squeals.

Breanne is sitting in Sunny's back seat when we leave for the service.

All summer I've been spending Saturday nights with Evan at his church. Evan's dad, Rev. Gedak, is the main pastor. Matt, the youth pastor, leads a contemporary service at 7:30 p.m. followed by a teen activity, like basketball or a movie. It's a welcome change from being around people who talk about partying and guys and sex. I don't mind going on a booze cruise with Kathy once in a while, but it's not my thing.

I don't fit in with Evan's crowd either. Some of his friends make no secret of the fact I'm not "saved." I don't let it bother me because God and I are on good terms – no matter what they think.

The tough part about going to Evan's church is Evan himself. Ever since I was his grad escort, he acts like I'm his girlfriend. He insists on paying if we go out for supper or to a show. He's hinted about being escort for my grad, but I haven't asked him yet. I just want to be friends, and things would be perfect if he'd settle for that.

"How'd tryouts go today?" he asks as I pull onto Souris Drive.

"Five girls got cut," I tell him.

"Anyone you know?"

"Amber Kowalski."

"That's too bad," he says, "but it shouldn't surprise you."

"I thought maybe there'd be a way for Sue to keep us all together."

"That's naïve, Jessie," he says.

"I guess."

"Are you worried about making the team?"

"I'll be okay." I find a spot to park in the lot beside the church. "I wish I could say the same for some of our forwards."

"Who?" Breanne asks, unbuckling her seat belt.

She's always listening when you think she isn't.

"Never mind, Short Stuff."

Jodi and Michelle are waiting for us in the lobby. They're dressed up because they're singing at the service. Two years ago I spent lots of time with Michelle, but she's made it clear I'm no longer part of her inner circle.

"Quick change for you," I say to Jodi, pointing to her black skirt. "Didn't you get off the ice an hour ago?"

"My hair's still wet." Jodi squeezes a handful of black curls. "I'm bagged after that fitness testing. Aren't you?"

"I had a nap," I tell her.

"We should go in," Michelle says impatiently.

We sit together in the second row. Evan takes the aisle so he can stretch out his long legs, and Breanne squirms into his lap. He slides closer to me and puts his arm around my shoulders. When people try to get inside my personal space, it makes me uncomfortable. I lean ahead and put my elbows on the pew in front, as if I'm trying to get a better look at Pastor Matt.

He's worth looking at. But I tune him out when he starts beating his "them and us" drum. I know I'm considered a "non-believer" because I haven't made the trip down the aisle to give my life to Jesus.

Instead I think about tryouts. Poor Amber. Maybe we never should have gone AAA. My thoughts wander to my future, which stretches out before me like an endless blank page. I still have no idea what I'm going to take at university next year. What if I can't play CIS hockey? What if I don't get back together with Mark in time for my grad?

I feel Jodi shifting in her seat next to me, and I realize it's time for her and Michelle to perform. When they go up to the front, Michelle slides behind the grand piano, and Jodi picks up her acoustic guitar and adjusts the microphone stand.

"We'd like to sing something new for you," Jodi says. "Many of you are headed back to school and have tough decisions to make as you face your future. Michelle and I believe these choices will be easier with Jesus in your heart. This song is called *Risk*."

Jodi and Michelle have been writing music together for two years. I think Michelle does most of the composing. She's got a knack for writing poetry and scoring it with a melody that lingers long after the song is over. But it's Jodi who gives life to Michelle's compositions. She's got this old school voice, childlike and seductive at the same time, not exactly suited for church music.

She opens her mouth, and the notes ripple out effortlessly, as if she was born to do it.

I connect with one of the verses.

> *I meet a faceless stranger*
> *Cellphones in our hands*
> *Our messages float in cyberspace*
> *But our gazes never land.*
> *We hurry on; the space between us*
> *Stretches a fine line.*
> *I've missed the chance to change his life*
> *He won't be changing mine.*

When Jodi and Michelle finish, the congregation explodes in enthusiastic applause and whistles. Jodi smiles and touches her hair self-consciously then acknowledges Michelle. Jodi's so different from the party girl I used to know.

Breanne climbs onto my knees and slumps against my chest, sighing loudly.

"What?" I whisper in her ear.

"I hate when Evan goes away," she says. "And when he's gone, I don't see you either."

I bear hug her in response. "You can come watch me play hockey."

She seems to take comfort in that.

I spend the rest of the service thinking about Evan. I sneak a glance every now and then at his profile. He's so good to me. Maybe the only reason I don't feel *that* way about him is he's not drop dead gorgeous like Mark. And if that's true, how shallow am I?

Here I am eating my heart out over a guy who belongs to somebody else, and missing out on something amazing, just because I'm focused on the wrong thing.

The wrong guy.

What am I doing, I think. What the hell am I doing?

# *chapter five*

**A** drive-in movie is planned for after the service. Pastor Matt had a permanent screen built at one end of the church parking lot, and everybody parks their vehicles in front of it and tunes in to the church radio station.

The movie, which is about talking dogs and cats, verges on annoying. Breanne falls asleep after a half hour, and Evan puts her in the backseat where she curls up, using my hoodie as a pillow.

Most of the time, conversation with Evan is easy. He always asks about my friends, and he cares about my hockey. Sometimes he gets judgmental about the girls' partying. It's strange because I don't like what they do, but I *hate* it when somebody else criticizes them.

Tonight Evan's quiet. He leans against the passenger door, his seat jammed as far back as it will go to accommodate his legs. He stares fixedly at the windshield, but I can tell he's not watching the movie because he doesn't react to anything on the screen.

"What're you thinking?" I ask.

He looks out the side window. "Nothing."

"Did I do something wrong?" I ask him.

"You couldn't," he says.

I know he feels helpless, the same way I feel about Mark. Evan can't control his own feelings, and he can't control mine either. Only one person can change that.

I think about Michelle and Jodi's song.

The strangers passing. Missing out. Risk.

"I think I want to go out with you," I say quietly.

He doesn't hear me because the movie soundtrack is too loud. No need to pull the words back.

Then I think about Mark and Holly. They probably have sex every time they're together. Just like the rest of the girls on my team do with their boyfriends.

And I'm alone.

"Evan, I want to go out with you," I say again, louder.

There's no chance he doesn't hear me this time.

"Jessie, don't," he says.

"I mean it." I say the words with conviction because at least half of me needs convincing.

"You're feeling bad because I'm leaving tomorrow," he says. "You're scared about what's going to happen with hockey and school next year."

I shake my head.

He stretches his long arms. "It's time to go home. I have to make an early start tomorrow." He looks over his left shoulder into the back seat. "Look at her," he says. "I miss her when I'm away."

That's when I do it. I lean right over and kiss him.

I don't know if Evan's ever been kissed before. I know he's never had sex because he says he's saving himself for marriage. It probably hasn't been difficult for him up to today.

I'm a rookie in the kissing department...not counting a June night long ago. I never had a serious boyfriend before Mark – and heaven knows Mark was a prude most of the time. If I knew *then* what I know about him *now*, I might have gotten him to loosen up.

So here I am kissing Evan, trying to convince him I'm serious about going out with him, and I'm thinking about Mark.

You shouldn't be doing this, that infuriating little voice warns me.

The voice that takes the fun out of everything.

Something about the way I'm kissing Evan must change his mind because suddenly his hands are tangled in my hair, holding me close, but not too close. He pulls back after a minute and takes a deep breath.

"Wow," he says, shaking his big head. "Where'd you learn to kiss like that?"

He's easily impressed, my little voice says. Wouldn't the truth shock him?

I ignore the voice, bent on pursuing this thrill ride on the SS Jessie Mac.

"I'm serious, Evan. I want to go out with you."

"I'm leaving for Calgary in less than twelve hours. You've had all summer. Why did you wait so long?"

"I didn't know it until a minute ago," I tell him.

"Look," he says, "I resigned myself to this 'friend' thing a long time ago. I didn't like it, but I had no power to change it." He holds both my hands and squeezes them gently. "Jessie, if you're not serious, please don't do this. It's not fair."

His last three words echo in my brain. Where did I hear them before? Who said that?

"I *am* serious." I lean over and kiss him again. To convince him I mean it.

To convince yourself, my little voice says.

You've been wrong before, I tell the voice. Why should I listen to your sanctimonious crap this time?

Evan lets me kiss him, and when I pull away, he takes a long, shuddering breath. "You better mean it."

"I do," I tell him.

Breanne stirs in the back seat then snores lightly.

"I think you should take us home," Evan says.

"I think we should *talk*." I grab one of his hands and squeeze it. "Then we should neck some more. How does that sound?"

His expression is priceless.

It feels wonderful to know how happy I'm going to make him.

# *chapter* *six*

**S**unday night.

The last scrimmage is history, and the final roster for the Estevan McGillicky Oilers is posted in the rink lobby.

Sue's cuts so far haven't been surprising. Amber Kowalski. Two girls from Stoughton who never showed for fitness testing yesterday morning. Some thirteen-year-olds from Estevan who were too light in the pants. A Radville girl with no hands at all. One from Redvers who couldn't do the drills.

Even so, I don't have the guts to look. Instead I stand a healthy distance away, equipment at my feet, and watch the girls' faces as they check the roster.

Kathy's first. The set of her shoulders is confident as she scans the names. She turns away after a second, catches my eye, and gives me a thumbs up. She high-fives Randi and Carla. Miranda sidles up, and Kathy throws an arm around her shoulders and points to her name.

So far so good.

A girl from Lignite moves closer, and they part to let her through. She scrutinizes the names for several long moments, and I can tell by the sudden droop in her shoulders that her name is missing. She pushes between Kathy and Carla, picks up her equipment by the door, and walks out.

Crystal, Larissa and some girls I don't know find their names on the list. They congratulate one another and exchange compliments. The team chemistry of the Estevan Oilers starts to evolve.

"I knew you'd make it."

"Anybody hear when our first practice is?"

"Can't wait for our first league game."

It's heartwarming – and sickening – at the same time.

Jodi finds her name. Jennifer and Amy find theirs.

A girl from Alameda doesn't make the cut. Nor does one of the Carnduff girls.

Teneil comes up the stairs, drops her hockey bag beside mine, gives me a nervous smile, and approaches the group. Scans the list of names, then scans it again. Miranda is smiling and talking to Randi. Obviously she never noticed her best friend's name is missing. Teneil's muttered curse is Miranda's first clue something's wrong. Miranda reaches out to touch her shoulder, but Teneil wrenches away, sobbing, and heads straight towards me.

"I'm sorry," I murmur.

She hoists her equipment onto her shoulder and scrapes her nose with the back of her hand.

"Why are *you* sorry?" she demands. "You made it, and I didn't! So much for controlling what we can control!"

Her parents are standing by the arena entrance. Mr. Howard has to step aside so she doesn't swipe him with her hockey bag as she swears and storms out. Mrs. Howard looks like she's been kicked in the stomach.

I think of the times I've carpooled with the Howards.

Shit.

Miranda approaches me. "It's not fair. Teneil should get to play her last year of Midget."

"Last season she always picked volleyball over hockey," I remind her. "Don't you think Sue remembers that?"

Miranda walks away, muttering.

I try to imagine a dressing room without Amber or Teneil.

But I can't.

# *chapter*
## *seven*

I t's the first day of my last year at Estevan Comprehensive School, and I'm headed over to Amber's house to pick her up. The morning is bright and beautiful and breezy. Since it's been raining steadily for the last three days, it sucks that we'll be cooped up inside the Comp for six hours.

I gave Amber a ride nearly every day last year. The kid asks the craziest questions. She totally cracks me up.

But today she doesn't say much.

"I'm sorry you got cut," I tell her right off.

"It's okay," she says. "I get it. I wasn't good enough. I'm going to play on one of the ladies' teams. I already talked to some people."

"You're going to play *senior* ladies?"

"You make them sound old," Amber says. "Some of them aren't much older than I am."

I check the traffic before making a right turn. "I didn't

know that."

"They practice once a week and have games on Fridays. They even go to tournaments. You don't have to feel sorry for me, Jessie. I'm on student council this year. And I'm getting a part-time job because I want to buy my own car."

"So you've got everything figured out." I give her a quick once-over to see if she's just saying this to make us both feel better.

But she looks happy.

By the time we get to the Comp parking lot, she's talked me into helping her out with the talent show next week. As I back into a spot, I wonder why I ever worried about her. Amber's one of those people who knows how to bounce – whether she gets rubbed out on the boards or served up a big helping of Reality.

On the other hand there's Teneil.

She's waiting for us in the courtyard, sitting at our "team" table. It's not like we won't let anyone who's not on the team sit with us. We're not a clique or anything. But nobody's ever been cut before.

As soon as Amber and I sit down, Teneil starts in. She doesn't even say hi. "So when's your first practice?"

"Monday."

"Found a head coach yet?"

"No."

She raises an eyebrow at Amber. "I was looking on the internet. Most AAA teams carry more than seventeen. Lots of them AP players."

Hard to guess where this is going.

Amber smiles and shrugs.

Teneil turns to me. "Did Sue ever say why she only wanted seventeen?"

"Not that I remember."

"How many out-of-town girls made the team?"

"I'm not sure."

Teneil's inquisition goes on until Miranda arrives. Then the two of them sit there and whisper while Amber tells me about potential part-time jobs, and I pretend to listen.

I'm relieved when the other girls show up.

And even more relieved when the buzzer sounds for first period.

English. Mrs. Buckingham. She's the greatest. I had her in Grade Eleven, and she doesn't disappoint. I don't think about hockey even once during her class.

After English, there's homeroom.

I'm still with Mr. Gervais down in the band room, and — surprise surprise — so is Amy Fox. She looks big, even with khaki shorts and a tank top replacing her pads. Her long brown hair is pulled back in a ponytail, and she doesn't wear a lick of makeup.

"Where are you billeting?" I ask her.

We're sitting on one of the carpeted tiers, legs stretched out in front of us.

"My aunt," she says. "That was the plan all along. I want a university scholarship next year, and I needed to transition to girls' hockey. Playing in Estevan means my dad won't have to pay someone to billet me."

I gather money is an issue for Amy's family. I know her dad raises cattle, and the beef market has been in trouble for a while.

"Bet he'll miss you on the farm," I tell her.

"I've got three brothers," she says.

"So where do you want to play next year?" I ask. "Best case scenario."

"An Ivy League school," she says. "I won't be choosy. No offence, but another reason we picked this team is because my numbers are going to look better if I get lots of shots."

Some other kids come over to talk, and I introduce them to Amy. While they're getting acquainted, I think about Amy's assessment of the Oilers.

Lots of shots on Amy means the opposition is blasting right past the defence.

My position.

And there's no way I want *that* to happen.

# *chapter eight*

I check the list of talent show entries on my clipboard. "I don't know why people bother to enter. Everybody knows Jodi's going to win."

"Yep, she always wins," Kathy agrees. "But I still say you should have played your flute. You're always telling us how good you were in junior high."

"I lied."

The guys on stage finish their air band routine, performed to "Smells Like Teen Spirit" and back off the stage, bowing and waving their arms like rock stars.

"I have no idea what that song's about," I say philosophically.

"Who's next?" Amber demands.

"Calm down, Kowalski." I check the clipboard again. "Liam MacArthur."

"He's Indian," Kathy says.

"You should say *First Nations,*" I correct.

Kathy tries to peer at my clipboard, but I pull it tight against my chest. "Can you at least tell me what he's doing?" she asks.

"Rope tricks," Amber says. "What would you expect from somebody in Rodeo Club?" She walks out on the stage to introduce him.

Liam enters from the opposite side, wearing Wranglers, a checked shirt, boots, a white Stetson and a huge, shiny belt buckle. He walks to centre stage, uncoiling a lariat. Kathy puts on a Keith Urban song, and Liam starts his routine. He keeps the rope in continual motion, twisting and snaking around him.

"He's good," Kathy says. "You know him?"

"He was in one of my math classes last year," I reply. "Talked to him a few times, but we're not friends."

"Of course you're not. You never let any guys get close to you," Kathy says.

"Do you blame me?" I ask. "They all know about that time I got drunk at Shauna's. I don't trust any of them."

"Jessie, that was a long time ago. Everybody but you has forgotten about it."

When Liam finishes his performance, the crowd cheers and hollers. He removes his hat and inclines his head, flashing a gap-toothed smile. His dark hair is cut short, with one big cowlick on his forehead.

He borrows the microphone from Amber. "For this next bit, I need a volunteer. Would someone from the audience..."

Kathy shoves me violently from behind, and I end up on hands and knees on stage, my clipboard skittering across the smooth surface.

Someone – it sounds like Randi – yells, "Way to go, Jessie!"

Liam bends over, picks up my clipboard, and hands it to Amber. "Thanks for volunteering."

"But..."

He's already stepping away from me, rearranging the coils of rope. "Would you mind standing very still?"

I get up and turn around, throwing daggers at Kathy. She grins and waves. I face Liam and stand very still indeed, my cheeks flaming while Liam shakes out a loop and begins. The rope whirs around me like a bumblebee, barely grazing my hair. I try to make eye contact with Liam, determined he should see how pissed I am, but his dark eyes register total concentration, and his thick black brows are beetled together.

The performance concludes – again to thunderous applause – with me trussed and hog-tied like a steer. Like a moron, I hop offstage, where Kathy and Amber are doubled over.

"Would you mind untying me?" I fume.

Naturally they think it's funnier to leave me in my

present state.

Liam jogs off the stage. "Are you finished with my rope?" He has to speak loudly because the audience hasn't stopped cheering and whistling.

Naturally that sends my two friends into hysterics. It's a wonder they don't pee their pants.

He unravels the rope in a few deft movements, setting me free. "Frankly I'm surprised you volunteered so quick. Usually it's a lot harder to coerce someone."

"Go take another bow!" Amber shouts.

Liam steps back out. The volume increases immediately.

"He's cute," Kathy says.

"He's not good looking," I say.

"I said he's *cute*. There's a difference," Kathy points out.

The audience starts chanting, "Jessie! Jessie!"

"And you said you didn't have a talent." Kathy puts her hands on my shoulder blades.

"Don't push!" I snarl at her.

Liam is suddenly back. "Come on!" He grabs my hand and pulls me to the middle of the stage, then drags my arm over my head, like I'm a prizefighter.

Right now I'd like to go a few rounds with him *and* Kathy – armed with my hockey stick.

"Encore!" someone shouts.

Liam leans over and murmurs in my ear. "Can I tie you

up again later?"

"What?" I rip my hand from his grasp.

Suddenly Amber's there, introducing the next act, another air band. The guys are dressed and painted up like the members of KISS.

I stalk off the stage, grabbing my clipboard from Kathy.

"Hey, I'm sorry!" She doesn't even sound apologetic. "He looked like your type."

"My *type?* I *have* a boyfriend! And besides, that guy is *sick!*"

Liam comes backstage. "Hey you...Hockey Girl!" he says.

"Get away from me!"

"I just wanted to find out if you'll do it!"

"You are twisted, you know that?"

His eyes widen in surprise, and he backs up a step.

"Kathy, this guy asked if he could *tie* me up later! Have you ever heard of anything so perverted?" My face is burning.

He looks just as embarrassed. "I didn't mean *that!* Honest! I was just wondering if you'd help if I advance to the final round."

I wish there was a trap door on this stage, so I could disappear through it. "Oh."

"Well, will you?" he asks.

"No," I say slowly and distinctly. "I won't."

Liam turns to Kathy. "How about you?" he asks.

"I have to run the music," she says sweetly. "Love to, but no."

He heaves a disappointed sigh and exits, using the back stairs.

"I still say he's cute." Kathy turns to the sound system and cues up the air band's CD.

"What's with you anyway?" I ask. "You've hounded me for two years to take Evan seriously. And now that I'm dating him, you try to throw some other guy in my face!"

Before Kathy can answer, Jodi comes backstage to get ready for her performance, and I push the incident with Liam to the back of my mind.

Good place for him, my little voice says.

# *chapter*
## *nine*

**R**utherford Rink. U of S campus. Saskatoon.

There's less than two minutes left in the period.

I'm lined up at centre ice.

We lead the U of S Rookies 5–4.

Kathy looks over her right shoulder and grins. She's having a great game, and so am I.

Why wouldn't we be? We don't have to make *this* team, *this* year.

But the girls we're playing want to.

Badly.

This is the second time I've been invited to attend the U of S Huskies' fall camp. Last year I got a decent evaluation, and this year, I plan to do even better.

Kathy wins the draw back to me, and the Rookie left winger skates right at me. I pass to my D-partner, who puts a move on the Rookie rightwing and fires the puck in deep.

The old dump and chase.

I like our chances.

**H**i, Jessie."

I turn around and see Holly Chamberlain, Mark's girlfriend, standing in the hallway between the Rutherford ice surface and the dressing rooms. She's wearing sweatshorts and a tank top, and she's got a green bandana tied around her short, feathery brown hair. Holly is a little bundle of dynamite, with muscles popping in her forearms and calves.

"Hey, I was hoping I'd see you this weekend," I tell her, trying to inject some sincerity into my tone. "How'd you know I was in Saskatoon?"

"I saw your status on Mainpage," she explains. "Thinking about coming to U of S next year?" she asks.

I nod.

"It'd be great if you made the Huskies."

Holly wrestles for the university team. Last year she was a CIS All-Canadian, and she's medalled two years in a row in her weight class at Nationals. Besides that, she's brilliant. She's working on a Bachelor of Science, majoring in microbiology.

"Next year when I come to this camp, I'll be coming as a rookie." The thought makes my insides twist and turn.

"Is that what Kathy's hoping for too?" Holly gestures at Parker, who's standing just outside the dressing room, schmoozing some of the Huskie vets.

"Yes." I pull off my helmet and tuck a sticky strand of hair behind my ears. "Seen Mark lately?"

A weird look crosses Holly's face. "Not for a little while."

Such mixed emotions. I do like Holly, and I know she's great for Mark. But there's a big part of me hoping their long distance relationship will eventually implode.

Correction, says my little voice, there *was* a part of you hoping. Now you're going out with Evan, and everything's different, right?

Right.

"Is your family here?" Holly asks.

"No, I came with Kathy and her mom."

Holly nods. "I was wondering if you wanted to get together this weekend – go for lunch or something. Will you have time?"

"Sure."

"Text me," she says.

After we're showered and dressed, Kathy and I pack up our equipment.

She pushes the dressing room door open. "Wish we could leave our stuff here to dry."

"We can air it out on the hotel balcony."

As we walk along the narrow walkway, headed for the rink entrance, I look up at Rutherford's roof, which looks every minute of its eighty-plus years. There are posts and exit signs everywhere, and spectator stands on one side only. The luxury boxes above us – I'm using that term loosely – give the best view of the ice. The place feels comfortable, even if it's not glamorous.

"Look who Mom's talking to," Kathy calls back to me.

I can't see past her, so I have to wait until the walkway widens.

Near the entrance, Mrs. Parker is standing with the Huskies' head coach.

Kathy stops and shifts her bag to her other shoulder. "I hope she's telling him how much we'd love to come to school here."

"No doubt," I say.

When we get there, we drop our equipment, so the coach can shake our hands. We make some small talk about the game, and then he says, "What're your plans for next year, girls?"

"University," I tell him. "And university hockey, if I can make the cut."

"Me too," Kathy says.

"Well, U of S has a lot to offer. You girls can't go wrong staying close to home to further your education – and to play."

He shakes hands with us again before moving on to another set of parents.

Mrs. Parker grins and gives us two thumbs up.

"He's just doing PR," Kathy says. "We shouldn't let it go to our heads."

"Right," I tell her.

Just the same, we throw down our bags outside the Rutherford and do a happy dance.

Mrs. Parker drives us downtown, where Kathy and I plan to start looking at grad dresses. Since my mom's not along, I won't be buying one, but I don't mind helping Kathy pick one out.

"You should strongly consider black and white," I tell her as we drive over the 25th Street Bridge.

"You think I'd look good in those colours?" Kathy asks.

"You and Brett the Ref will match. He won't even have to rent a tux."

She nails me in the shoulder so hard it brings tears to my eyes. "Keep your chirps to yourself," she says.

The next day Holly picks me up at the rink after our skills session. She drives an awesome shiny blue and white striped MINI Cooper. It even has a stick shift.

As soon as I open the passenger door, I can see she's upgraded her look. She's got on jeans, a bright yellow tank top and a white shirt. She's even wearing makeup, and she's flat-ironed her hair.

"You look nice," I tell her, sliding into the seat. I reach for the lever to push it back as far as it will go.

"Thanks," she says. "After I drop you off, I'm headed to the library to do some reading."

"Do you always dress up for that?" I ask.

"I'm dressed up for *lunch,*" Holly replies.

I look at the stack of textbooks behind us. "Wow. Do you plan to read all that this afternoon?"

"No!" She laughs. "I just picked those up from the book-store, and I want to get a head start. Classes start Wednesday." She waits for me to buckle my seatbelt before rocketing us onto Campus Drive.

It's my first time driving with her, and I find out pretty quick she's one of those aggressive city drivers. Must come from growing up in Calgary. I brace my feet on the floor, and my hand on the armrest, as she swerves in and out of traffic. She keeps up a steady chitchat the entire time, telling me about her summer job as a camp counselor for deaf kids.

"You know sign language?" I ask, amazed.

"It might sound mercenary, but the summer job will look great on my pharmacy application. I enjoy the kids, and I know I'm good at it, so I try not to feel bad about some of my motives."

"You gotta do what you gotta do," I tell her. But inside I'm wondering, does she have the faintest clue how to do *anything* wrong?

After we get to the restaurant and place our order, she quits making small talk and gets down to business. "I need to talk about Mark," she says.

I try to keep my face expressionless. Has she suspected I still like him?

"I'm worried about him." She leans closer, as if she's exposing a state secret. "His whole focus has changed."

"Should that be a surprise?" I point out. "With his dad being sick, his world must be pretty shook up."

"It's more than that," Holly says. "He thinks he can make his dad better by having a great year with the Hitmen."

"That's crazy," I tell her. "You can't believe he thinks that way."

"I do, and so does Maggie."

Mark and his mom are very close, but right now she's managing an art gallery in Ontario while Mark lives in Calgary with his dad and his dad's partner.

"We've all tried to talk some sense into him," Holly continues, "but he won't listen. He says he knows what he's doing." She pauses to take a sip of her water. "I don't think he's preparing himself for the worst. And he's messing with his future."

What about Mark's future? Will he and Holly live in Calgary, juggling two careers and raising their kids? Will he ever think about me, and the time we spent together?

You know he won't, my little voice says.

"Jessie, are you listening?" Her brown eyes are looking right through me.

"Sorry, yes." I give myself a mental shake. "Do you want me to talk to him?"

"It wouldn't hurt." She sighs. "Just don't make it sound like I put you up to it. He doesn't like me meddling."

"How's his dad doing anyway? I know he had surgery to remove part of his stomach, but I don't know anything else."

"They removed some lymph nodes as well, and part of his pancreas," Holly explains. "He finished his last round of chemotherapy a few weeks ago. We're all praying he'll get a good report at his next checkup."

"So what does *he* say about Mark not going to university this fall?"

"To be honest, I think he's looking forward to watching Mark play another year of Major Junior. At least Mark's taking some university classes." Her fine chestnut brows furrow. "It's tough for us, living in two different cities, trying to do university *and* a sport." Holly rolls up the remains of her chicken wrap and stuffs it in the satchel beside her chair. "Will you call him? He values your friendship."

Yeah, Holly, he values it so much I haven't talked to him for ages. My stomach twists at the thought.

"Okay."

"You're a good friend – to both of us. " She folds her arms and leans on the edge of the table. "Now let's hear the skinny on you. Is there a guy in your life?"

I tell her about Evan and Evan's basketball. I'm a little embarrassed because I find myself faking some of my answers to her questions.

You should know these answers, my little voice tells me.

"He sounds terrific," Holly says when I'm finished. "I know Mark's mentioned him once or twice. How long have you been going out?"

"Just a few weeks."

She gives me a quirky smile. "So I'm not the only one juggling a long distance romance."

"It won't be so bad – with Skype and texting and stuff," I tell her.

"Well, I hope you two can hold things together."

"Have you heard my hockey team went AAA this year?" I ask.

"No, I didn't. Does that mean big changes?"

I nod. "Lots more practices. Time at the gym. Weekends on the road. A new coach to get used to."

Holly raises an eyebrow. "Who is it?"

As I tell her about our situation, I get the idea she's not listening. I drop the subject and suggest we leave because I can tell she's preoccupied with thoughts of Mark.

Yeah, I know the feeling.

After she drops me off at the hotel, I remember my promise to call him. My hands get sweaty.

Stop it, I tell myself, before my little voice can kick in.

Stop it.

# chapter ten

**H**ow was practice?" Mom asks at supper on Thursday night.

"Yeah, how do the Oilers look?" Dad's scrolling on his Blackberry with one hand and picking at his supper with the other.

Who says adults can't multi-task?

"Good," I reply.

"Just *good?*" Dad sets down his phone and looks at me.

"We've only had *two* practices."

"Define *good.*" Mom sits down across from me and unfolds her napkin.

"Goaltending is good. Defence is good. Offence is good."

"Thanks." Dad's voice is dripping with sarcasm. "How does the team compare to last year's?"

"We'll find out when we play Weyburn next week."

"How does Jodi look?" Dad asks.

"About eighty per cent of what she used to be," I tell

him. "But she's still our best forward."

"Tell us about the new girls," Mom says.

While I'm describing them, Courtney keeps making these annoying noises, sighing loudly, dropping her fork on the floor, shifting her chair. It's hard to concentrate.

"What's with you?" I ask her, exasperated.

"I'm not figure skating this year," she announces.

Mom drops *her* fork. Dad raises both eyebrows.

Courtney's been in Grade Six less than two weeks, and she's already charting a new course. Because she's the only Grade Six girl interested in playing volleyball, her principal told her she could move up to the Grade Seven and Eight girls' team. Apparently the older girls have been awesome. Courtney's been hanging out with them on the playground and after school. She talks about them all the time. Meanwhile her classmates, the ones Mom nicknamed the Coven because they're all little witches, have laid off the teasing and bullying. Courtney's walking on Cloud Nine.

At least I'm pretty sure she is. Between *my* hockey and *her* volleyball, we're lucky if we see each other an hour a day.

"Then what are you going to do all winter?" Dad is asking her.

"I'm going to play hockey," Courtney says. "I'm grown up, and I can make my own decisions."

Whoa.

"Hockey?" Dad acts like he's never heard the word before.

Mom shakes her head repeatedly.

I wonder if she's experiencing déjà vu. I sure am. Three years ago. Same location. Only that time Mom told me I *had* to play hockey, and I told her I wouldn't. Lucky for me she won *that* round.

"What brought this on?" Mom's tone is prickly.

Courtney shrugs.

"It would help if you opened your mouth," I say to her.

She sticks her tongue out at me.

"Oh, not so grown up after all," I say.

"This is none of your business!" she retorts. "This is between Mom and Dad and me!"

"That makes sense." I pick up a forkful of potatoes. "I know nothing about hockey."

"Jessie, stop," Dad says quietly.

Mom's staring at the ceiling. I can see the dollar signs flipping, as she tallies the money spent on figure skating this past spring and summer while Courtney worked on her free skate, skills and dance.

"I just bought you new skates," Mom says vaguely. "They've only been sharpened once."

Courtney shrugs again.

"There's no peewee girls' team. You'll be playing with

girls two years older than you," I say. "What did Gia say when you told her you wanted to play?"

Gia's got talent. She tried out for the Oilers, but she got cut — I assume — because she's only in Grade Eight. She's on Courtney's volleyball team, and she's the girl Courtney talks about the most.

"She doesn't mind." Courtney gives me a sideways glance. "She wants you and Kathy to help her dad with practices. There'll be a few girls who've never played hockey before."

"You make it sound like you're not one of them," Dad observes.

No wonder he's cynical. He thought I was making the switch from ringette to hockey too late when I started playing in Grade Nine. But I proved him wrong.

"You also make it sound like you're *already* on the hockey team...which you're not," I point out.

Courtney ignores me. "Dad, I'm a good *skater*. I won't be like those other girls who've never worn hockey skates."

"You've never worn hockey skates," I point out.

She rolls her eyes at me.

"Jessie," Dad says again.

"Hockey skates aren't figure skates. The stride is way different. Then there's the equipment and the stick and the puck. And all those people who aren't afraid to run into you.

It won't be as easy as you make it sound."

Courtney stands up, knocking over her chair.

"Dramatic exit, coming right up," I say.

"Shut up!" she screams. "You're just afraid I'll be *better* than you! That *I'll* be the centre of attention for once!" She looks down her nose at me. "Mom and Dad think it's okay. Why can't you be happy for me?!"

I look at Dad. "Did I say I wasn't happy?"

Dad lays a hand firmly on mine and shakes his head. Poor man. Living in a household with three women, he's tossed like a cork in the maelstrom of our overlapping menstrual cycles.

"Courtney, we need to talk some more," Mom says.

"I'm sick of this bullshit!"

"Watch your language," Mom warns.

"I don't care!" Courtney wails. "You treat me like a slave, and I'm sick of it!"

"Slave?" I laugh out loud. "You won't even do the dishes on your night!"

"Jessie, please," Mom says.

Courtney bolts out of the kitchen and up the stairs. Her bedroom door slams like an exclamation point.

Dad picks up Courtney's chair and positions it under the table, then sits down and resumes carving his steak. "What in the hell was *that* about?"

"Puberty," Mom says.

"There's lots of time for Courtney to finish her dances," I say.

"She'll never go back to figure skating." Mom massages her temples with her fingertips. "She'll get the hockey bug – just like you did."

"She may not like it so much," Dad says. "In fact, a few practices might be enough to convince her she's not cut out for hockey." He pauses to chew and swallow a piece of steak. "That's why I'm not buying her any equipment. Not yet anyway." He looks at me significantly.

My appetite abruptly disappears. "So she's going to wear *mine?*"

"She's nearly as tall as you are," Dad replies. "Makes sense to me."

I pick up my plate and move over to the sink.

"Thanks, Jessie," Mom says. "You're a trooper."

I hate the way they interpret silence as agreement.

"She's not wearing my equipment," I say quietly.

"Not even once?" Mom wheedles.

"So now *you're* on board with this hockey thing?"

Mom rubs her neck muscles. "I don't want to be. But she's finally got some decent friends. Would it be so terrible?"

"She has Pam," I point out.

"Pam doesn't go to her school, Jessie. You know how miserable Courtney was last year. Isn't it great she's *happy?*"

I pause so we can all listen to Courtney stomp around in her bedroom. "Does that sound like happiness to you?"

"Come on, Jessie," Dad says. "Once upon a time, I let you borrow my hockey socks."

I turn on the garburator. "She better not wreck or lose any of it!" I shout.

When I shut it off, Mom says to Dad, "How much will it cost to outfit her for hockey – if she *does* end up liking it?"

"We'll pick up some used skates at JL's," Dad says.

"Sports are supposed to be cheaper than bail or lawyers." Mom sits back and folds her arms. "But sometimes I wonder if it's all worth it."

"Are you going up to tell her the good news?" Dad asks.

"Why don't you do it?" Mom replies.

"I'm not done eating," Dad says.

I pick up Courtney's plate and carry it to the dishwasher. I turn my back on both of them and fire a handful of forks and knives into the cutlery receptacle.

"Careful," Dad cautions.

Mom pushes back her chair. "No time like the present."

After she's gone, I put the stopper in the sink and turn on the hot water, thinking about how my shoulder and elbow pads are going to be wet and stinky every Tuesday, since Courtney's practices will precede mine.

The phone in my pocket vibrates, and I look at it.

Evan.

Call me, he says.

I tell myself I'm ignoring him because I promised Holly I'd talk to Mark, and that's exactly what I'm going to do. Tonight. I've been thinking about it all day. About what I'll say to him.

Apply now. Get into university in January. Take a full load of maths and sciences. Get ready for engineering.

Me = Mark's hero.

I leave Dad to finish his supper. He's pretty much hypnotized by his Crackberry anyway. I grab my phone and go upstairs. As I walk by Courtney's room, I can see Mom and my sister lying on her bed, shoulder to shoulder, deep in conversation.

Peace is restored in our happy home.

I go into my room and close the door. By the time Mark picks up on the other end, my palms are moist, and my stomach is twisting.

"Hey!" he says. "We were just talking about you."

"Who was?"

"Evan and me. He hung up a while ago. Said he was going to call you. So, what's up?" Mark's voice sounds friendly and natural.

"Not much. I just got home from the U of S fall camp."

"How'd it go?"

"My evaluation says I'm supposed to work on foot speed."

He laughs. "Figures. They all say that." He pauses and clears his throat. "Are you going to U of S next year?"

"I don't know. Do you think I should?"

"You could do a hell of a lot worse. For a Saskatchewan girl, there isn't anything better than CIS hockey – except the National program."

"So what university classes are you taking this fall?" I ask.

"Who told you I'm taking classes?" he responds, a note of suspicion in his voice.

"I don't know. Evan maybe."

"Did you see Holly in Saskatoon?"

Caught. Like a rat in a trap.

"Yes."

"She told you to call me, didn't she?"

"No."

"She told you to get on my case about quitting Major Junior and going to school full time." He pauses for so long I think he's put the phone down and walked away. "I have a once in a lifetime opportunity, Jessie. I'm not screwing it up. It means too much to my dad."

"Mark, you don't believe there's a connection between your hockey and your dad getting well, do you?"

"Is that what Holly told you?"

"I don't remember."

"Well, Holly's exaggerating, as usual. She figures she needs to be my mother *and* my girlfriend since Mom's out East. Every guy on my team has a demon on his back. My D-partner should have shoulder surgery, but he's putting it off. My captain lost his mom to breast cancer last year. Playing through pain and personal stuff comes with the territory, Jessie. Next time you talk to Holly, ask her about her ankle sprain. It doesn't seem to be holding *her* back."

When I hang up a minute later, I feel like a total dork. Kathy always says, "Before you jump in a hole, make sure you know how deep the shit is at the bottom."

I'm up to my ankles.

There's a knock at the door, and Courtney sticks her head in before I have a chance to answer.

"Thanks for letting me borrow your equipment," she says sweetly. "I'll make it up to you."

The phone rings downstairs.

I know who it is even before I hear Dad shout, "Jessie! It's Evan."

"I'll get the cordless for you," Courtney volunteers.

The last thing I want to do is talk to him, but I know I have to. It's been a week since we Skyped.

"Sure, Court," I tell her.

She bounces out of the room.

# chapter
## eleven

I hardly get any sleep the night before our first exhibition game against the Weyburn Gold Wings. After school I have a nap, then drive to the rink at five thirty.

We were hoping we'd get our own dressing room in the new arena, but no such luck.

Then again, I'd sooner have a full-time coach. So far Sue has run two out of four practices. Two Bruins ran the others, but Whitney was so busy flirting with them, we didn't get much accomplished.

Furthermore, Mr. Johnstone isn't holding up his end of the deal as team manager. We don't have uniforms, but he promises they'll be here for our first league game in October. Tonight we'll be decked out in our old Rafferty Rage unies.

Normally Kathy's cocky in the dressing room on Game Day, especially when we're playing Weyburn, but today she's quiet. Carla's *always* reserved, so the three of us don't talk much until the rest of the girls show up.

The Rookies are starting to fit in. The ones who go to the Comp sit with us at lunch, and that makes it easier to get to know them. The only player who doesn't hang out with us at lunch or say much in the dressing room is Jodi. She's so totally *un*like the Jodi I played with two years ago I sometimes forget she's there.

But I can't say that about her on the ice. Jodi's lost a little of her jump, but she sees the ice better than anyone else, and her hands are pure gold. As much as I hate the thought of her getting hurt again, we'd be screwed without her.

"Talk to Evan lately?" Kathy asks me.

"On the weekend."

"How's his season going?"

"Okay. There's no league games until mid-October."

"It sucks we don't have uniforms yet," Randi says.

Miranda walks in, carrying a doll wearing a blue sleeper. A receiving blanket hangs over her shoulder.

"What the hell," Kathy says.

"Everybody, meet Jake." Miranda holds up the doll so it's looking at all of us. "Jake, this is everybody."

"Are you kidding us, Ebberts?" Carla asks.

"It's part of my Psych 30 class," Miranda says. "I'm learning what it feels like to be a mom."

Jake starts crying, a pathetic whimpering noise.

"Shut it off," Kathy says. "Dolls are creepy."

"What about clowns?" Randi asks. "I hate going to the circus because of the clowns."

*"You're* a clown," Kathy says.

Jake keeps on whimpering. Miranda paces and jostles and pats him, but the robotic cries persist.

"Maybe he needs changing," Larissa suggests.

"I did that already," Miranda says. "And I fed him too. Nothing helps. He woke up at three this morning and started bawling. None of us got any sleep. And then I couldn't find a sitter, so I had to call Sue and tell her I couldn't warm the bench today."

"And you brought him down here so we could all be miserable with you," Kathy says.

"Thanks a lot, Ebberts," Carla says.

Miranda yawns loudly.

"Give 'im here." Amy beckons with one finger.

"But I'm supposed to be the one who settles him," says Miranda. "I'm getting graded on this."

Amy gestures again. "Hand him over. Nobody's gonna know."

Miranda does as she's told, but she's not happy. There's tension between her and Amy – although if you ask me, it's Miranda who's tense. Amy treats Miranda like she treats everyone else.

Amy places Jake on her knees and gently massages his back. He gives a loud mechanical burp, and the cries desist.

"Gas," Amy explains.

"Kid must be a hockey player," Kathy says. "And speaking of gas..."

"Don't." Carla raises a warning finger. "If you release any toxins, you're going to be very sorry."

"Correction." Kathy points back. *"You'll* be sorry."

"Can I have him now?" Miranda demands.

"Sure." Amy hands Jake over and goes back to lacing her goalie skates.

Miranda cuddles the doll as she crosses the dressing room and sits down next to Kathy. "Who's your momma now, Jake?" she coos.

"Jake must take after his daddy," Carla says, "because he doesn't quite have your colouring, Ebberts."

Miranda ignores her and starts singing "The Good Ol' Hockey Game" in her peculiar Minnesota drawl. She gets some of the words wrong, as she always does.

"Why don't you leave the singing to Jodi?" Carla asks.

"Shut up, Bisonhead," Miranda says.

Whitney throws open the door and makes an entrance. "Hey, girls! Want to know which Bruin I had last night?"

"Let me guess." Kathy taps her lower lip. *"All* of them?"

The remark doesn't fizz on Whitney, who launches a

detailed account of her date with the Bruins' seventh defenceman. I try not to listen. None of the other girls talk about sex in the dressing room, even though I know most of them are on birth control.

Jake farts, and we start howling.

Whitney's pissed that she never gets to finish her story. She gestures at the doll. "What *is* that?"

"It's a baby, Johnstone," Kathy says. "That's what *you'll* get if you keep screwing the Bruins."

"Jealous?" Whitney asks, fluttering those beautiful eye-lashes.

Fortunately Jodi walks in then, and we put on their game faces. Kathy manages not to stir anything else up before Sue arrives for our pregame pep talk.

Mr. Johnstone is one step behind her.

"I apologize to you ladies for making you play in these old uniforms," he says. "Your new ones will be here soon, I promise."

Jake starts crying, and Miranda does her best to quiet him.

Sue stares at the doll and wrinkles her nose.

"He comes equipped with smell *too?*" Kathy demands.

Miranda hustles him out, and Sue runs through the lines. She's got me paired up with Jennifer on D while Carla gets a Rookie. Jodi and Kathy are our centres, but Jodi will also drop back to quarterback our first power play unit.

Mr. Johnstone interrupts Sue to offer us some advice. He knows his hockey, but he sure doesn't know his place. The second time he does it, she asks him to go find a new marker for her whiteboard.

During the warm-up, I try to concentrate on the drills and not gawk at the Weyburn girls at the other end of the ice. They look big and fast and confident.

"Hey, you've got fans! Did you notice?" One of the Rookies taps me on the shoulder and points into the stands.

There're two guys up there, with signs. One of them says, "Hockey Girl, I'm having your baby."

"Who are those guys?" I ask.

The Rookie shrugs.

I take a closer look. The guy with the sign could be Liam MacArthur. I haven't talked to him since the talent show.

"Looks like somebody thinks *you're* cute," Kathy murmurs in my ear.

I skate away.

*O*pening faceoff.

I look at Number 19, lined up across from Kathy at centre ice. She doesn't look big enough to be last year's runner-up in the SFMAAAL scoring race. She wins the puck back to her left D and steps around Kathy like she's standing still, pounding her blade for a pass. She comes straight at me, and I try to poke check, but she puts the puck between my legs, glides past me, and blisters a shot off the crossbar.

I hurtle into the corner, arriving just ahead of Number 19. I turn myself to get body position and hold her off while I use my feet to inch the puck along the boards. Now there're two sticks gouging at my skates, and it's all I can do to stay on them. Somebody elbows me in the ear, and my head bangs the Plexiglas. The ref is yelling at us to play the puck. Kathy barrels in, using her ass to block the two Gold Wings, and fishes out the rubber. Before she can do anything with it, 19's got it back. She fires on her backhand, but Amy deflects it with her blocker. The juicy rebound falls on 19's blade and she stuffs it in.

While the Wings celebrate, there's nothing for us but the walk of shame back to the players' box.

My next shift starts on the fly with Jodi taking the puck deep into Weyburn's end. One of their D-men smacks the puck away from her and tries to chip it over the blue line. I arrive just in time to pinch along the boards, cycling to Larissa. She passes to Whitney, who stickhandles in a tight circle, looking for an opening, and then passes back to me. I slide the puck to Jennifer, and she fires it right back. My slap-shot hits the Weyburn left-winger square in the shin. While she goes down squealing, 19 picks up the puck and blasts down the ice on a breakaway, with me on her heels.

Not a chance of catching her.

Amy skates out to meet her, and 19 takes a wrist shot, glove side.

Right where Amy likes it.

She does the splits and snaps the puck out of the air.

I love this girl.

Line change.

Back at the bench, Sue draws me aside and shows me a play she's drawn up on her whiteboard. I get the feeling she thinks I forgot some basic defensive rules over the summer.

You are the weakest link, my little voice tells me.

A few minutes later Kathy takes a roughing penalty. We get trapped in our end for the whole PK. When Weyburn's biggest D-man lines up a slapshot, I block it with my belly.

Carla says blocking a shot gives her as much of a rush as scoring a goal. Frankly, I find shot-blocking to be mostly painful.

This time is no exception. Especially since I end up on top of the puck, with three different players trying to gouge it out with their sticks. Mercifully the ref blows down the play, and I skate back to the bench, holding my stomach.

Jennifer pounds my shoulder blades the whole way. "Way to take one for the team, Mac!"

The guys with the signs are going crazy in the stands. Liam's yelling, but I can't make out the words.

Sue gives me a pat on the head as I come off while Crystal's mom, our trainer, waves me over. I know I'm going to have some major bruises. Good thing I took out my belly button ring.

After the penalty, it takes a while for us to get some momentum. Then Jodi dekes the Gold Wing's goalie into oblivion and scores unassisted, popping the water bottle. It's her first goal in almost two years, and it's an amazing moment. Strangely, Jodi doesn't seem that excited as she skates by to receive our high-fives.

"I can't believe how good she is," the Rookie D says when I meet her on my way back out.

"Believe it," I say.

Then Whitney nearly runs into me. "That wasn't unassisted! I should have gotten a point!" she pouts.

Sue always says it takes all kinds of players to make a team. Why do some of them have to be such prima donnas?

**A**my stands on her head, and Jodi gets a hat trick. We beat Weyburn 3–1, even though the shots are 37–21 for the Wings. As we line up to shake hands, I can tell they're choked.

"Good game," I tell Number 19, who brings up the rear.

"We'll get you next time," she says. "Your refs are friggin' homers."

I watch her skate away. Liam leans over the glass and smacks our helmets as we exit the ice. Mr. Parker, who's been manning the booth, announces the three game stars: Jodi, Amy and me.

I am blown away.

"Don't let it go to your heads," Sue tells us in the dressing room. "You've got your work cut out in this league. Eat properly. Stretch. Hydrate. Work hard in practice."

"Will you be there this week?" I ask.

She shakes her head.

Great.

# chapter twelve

I dip my brush in the shiny orange acrylic paint and brush it on the wall, managing not to drip any on my coveralls. Painting the outside of the Sarcan Recycling building is part of a project for my senior art class. One of my classmates came up with the colourful design of crushed cans and geometric shapes.

I'm happy just to be applying paint, and not having to freehand the objects on the storefront.

"Would you mind staying until four thirty?" Mr. Tilson, our visual arts teacher, stares up at the sky, frowning. "There's rain in the forecast tonight. I'd like to finish this part today."

"I have hockey practice right after school." I hastily add, "I'm sorry."

He steps back and looks up at Kathy, who's standing on the scaffolding above me. "What about you, Kathy? Can you stay?"

When she gives him the same excuse, he stalks off, obviously frustrated.

I'm frustrated too. Sue won't be at practice again, which means Whitney will goof off to impress the Bruins, and the Rookies will follow suit. The Regina Rebels are hosting us in an exhibition game on Saturday, and I doubt we're ready for them.

"I don't know why Whitney's so confident we'll beat the Rebels," I say loudly. "She dicks around too much in practice."

Kathy's face suddenly appears, inverted, as she peers at me from the scaffolding overhead. Her long blonde hair is dangling below her face. "How're you getting to Regina?"

"I'm going up with the Gedaks after school tomorrow. Evan's game is at seven."

"Will Evan get to play much?"

"I don't know. He hasn't cracked the starting lineup yet."

"Your parents aren't going?"

"They're coming up Saturday morning."

"Where are you staying Friday night?"

"With the Gedaks — at the same hotel as the Dinos. I'm not sure which one."

The sound of a loud muffler makes us both start. An old pickup pulls in and lets out a loud, rattling cough as the engine dies. A guy in a baseball cap jumps out and climbs onto the rear bumper, leaning way over to grab some garbage bags.

"Nothing says 'hug my buns' like a pair of Wranglers," Kathy observes.

"Parker!"

"Come on, Mac. Get a load of that caboose."

I let my eyes wander in his direction. Not bad, at all.

Kathy pulls off her paint gloves, puts her forefingers in her mouth, and wolf whistles. The guy straightens and looks over his shoulder at us.

It's Liam MacArthur. My nemesis.

I turn my back and start painting.

"Your caboose isn't half-bad either," he says as he walks past. I hear the automatic door swish open and shut behind him.

Kathy throws herself down on the scaffolding above me, beating it with her palms and soles, laughing hysterically. Finally she leans over to look at me.

"So whose caboose did he mean? Yours or mine?" she asks, breathless.

"Since I'm wearing coveralls, and you're not, my guess is *you*," I tell her.

We resume painting, but I keep listening for the sound of the door. A while later it swishes, and a voice behind me asks, "Trying to get on full time?"

I turn and open my mouth to say something smart-assed. Then the meaning of his question registers.

You see, Sarcan employs individuals with mental challenges.

"It's rude to make fun of the people who work here," I say.

His gap-toothed grin vanishes. "That's not what I meant."

I turn my back and resume painting.

"Tell her she's got the wrong idea." From the increased volume of his voice, I gather he's directing this comment at Kathy. "I don't go around insulting hockey girls or people with mental handicaps."

"Challenges!" I call over my shoulder.

"You girls played great the other night," he says. "Especially you, Jessie."

I keep painting.

"I better get going," he says. "See you, hockey girls."

I hear the sound of boots on gravel. A truck door creaks open, slams shut, the truck coughs again as it ignites, and the loud muffler gradually disappears in the distance.

"I don't think he meant to insult you." Kathy climbs down from the scaffolding and joins me at ground level. She picks up some mineral spirits and begins cleaning her brush with a rag.

My pocket beeps. I wipe the paint off my fingers and pull out my phone. It's a text from Mom, asking me to pick up Courtney and drive her to volleyball.

"Is it from Evan?" Kathy asks.

"No, my mom."

"When's the last time you talked to him?" Kathy asks.

"I told you I'm seeing him this weekend," I respond, irritated.

"Look, Jessie, if you're having second thoughts about going out with him, you should tell him right away. Don't keep stringing him along."

"I'm *not* having second thoughts, and I am *not* stringing him along." I drop my phone in my pocket. "I have to go."

I wait twenty minutes for Courtney to come out of the school. At this rate, I'm going to have a tough time being on the ice at five. Not that the Bruins will care.

When Courtney finally appears, she's got Gia with her. They're breathless with laughter. Too bad I'm immune to their good mood.

"Can you give Gia a ride too?" Courtney asks, opening the passenger door and flipping the seat forward.

"Why not?"

Before I know it, both of them are in the back. Gia's got her auburn dyed hair pulled up into two perky ponytails that stand straight up in the rearview mirror. Even though she's two years older than Courtney, she's a full head shorter.

On the way over to Spruce Ridge, I try to focus on my driving and forget about the fact that in a few weeks, I'll be chauffeuring Courtney, Gia and *my* hockey equipment to bantam girls' practice.

"Hey, Jess, can I borrow your Bruin jersey to wear to the game tonight?" Courtney asks as we pull into the Spruce Ridge parking lot.

"Sure. Who're they playing?"

"Yorkton," Gia supplies. "Are you going to the game, Jessie?"

"Yeah," Courtney says. "We need a ride."

"Did Mom say you could go out on a school night?" I look at my sister in the rearview mirror.

Courtney squints back at me. "None of your business."

"Putting on a show for Gia, are we?" I ask.

That shuts her down.

As I pull up to the main entrance, they gather their stuff and climb out, never saying thank you or goodbye.

I guess I know what I am to Courtney now.

A driver's licence.

# chapter thirteen

A t lunch on Friday, the Oilers are pumped about playing the Regina Rebels.

"Have you seen the rink they play in, girl-friends?" Miranda pauses for emphasis. "So cool."

"Quit livin' in the past," Kathy says. "Nobody calls *anybody* 'girlfriend' anymore."

Miranda sticks out her bottom lip.

"It *is* cool," I say, changing the subject back to the Rebels' home rink. "I can't wait."

The Co-operators Centre at Evraz Place is an impressive facility with multiple ice surfaces. Both University of Regina hockey teams play there, as well as the Rebels.

"It's going to be fun beating them in their own rink," Whitney says.

"What makes you so sure we're going to beat them?" Larissa asks.

"Look how well we played against Weyburn," Whitney says.

"Look how well *Jodi* and *Amy* played against Weyburn," I say.

"You played good too, Jessie," one of the Rookies says.

"Is this table Hockey Girls Only?" a voice behind me asks.

"Hi, Liam," Amy says. She grabs a chair from another table and pulls it over.

Liam sets down his cafeteria tray with one hand and slides into the seat next to me. I make a point of not looking at him.

"You girls nervous about the big game tomorrow?" he asks.

"Not a bit," Whitney says confidently. "We're aiming to improve our record to 2–0 in the preseason. It'll be a good warm-up for our double-header against Swift Current the weekend after."

"What happened to your arm?" Larissa asks, pointing.

I look over at Liam. The collared shirt he's wearing over a T-shirt hangs loosely from his right shoulder. Underneath, his arm is bound by a tensor to his ribs.

"No more football for you," Amy says.

Liam shrugs, then winces. "It's just a sprain."

"You play football?" I ask.

Everyone stares at me.

"Liam scored the Elecs' only touchdown last year," Kathy says. "Did you never go to a game?"

I shake my head.

"Will this mess up your plans for Agribition?" Amy

asks Liam.

"I hope not," he says.

"How do you two know each other?" I ask Amy.

"Liam's done some team roping with my brother Tim," Amy explains. "We go way back, don't we, MacArthur?"

"We're just one big rodeo family." Liam picks up his knife and fork and in his left hand and holds them out to me. "Would you mind cutting my meat?" He points to the chicken breast on his plate.

"I *would* mind," I say.

"McIntyre, are you kicking a man when he's down?" Kathy asks.

"Won't be the first time," Miranda observes.

Kathy and Miranda high-five.

Liam looks confused. "Am I missing something?"

"Never mind. It's a long story." I stand up and pick up my own tray. "Somebody else can help you. I have to study."

"Why're you so angry all the time?" His dark eyes are perplexed.

Kathy's right. He *is* cute.

"I'm not angry," I reply. "I'm just too busy for this."

I don't say goodbye to Liam or the girls. I just jam my tray onto the cafeteria cart and walk away.

**W**hen I get home after school, Courtney greets me in the back entrance, a grin splitting her face.

"Mom said I can go with you to Regina," she informs me, "and Gia's coming too!"

"Really, and where do you plan to sleep?"

"At Gia's auntie's," she says.

"It's short notice, Courtney."

She opens the floodgates. "I hardly ever get to go to Regina! I have volleyball next weekend, and it's Thanksgiving after that, and then hockey will start!"

"This isn't my call," I tell her. "I don't know if the Gedaks have room for both of you."

"Mom already talked to Evan's mom," Courtney says, calmer. "It's all arranged."

Mrs. Gedak and my mom work at the same law firm. Mrs. Gedak's got a soft spot for Courtney because she helped out with babysitting Breanne last summer.

I check my watch. 3:45. I start stripping off my coveralls.

"Are you packed?"

Courtney points impatiently at the duffle bag sitting on the kitchen table. "Gia's coming over right away, so we'll be ready when Breanne's mom and dad get here. Go get changed!"

I shower, but I don't have a chance to dry my hair because the Gedaks drive up just as I'm yanking on my jeans and the

Dino T-shirt Evan gave me. I can't find my Sketchers at the back door and have to settle for my old Nikes. I'm halfway down my driveway before I realize I forgot to put on the emerald earrings.

No time for that now.

When I open the rear passenger door of the Gedaks' van, the first person I see is Breanne. Rev. Gedak is driving, and Mrs. Gedak is shotgun. Gia and Courtney are in the very back, though I can hardly see either of them for all the stuff packed around them.

"How are you, Jessie?" Rev. Gedak asks. He's a big man with a dark beard, moustache, and sideburns. Today he's wearing a red U of C Dino hoodie.

"Great, thanks." I set my bag and purse on top of the cardboard box crammed between the seats and hop in.

"Hi, Jessie," Breanne says.

Mrs. Gedak reaches around and pats my knee. "Hope we didn't rush you too much," she says. "We thought we'd grab something to eat in Weyburn."

"Fine by me."

Then I look down and see one of my Sketchers propped on top of my bag. I shift in my seat so I can see the other one. I turn right around and see Courtney's wearing one of my shirts too.

"Nice outfit," I say.

She smiles. She knows I won't get into an argument in front of Evan's parents.

"Thanks for letting us come, Mr. and Mrs. Gedak," Gia says. "We appreciate it."

"The more, the merrier," Rev. Gedak says.

*R*ev. and Mrs. Gedak talk basketball and religion all the way to Regina. The two subjects are so intertwined I'm not sure where one ends and the other starts. Breanne reads to me from an assortment of school and library books in her backpack. She's a good reader, considering she just started Grade Two. Behind me, Courtney and Gia listen to each other's iPods and play on Gia's iPhone. The kid has everything.

"So where does your auntie live?" I ask Gia while Breanne's digging in her Taylor Swift backpack.

"Not far from the university," Gia replies. "She's going to pick us up at 8:30. Is that okay?"

"Sure. Got any plans for tonight?"

"Just watching movies and hanging out."

"And that's why you're wearing my shirt?" I ask Courtney.

My view of her is suddenly blocked by *The Berenstain Bears Visit the Dentist.* "I'm ready!" Breanne says.

We stop at Dairy Queen in Weyburn to grab some takeout. When it comes times to pay, Gia reaches in her purse and comes out with a hundred dollar bill.

Meanwhile I have to pay for Courtney's supper.

"Mom said you're supposed to give me money," Courtney says. "She'll pay you back tomorrow."

I stare at her, and she boldly returns my gaze.

"You'll have to wait until I find an ATM," I say.

While we're waiting for the Gedaks to get their order, Courtney and Gia disappear into the bathroom. When Courtney comes out, her eyes are made up with black liner, just like Gia's.

"You look ridiculous," I hiss. "Go wash that off."

Courtney tosses her head.

As I follow her to the van, I wonder if this is an improvement: Courtney moving from the Coven to Gia.

My gut says...

Not likely.

# chapter
## fourteen

**T**he Regina Cougars men's basketball team play their home games at the complex attached to the Education building on campus. We don't arrive in time to see much of the warm-up, but there's a huge crowd wearing Cougar green and gold that does. For a while it looks like we could be the only people cheering for Calgary, but Rev. Gedak manages to sniff out some other Dino parents. He introduces me to Mr. and Mrs. Blah-Blah-Blah, whose son is Blah-Blah Blah-Blah-Blah.

When we go into the gym, Breanne and I sit to the left of her parents while Courtney and Gia sit in front of me.

I look for Evan on the court and he's there, focused on executing the drills. He's put on some muscle since I saw him last. Before he goes to the bench, he looks up at the crowd, as if he's trying to find us.

"Wave at him, Jessie!" Mrs. Gedak urges me.

I stand up and flail my arms.

"Call out to him!"

"The music's too loud." I sit down again. "He'd never hear me anyway."

"I hope he gets lots of court time," Rev. Gedak says. "He did at the Lethbridge tournament. Too bad you couldn't come."

"It was the weekend after the U of S fall camp. I didn't want to miss another day of school so early in the year, not with all the classes I'm going to miss because of hockey."

You wouldn't have cared if Mark had invited you to watch *him* play, my little voice says. You're only going out with Evan because he's safe. He's too religious to push the physical stuff.

I make Evan happy.

My little voice chirps in my ear, you don't call Evan. And sometimes you ignore his texts.

I'm very busy with school and hockey. I never dreamed we'd have to practice so much in AAA.

The voice whispers, you're going to have to kiss him later.

Of course I will. And I'll let him hold my hand and put his arm around me. If I spend enough time with him, eventually I'm going to start to feel about him the way I used to feel about Mark.

*Used* to feel?

"Basketball is a lot like hockey, isn't it?" Mrs. Gedak observes. "Minus the skates and the goaltender."

"Evan wants to be like Steve Nash," Breanne says. "He watches Steve Nash all the time." She yawns. "I hate Steve Nash."

"Steve Nash is the best point guard in the NBA," says Mrs. Gedak.

"Breanne, do you know what a quarterback does in football?" Rev. Gedak asks his daughter.

Breanne nods her head uncertainly.

"Well, a point guard is like a quarterback. It's his job to know the game plan and execute it. He needs to be able to speed up or slow down the game and set up plays. He needs to have great ball-handling skills, especially in heavy traffic."

While he's telling her this, I think about how closely this relates to defence in hockey. I want to be exactly like a point guard. I want to be the smartest and most skilled player on the ice. I want to quarterback the power play, like Jodi does. I want to play shutdown defence and bust-their-balls offence.

While the Gedaks continue to educate Breanne about basketball, some university guys sit next to me. At least I assume they're in university because they've got their faces painted and they're carrying noisemakers. One of them asks if he can look at my program, and we strike up a conversation. It turns out one of the Cougars is from his hometown, and Indian Head Guy is there to cheer him on.

Courtney stands up and asks if she can borrow some money for licorice. I give her a twenty.

"When are you going to get me some money?" she asks.

"I just gave you some," I reply.

Courtney and Gia leave.

A loud buzzer sounds, and the teams go to the sidelines, towel off, and get ready. While his coach issues last minute instructions, Evan stands near the bench, facing the court, so I gather he isn't starting. The Cougar fans start cheering, and the guys sitting next to me fire up their noisemakers.

Since Evan isn't on the court, and since Indian Head Guy is playing "Twenty Questions," I don't pay much attention to the game once it's underway. I do notice that the Cougars jump out in front early in the first quarter, and the Dinos struggle to find their stride.

Breanne yawns repeatedly and moves to her dad's lap, which apparently is more comfortable than mine.

Once Indian Head Guy learns I play hockey, he starts asking about my team. The basketball game is well into the second quarter before I notice Courtney and Gia aren't back from their licorice expedition.

As I reach for my phone to text Gia, I remember I don't have her number. Courtney doesn't have a phone, so I have no choice but to go look for them. I excuse myself and head for the concession, but I don't see them.

I comb the building. No sign of them anywhere.

On a hunch, I check outside.

They're shivering in their hoodies, talking to two guys who are clearly high school age and who are also smoking. As I approach, Gia appears to be doing most of the talking when she's not sucking on a cancer stick of her own.

I barge right into the midst of them. "Hey, I've been looking all over for you guys! I see you got the licorice!" I grab the bag with one hand and Courtney's elbow with the other. "You're missing a great game. Let's go back inside."

Gia checks her phone and takes a drag of her cigarette. "My auntie's going to be here right away. There's no point."

"Okay." I take a bite of licorice. "I'll just hang out until she gets here."

Gia is pissed, but she doesn't say anything while I quiz the guys about their high school basketball team.

Eventually they go back inside.

I hold out my hand. "Gia, give me your cell number. That way I can text you if I need to get hold of Courtney."

"Sure." Gia's eyes measure me. "Give me your phone, and I'll program it in."

I hand it to her. "Need me to hold your cigarette?"

She gives me her smoke, and I drop it on the cement and crush it under my heel.

"Hey!" she exclaims.

"I don't appreciate you smoking around my little sister," I tell her.

Courtney smacks my arm. "Jessie! Quit trying to be Mom!"

"Were you planning to leave without saying goodbye?" I ask. "The Gedaks were thoughtful enough to let you come along, and *this* is how you repay them?"

"I thanked them on the way up," Gia says defensively. "Didn't you *hear* me thank them?"

We stand there and bicker with each other until Gia's auntie finally gets there. By the time I get back to the gym, there's only two minutes left in the fourth quarter. When I look down at the court, Evan is lined up at the free throw line, readying himself for a foul shot.

I'm going to kill Gia and Courtney.

# *chapter*
## *fifteen*

I stand still long enough to watch Evan score two points. I check the clock.

85–79 for the Cougars.

I apologize like crazy to Mrs. Gedak as I slide into my seat. No sign of Indian Head Guy and his friends. Rev. Gedak is so engrossed he doesn't seem aware of Breanne, who's fast asleep in his arms.

Evan's bringing the ball up the court, dribbling with his left hand and directing his teammates with the other.

"When did Evan sub in?" I ask his mom.

"A long time ago," she says pointedly. "Where have *you* been?"

"I'll tell you later."

Evan sinks a three-pointer, and his parents go crazy. Rev. Gedak shifts Breanne to his shoulder, and she doesn't even wake up.

The Dinos are in the midst of mounting a last minute

rally, when my cellphone begins vibrating again.

It's a text from Gia.

The noise around me is growing in volume and intensity as the Cougar fans rally their team to hold off a Dino come-from-behind victory.

Sorry, Gia says.

I look up just in time to see Evan's teammates mobbing him. The Gedaks and the other Calgary parents are on their feet, cheering. Breanne is slumped over her dad's shoulder like a sack of potatoes.

"What happened?" I ask.

"Evan just sank another three-pointer!" Mrs. Gedak shouts. "Didn't you see?"

The buzzer sounds to end the game. I take a quick look at the scoreboard again.

The Dinos lost by one point.

And Evan — with 22 points — is named Game MVP.

It's mortifying I wasn't at least a spectator.

His parents are bursting with pride as we wait for him to come out of the dressing room.

"That boy is going to be a CIS All-Star," a Dino dad tells me. "Too bad the coach is a train wreck."

"Are you serious?" I ask. "What's wrong with him?"

He doesn't have a chance to tell me because Evan arrives at that moment. He's wearing a bad-fitting suit and a tie that appears to be choking him.

He smiles when he sees me and hugs me hard. His mom has to tap him on the shoulder to get his attention. Evan turns around and hugs her too and shakes hands with his dad. Breanne's standing there, rubbing her eyes and looking like she has no idea where she is. Evan reaches down and picks her up, and she snuggles her head against his neck.

Mrs. Gedak says, "Good game," and a dark cloud rolls over Evan's face. I hope it's not because of me.

"Your little sister and her friend found their ride?" Rev. Gedak asks me as we leave the complex. He's got Breanne bundled in his jacket to protect her from the raw northwest wind.

"Yes." I extract my hand from Evan's grasp to pull my hood up. "That's why I was gone so long in the second half. I was just making sure Court and Gia got picked up." I sneak a quick look at Evan's face. "Sorry I didn't see more of your game. I'll make it up to you."

He leans over and murmurs in my ear. "You sure can."

The remark takes me off guard.

He laughs and grabs my hand again. "I'm kidding! I have an eleven o'clock curfew. We'll have just enough time to eat."

We have supper at a nearby restaurant. Evan and his parents spend most of it picking apart and replaying every second of the game. My eyelids get droopy, and I fight to stay awake. I envy Breanne, who falls asleep with her head on the table, still clutching a quarter of her grilled cheese sandwich.

I hold hands with Evan in the back seat all the way to the hotel, even though he's got his little sister sprawled across him. Once we're there his parents take Breanne upstairs to our room. Evan and I sit down on the comfy couches in the hotel lobby, so we can talk. It's 10:45, so we only have a few minutes.

"I'm sorry about tonight," I tell him.

He leans towards me. "It doesn't matter. I'm just so glad to see you — for real."

A couple of his teammates sweep in through the automatic doors. "Hey Preacher, get a room!" one of them shouts.

Evan blushes, but he looks pleased. He introduces me to them, and they hang around to make small talk. Before we know it, it's curfew. He walks me to the room and kisses me gently before heading off to his own. As I watch him lumber away, I feel inexplicably sad.

I *will* make it up to him tomorrow, I think.

I really am going to kill Gia and Courtney.

# chapter sixteen

**E**van meets us downstairs for continental breakfast, but since his mom and dad and Breanne are there the whole time, we don't get to talk much. He manages to squeeze in a few questions about my hockey team.

At 9:45, Evan looks at his phone. "I have a team meeting in fifteen minutes. I should get changed." He stands up. "Want to walk me to my room, Jessie?"

"Sure."

Breanne stands up too.

"Not this time, Squirt," Evan says.

Breanne sinks, crestfallen.

We take the stairs, instead of the elevator. At the second floor landing, he holds out an arm to stop me, checks above and below, then pulls me into his arms and kisses me.

I try to concentrate on him and forget about details like – is there bran muffin caught in my teeth and what does yogurt taste like on his end?

A door above us opens, and three of Evan's teammates come barreling down the stairs. I start to pull away, but Evan won't let me go, so they catch us red-handed.

"Hey, Preacher, didn't we tell you to get a *room?*"

"Got any friends in town, Flatlander?"

"We'll tell Coach you're gonna be late!"

Fortunately they keep moving, and we're alone again.

"I don't want you to get in trouble with your coach," I tell Evan.

"I don't want to talk about him. That guy's got too many issues. I want to talk about us." He pulls me closer. "Do you miss me?"

"Of course I miss you." The intensity of his gaze is making me uncomfortable.

"Jessie, I think about you all the time. You're the only thing in my life that makes sense. I don't call you as often as I'd like to, but it doesn't mean I don't care about you, okay?"

"Okay." He calls and texts me all the time. How could I get the impression he doesn't care about me? "How are your classes going?"

"What am I doing, killing myself to get good grades, when the person I care about most is back home."

An alarm starts ringing inside my head. This guy is way too serious, Jessie. You're not anywhere near as serious as he is.

I have no idea what to say. All I know is that he better not

**115**

be late for his team meeting. Not if he's already having a personality conflict with his coach.

"Evan, you should go. We'll talk later."

"When?" He still hasn't let go of me.

"After my game. I'll get my parents to bring me back to the hotel. We'll go for supper, and we'll talk then."

"Okay." He rests his chin on top of my head. "You smell so good."

After he leaves for his meeting, I go shopping with Mrs. Gedak and Breanne because I don't have to be at the rink until two o'clock. Breanne natters away to me, excited to have me all to herself, but all I can think about is Evan. He's put himself under so much pressure to excel at everything, at school and at basketball, and his parents seem to be oblivious to it. What happens if he *snaps?*

He's too sensible, I tell myself. That's not going to happen.

Part of me is also worried about Courtney and the direction her life seems to be taking. I text Gia a couple of times, but she doesn't answer.

Just before two o'clock, the Gedaks drop me off at the Co-operators Centre. I'm not sure where the dressing rooms are, but as I walk through the main entrance, I see Kathy's dad standing near Tim Horton's.

"Right in there, Jessie," Mr. Parker says, pointing.

"Have a great game," Amy's dad says. "And don't be afraid

to jump into the play. Take some chances."

"I'll try," I tell him.

Most of the girls are already in the dressing room. I sit down next to Jodi, who's by herself, as usual.

"How was Evan's basketball game?" Jodi asks.

I tell her about it, sticking to the details of the game. I don't feel like talking about Courtney and Gia.

"Sue's not coming today," Whitney announces.

"She told us that last practice," says Kathy. "Do you think we're deaf?"

"I just wanted to make sure everybody knew. Is that a crime?" Whitney snaps.

"So who's behind the bench – besides Mr. Johnstone?" I ask.

"Mr. Parker," Kathy says. "But I'll just call him Dad, if that's all right."

"And I'll call him Loverboy," Carla says.

Kathy wings a roll of sock tape at her head, but Carla ducks and laughs.

"So, Jessie, what's the deal between you and Liam?" Amy asks, pulling her Under Armor over her head. "You were plain nasty to him at lunch yesterday."

"Do ya think?" Kathy asks.

"I wasn't nasty," I tell her. "I was in a hurry."

All the girls are looking at me now.

"He was rude to me first." I sound like I'm whining.

"The other day, at Sarcan, he implied I'm mentally handicapped."

"Liam wouldn't do that," Amy says.

"How would you know? You weren't there." I turn to Kathy. "He was rude to me, wasn't he?"

Kathy flings one of her shoes into her hockey bag. "No, he wasn't. He was just trying to make conversation, and you twisted his meaning. You've been mad at him ever since the talent show."

I open my mouth to argue with her.

She's right and you know it, my little voice says. Dead right.

"You think every guy in this school is a loser because some of them said sick things to you," Kathy continues. "Well, Liam's not one of them."

"Liam would never make a crack about you being mentally handicapped," Amy says. "His brother Russell works at Sarcan. He lives in a group home."

Oh damn.

"His brother is...?"

"Yes," Amy says.

"I'll be nicer to him from now on," I promise. "I didn't realize...I never thought I was being like that."

I go for a run in the stands for my off-ice warm-up. A little oxygen goes a long way to clear my head. The main arena is brightly lit, and the metallic bleachers clang and clunk as I do the stairs. Hockey is where you need to be right now, I keep telling myself.

Afterwards, I quickly suit up, avoiding eye contact or conversation. I'm good now, I tell myself. I'm going to have a great game. I head into the hallway to make my way to the ice surface. But when I stop to put my extra stick in the rack by the door, Kathy's right behind me.

"Somebody might get the idea you're afraid of Liam," she says. "Maybe you like him more than you want to admit. Maybe you think it was a mistake to start going out with Evan."

"*Like* Liam?" I scoff. "I hardly know him! And believe me, this has nothing to do with Evan. It has to do with all the loser guys at school."

"I don't buy it." Her blue eyes are measuring me. "You better look yourself long and hard in the mirror and ask yourself why you hooked up with Evan in the first place. The guy lives in another province, conveniently out of the picture, and in reality, you don't think about him much, do you?"

"You're wrong," I tell her.

"Well, you're stupid," Kathy says.

"I don't care what you think," I whisper.

A door closes down the hall. The other girls are coming.

Kathy leans closer. "You're stupid and you're dangerous." She disappears through the door to the players' box, so I don't have a chance to defend myself.

I'm in a blind rage when I step on the ice, and I can't concentrate on any of the drills. How could she say that? She's supposed to be my friend.

On-ice warm-up is a total blur.

But one thing is abundantly clear.

I'm going to play like shit.

# chapter
## seventeen

**W**e crash and burn against Regina on the road to a 9–1 loss.

I take two penalties in the first period, and the Rebels score on both power plays. I'm on the ice for the next three Regina goals. On the first one, I get undressed by Number 22, who snipes one past Miranda's outstretched glove. Another time I attempt a saucer pass to Jennifer in our end, and the Rebel centre picks it, then fires low blocker. A Regina winger pounces on Miranda's juicy rebound and pokes it in. On my next shift, I put the puck in all by myself when I'm trying to clear the trash around the net.

Miranda snaps at me when I apologize. "McIntyre, keep your *ass* outta my face!"

I'd bench *myself* if I had any choice in the matter.

It's a brutal game. The worst.

We are outplayed, outshot and outscored.

With three minutes left, Jodi scores on a breakaway, but it's not enough to lift our spirits.

After the game we start picking at each other as soon as Mr. Johnstone and Mr. Parker leave the dressing room. The offence blames the defence. The defence blames the offence. No one blames Miranda, but this notion is etched on everybody's face: if Amy had been playing net, the score would have been a lot closer.

Ugly. Ugly. Ugly.

I do the only thing I can do.

"Look," I say, "I know I could have played better today. I'm sorry for letting you all down."

Most of the girls jump on the "Oh, it's okay. We're all at fault" bandwagon right away.

Except for Whitney, Jodi and Kathy.

On the way back to Estevan, Mom and Dad thankfully do not grill me about the game. Courtney's puffy around the eyes while Gia's sunglasses conceal hers. Gia falls asleep with her head on my shoulder.

"So Evan got to play lots?" Courtney asks out of the blue.

"Quit sucking up," I tell her. "You girls have a late night?"

"We stayed up and talked," Courtney says.

"Get any shopping done?"

Courtney shakes her head. "We were too tired."

"I thought that was the whole point of going to Regina

in the first place," I persist.

Courtney leans around Gia so she's looking right at me. "Mom already talked to Gia and me about taking off on you last night, and we're sorry, okay? Enough with the inquisition."

"Such a big word," I reply sarcastically. "How about this one? Do you know what *manipulation* means?"

"Yes," she says.

"You manipulated me *and* the Gedaks so you could go to Regina, and then you tried to dump us without any explanation. I missed watching Evan play because of you."

"Give it a rest, Jessie," Mom says. "We'll talk about it when we get home."

"Yeah, Jessie." Courtney yawns and curls up against the window.

I put on my iPod, pull my hoodie over my head, and pretend I've fallen asleep too.

But I'm definitely not.

Sleeping, that is.

My head is swarming with images of my bad choices on – and off – the ice. I'm still not talking to Kathy.

Not after what she said to me about Liam and Evan.

Evan.

My stomach drops to my shoes.

I was supposed to go for supper with him tonight, after my game. I was supposed to get a ride home with his parents.

I dig in my purse for my phone and discover it's shut off. It's been shut off for hours.

As soon as I turn it on, the text messages pour in.

Where r u?

See u later?

Call me.

Please call.

I'm such a loser. How could I forget about him?

I want to call him, here and now, but everyone will overhear, and Mom will ask a thousand questions. I send him a quick text, telling him I'll call later and explain everything. Even as I'm texting, I'm wondering, how can I *possibly* explain?

Maybe Kathy's right, my little voice says. Maybe it was a mistake to start going out with Evan.

Shut up.

After we drop Gia off at her mom's, Mom and Dad take Courtney into the living room for a "chat" while I go up to my room to touch base with Evan.

I thought he'd be angry, but he's totally understanding, which makes me feel even worse.

"You don't have to apologize," he says. "Sometimes things don't work out the way you'd like."

He doesn't sound upset at all — a total change from his mood this morning. I quiz him about *his* game, trying to get a read on his relationship with his coach, but he ignores the questions, directing the conversation back to me.

And I let him. I need to talk to somebody who's *not* on my team.

. I pour out my heart, telling him about everything that's lousy on our team until I hear Courtney moving around in her room.

No fireworks. No tantrum. Amazing.

"I've got to go," I tell Evan. "I'll talk to you later this week."

"See you soon," he says.

When I go next door, Courtney's lying on her bed, listening to her iPod and flipping through a magazine.

"So what's the scoop?" I ask her.

She stares at me.

"You grounded or what?"

She yanks one ear bud out. "For a week. No going out for two weekends." She pauses for effect. "I'm sick of you trying to be the mom. You're not, okay?" She flips a magazine page, tearing it. "This is my room, and I don't want you in here. Leave me alone."

As I leave, I feel somewhat vindicated, even though I'd still like to throttle her.

Maybe Mom and Dad aren't losing their minds.

**W**hich is why my mind is blown when Mom comes home the following week with a brand new cellphone for Courtney. I find out about it after supper when Mom takes it out to show Dad.

Courtney's upstairs in her room, supposedly doing homework.

And I am stupefied.

"You're going to give her a cellphone." I start stacking the dinner plates, and I'm not gentle about it.

Mom takes the phone out of the box and powers it up. "It won't actually be hers. We're just giving it to her so we'll know where she is."

"You're kidding."

Dad empties the remains in the salad bowl onto his plate. "You don't think it's fair that she's getting one right now when you had to wait so long."

"Don't get me started," I tell him.

"Things are different now, Jessie," Mom says. "We could have rough seas ahead with Courtney, and we have to hold her accountable for her actions."

"How are you going to manage that — when you don't even make her do her chores?" I demand. "It's her night to do dishes!"

"She had too much homework," Mom says. "She can do dishes for the next two nights."

I scrape the leftover mashed potatoes into a plastic container and snap on the lid. "She needs an ankle bracelet, not a phone."

"I'm sorry you feel that way, but you're not the parent. Your mother and I discussed it for a long time," Dad explains. "It wasn't a hasty decision."

Mom tries to appease me. "We'll know where she is. We won't have to rely on one of her friend's cellphones."

I correct her. "You'll know where she *says* she is! She and her phone could be *anywhere!*"

"Thanks for your input," Dad says. "The subject is now closed."

And that's that.

They *are* losing their minds.

# chapter eighteen

I survey the girls assembled in the dressing room on Tuesday night. There're six of us in our final year of Midget – Carla, Kathy, Miranda, Jodi, Amy and me. For second years, there's Jennifer, Crystal, Larissa and Whitney. The first years are Randi and the rest of the Rookies.

We're in our street clothes because there's no practice, just an organizational meeting for our parents upstairs, followed by one-on-twos with our coaches.

We're all nervous and excited; a head coach has finally been found. And not a minute too soon. Our first league games are this weekend.

One of the other key items on the agenda is choosing a team captain and three assistant captains. Sue says we're voting on it later.

Whitney is clearly campaigning. "Rookie party this weekend at my place," she announces, "but don't worry. We won't go rough on you Rooks."

The Rookies exchange apprehensive glances.

"This weekend?" I ask. "We're playing a double-header, remember?"

Whitney rolls her eyes. "So?"

"Just when were you planning to have this party?" Kathy's tone perfectly mimics mine.

"Saturday night."

"But we play Sunday," I say.

"Not until two in the afternoon," Whitney says. "You can all sleep over at my place. We've got plenty of room. It'll be a blast."

"It's lousy timing," I say. "We should have the party another time."

"But next weekend is Thanksgiving, and then we go to North Battleford and Prince Albert. It'll be November before we know it. How are we supposed to bond as a team?"

"Good point," Kathy says.

"Okay," I say, "but no booze. And no Bruins."

Annoyance flickers across Whitney's face, but she doesn't argue.

I feel Kathy's eyes on me. She's tried to be nice to me at school, but I'm still mad at her. Let her pay for shooting her mouth off one too many times.

The door opens. Sue and Mrs. Jordan, Crystal's mom, walk in.

"Evening, ladies," Sue says, sitting on the bench between Carla and me.

Mrs. Jordan closes the door and stands next to it.

"How'd the meeting go?" Kathy asks.

"Great." Sue almost smiles. "Estevan Minor Hockey approved the most recent applicant for the head coaching position and hired him on the spot. He'll be down in a few minutes."

*"He?"* Carla pounces on the pronoun.

"Who is it?" Whitney demands.

"Be patient," Sue says. "I'm sure you'll be happy with the choice. He has lots of coaching experience."

There's a light knock on the door, and Mrs. Jordan opens it.

Bud Prentice walks in.

"Hey, Bud!" Kathy shouts. "What brings you to town?"

Bud smiles broadly. "You'll never believe it, Parker. I heard you girls were looking for a head coach, and I decided to apply."

My heart sinks. "But it's too late, Bud. Minor Hockey already hired somebody."

"I know," Bud says patiently. "They hired *me.*"

"Bud – are you crazy?" I ask him. "You live in Regina!"

Bud sits down beside Carla and rubs his round belly. "I've relocated. I'm staying with my daughter in North Portal until the end of April. Family stuff," he explains.

Half the girls look totally confused because they don't know Bud. But the ones who *do* know him are thrilled.

"That's awesome, Bud," Kathy says. "This means a lot to us."

"Don't get sentimental on me, Parker," Bud says.

I take a deep breath and let it out slowly. Finally. The hockey gods have thrown us a bone.

Sue briefly outlines Bud's coaching credentials – they are considerable – then Bud addresses us.

"I'm not expecting you to win every game, but I do expect you to improve," he says. "Let the points fall where they may. Let's play with passion. Let's play with confidence. Let's support our teammates."

"Anything else you ladies want to say – or ask – before we meet with each of you individually?" Sue asks.

Miranda raises her hand. "Is it true we're doing a barbecue fundraiser?"

Sue threads her fingers through her short blonde hair. "Looks like it. Amy's parents have volunteered to donate the meat." She fills us in on the rest of the details. "How does that sound?"

"Sounds delicious," Kathy says.

"Anything to add, Jaclyn?" Bud asks Crystal's mom.

Mrs. Jordan smiles nervously. "Just be honest with your coaches, girls. Tell us who you want for leaders."

Bud stands up slowly. "Go straight home after you meet with us. No texting each other as you leave. No 'I said, they said.' That's going to be very important as this team moves forward." He backs towards the door. "Bear in mind – there's no changing your vote tomorrow or the week after tomorrow. You have to live with the decisions you make, so make the best ones you can."

One by one Bud and Sue start taking players into the referees' room down the hall to get input on who should be wearing letters. We'll each have the opportunity to air our concerns, ask questions, and in the end, name some names.

They start with the younger girls and work their way up to the senior players.

"This is going to take forever," Jennifer moans.

But surprisingly, it doesn't. After forty-five minutes, Mrs. Jordan comes to get Amy, and it's just Kathy and me left in the dressing room. As far as we can tell, the girls have all lived up to their promise of leaving with their parents right after the meeting.

"What do you think our chances are?" Kathy says.

"I don't know," I tell her. "I don't care if I wear a letter, as long as Whitney doesn't have one."

"I was referring to the team," Kathy says dryly.

"I feel a lot better than I did when I came in here." I slump back against the wall, feeling the cool brick through my T-shirt. "Bud's going to be awesome."

"Yes, he is."

Silence.

You need to help her understand about Evan, my little voice says. Now is the time. The longer you wait, the harder it will be.

My pulse vibrates in my neck.

I don't say anything.

And neither does she.

When Mrs. Jordan comes to get her, I am left alone. I sit. I pace. I stand.

"I'm not afraid," I say to the door.

The brick walls absorb my words. I pull out my phone, tempted to check for texts from the other girls or to go to Mainpage, where some will have posted stuff already.

Mrs. Jordan's at the door. I follow her down the hallway, which is much colder than the dressing room. I gratefully slip into the referees' room and close the door behind me.

Sue and Bud are waiting.

"Okay, Jessie." Sue turns over the clipboard she's holding. "Fire away."

I gather they're expecting me to be full of questions, but I have only two. "Is Jodi okay to play?"

"Her GP and specialist say she is." Sue stands up and sets her clipboard on the counter. "Jodi deserves a chance to play again." She gives me a wry smile. "Anything else?"

"Did you have to cut Amber? Would it have hurt the team to carry *one* more forward?"

A ripple of emotion crosses Sue's face. "It would have hurt Amber, Jessie."

"Why?"

"She can't play AAA," Sue says. "She doesn't have the physical skills or hockey sense. It wasn't fair to ask her to give up so much of her time – hours and hours a week – to sit on the bench. And it's not fair to put her on the ice when she isn't as good as the other girls. Do you see?"

"I guess so," I say.

"Notre Dame and Saskatoon and Weyburn are strong teams. To coin one of Kathy's colourful phrases, we'll probably get shit pumped for the first season. But even so, we need to give those younger girls an opportunity to improve, so they can be successful after you and Jodi and Kathy and Carla are gone."

"What do you think, Bud?" I ask.

"I think any team can beat any team on any given day," Bud says, rubbing his bald dome. "That's why we play the games, all thirty-two of them." He pauses and jams his cap back on his head. "Now, who would you like to have for a captain?"

I take a deep breath. "Jodi."

*A*ll the way home, I quiz Mom about the parents' meeting, but her responses are maddeningly vague.

"Mr. Johnstone tried to charm the hell out of everyone, didn't he?" I ask.

"He was persuasive," Mom says.

"Do you think he's going to try to get on the bench with Sue and Bud?"

"I never got that impression," Mom says.

"Why didn't he just send Whitney to Notre Dame?" I take a drink of water before continuing. "He can afford it."

"I think you should stop worrying about Mr. Johnstone, and start thinking about how you're going to balance this AAA commitment with your school work," Mom says. "Bud's going to run a tight ship."

"Speaking of Bud – how come he's moving to North Portal?" I picture Zack, Bud's grandson. "His daughter's marriage didn't break up, did it?"

"Nothing like that," Mom says. "His son-in-law's going to university in Regina, finishing an education degree. He was living with Bud to save expenses, but Bud's daughter was having a tough go of it back in North Portal, juggling her job and three little kids. She asked Bud to move in and help out for a while."

"Wow," I say.

"Sue said Bud's been pretty lonely, since his wife passed

away," Mom explains. "This is a good move for everybody."

"Including us," I say.

"Including us," Mom agrees. She doesn't say anything else until we pull into our driveway. "When will you find out how the vote went?"

"Bud said he'd call before ten."

My stomach starts rolling.

The gloves will come off as soon as somebody gets, or doesn't get, an A. Sue created a monster when she put one on Whitney last season. It totally went to her head. No surprise our coaches have decided to let us vote on the letters this year.

"I wonder why your dad left the Prius parked on the street," Mom says as we wait for the garage door to open.

Then we see Courtney and Gia. They've got my road hockey net set up where the Prius is normally parked, and they're shooting on it. I notice right away Courtney's using Rambo, my favourite weapon on penalty kills. Chopping a stick in half diffuses a power play damn quick.

"Hi Mrs. McIntyre! Hi Jessie!" Gia calls as Mom and I climb out of the Explorer. "How did the meeting go?"

"I don't know yet." I come around the back of the vehicle, so I'm standing right beside Courtney. "What's up with using my stick?"

Courtney shrugs.

"Those blades are expensive, and I buy them with my own money. If you're going to use the shaft out here, at least put on a plastic blade." I wrest Rambo from her hands. "Next time, ask permission."

"Sor-ry." Courtney's apology doesn't sound sincere. "I didn't know you'd be so touchy."

"Well, now you know." I turn Rambo over and examine the blade.

"Where did those energy drinks come from?" Mom asks, pointing at some cans sitting on the step.

"I brought them, Mrs. McIntyre," says Gia.

"They're loaded with sugar and caffeine." Mom picks up one of the cans and examines the label. "Jessie and Courtney aren't allowed to drink these."

How refreshing to be lumped with my baby sister.

"My mom doesn't mind me drinking them." Gia exchanges glances with Courtney. "I'm sorry. I didn't know you'd disapprove."

Mom looks at her watch. "It's time for you to go home, Gia. It's a school night."

"Sure, Mrs. McIntyre. See you tomorrow, Courtney." Gia picks up her bike, which is lying on the front lawn, and glides into the twilight.

"You know the rule," Mom says to Courtney.

"I know *all* the rules," Courtney says.

"What's that supposed to mean?"

"Nothing." Courtney yawns and stretches. "I'm going to bed. Okay?"

Mom points at the energy drinks.

Courtney picks them up and tosses them in the recycling bin before climbing the stairs to go into the house.

"Nighty night!" I call out to her. "Good luck sleeping after two of those!"

Courtney gives me the finger before she disappears inside, but Mom doesn't notice.

You are *so* going to pay for that, I think.

"Gia knew she was breaking one of your rules," I tell Mom. "She's a bad influence on Courtney."

"She was respectful enough," Mom says. "Don't be so hard on her."

The phone rings inside, and Mom and I look at one another.

"Do you think you'll be wearing a letter?" Mom asks.

"Judging from the talk in the dressing room before the vote, I think Kathy and Jodi are for sure," I tell her.

The door opens. Courtney's standing there holding the cordless phone. "It's some old guy," she says. "He wants to talk to Jessie."

I reach up and take it from her.

It's Bud.

"Tell your mom to go down to JL's and pick up a letter," he says. "Make sure it's a C."

"You're kidding," I say.

"I'm not. Kathy, Carla, and Jodi get the A's. I'll email you a list of duties," Bud says. "I hope you like meetings."

# *chapter nineteen*

**W**ednesday morning I pick up Amber earlier than usual because she's got a student council meeting. When I get to the courtyard, Teneil's at our table.

Waiting.

I try to be polite to Teneil. She's been my friend a long time, even if she isn't acting like one lately.

"Don't you have volleyball practice?" I ask.

Teneil gives me a smug look. "You talked to Kathy yet?"

I sit down across from her and pull my calculus textbook out of my bookbag. "Want to help me study for my quiz?"

She ignores my obvious ploy to change the subject. "Kathy's pissed at you." The only thing that seems to delight her more than this news is the fact she gets to deliver it.

My heart quickens. "Is that right?"

She leans across the table. "She told Miranda you got voted captain because you sucked up to the new girls."

"Hi," a voice says.

Amy sits down beside me, stuffing her knapsack and long legs under the table.

"Hey, Amy." I push my textbook aside.

Teneil narrows her eyes at Amy. "No offence, Amy, but this is a private conversation."

"No offence, Teneil, but it's not," I say.

Teneil glares at me. "Maybe you should think about who your *real* friends are."

"Maybe you should think about growing up."

Teneil picks up her stuff, swears under her breath, and stomps off.

Hell hath no fury like a scorned hockey player.

"I'm sorry," Amy says.

"It's not your fault."

The other girls start drifting in a few minutes later. Kathy's tight-lipped when she sits down across from me. Oh she *is* pissed, I think.

Everyone steers clear of the topic of letters. Instead, they talk about mice. It seems Crystal's parents are doing a major reno, and Crystal has been banished to the basement storage room, which is frequented by the little rodents.

"It's like living in a prison movie. I can hear them romping across the ceiling tiles at night. It's grossing me out," she explains.

The Rookies offer solutions: poison, sticky pads, traps

baited with cheddar cheese or peanut butter. Kathy watches the girls, more like a cat than a mouse. But there's one person she's definitely *not* looking at.

Me.

I need to do something. Right now. Before it's too late.

"Hey, Parker," I say.

She continues staring at Amy, who's describing how rats are treated at her farm.

"Parker," I say louder.

When her gaze meets mine, her eyes are little discs of blue steel.

"I don't know why the girls went the way they did." My heart is hammering in my ears. *"I voted for you."*

I hope you don't have to pay for that lie, my little voice says.

"And I voted for you," Kathy says slowly. "After all, I can't vote for myself. But I never thought..." She pauses and clears her throat. "It sucks to get demoted."

"I'm sorry," I tell her. "I don't agree with everything you say, but you're still my friend. And I'll need your help this year. Big time."

She nods once and lifts her lips in a half smile.

We're going to be okay.

Then Whitney sweeps in, plunking herself down at the end of the table. She's clearly got her gitch in a knot.

"Hey, Whitney, what's up?" Larissa asks.

"Nothing," she says.

"Looking forward to that rookie party this weekend," Randi says.

Whitney shrugs.

"What? You've changed your mind about the big sleep-over?" Crystal asks, clearly disappointed.

Whitney shrugs again.

"It's just as well," I say. "We can't afford a bad night's sleep factoring in for Game Two of that double-header."

Whitney shoots me a look. "I never said I was cancelling," she says. Then she throws down the gauntlet. "Or, as team captain, are you telling me I *have* to cancel."

So *that's* the bug up your ass, I think.

Careful, Jessie, my little voice says.

"I'm sure you'll use good judgment," I respond.

Whitney launches into a description of her plans for the party, giving the girls directions to her acreage.

Kathy catches my eye across the table and mouths, "Good luck."

"Thanks," I mouth back.

**B**efore our home opener on Saturday, Bud, Sue and Mrs. Jordan hand out the new jerseys.

"Hot off the press," Bud says. "You girls wearing letters will have to tape up for now."

Black, orange and white, with a modified Oilers' symbol on the front. We wear white for home games.

Although their styles are different, Bud and Sue are a great team in the dressing room. Bud has a lifetime of experience coaching both boys and girls. He's jovial, positive, and has a bottomless bag of hockey platitudes. We call them Budisms. On the other hand, Sue is heavy on strategy and sparing with praise. I've learned to pay close attention to every single word. If she says I played a good game, I know I did.

Thursday night we had our first practice with Bud. Mom was so right when she said Bud runs a tight ship. When some Bruins showed up to help, Bud told them he could handle things on his own.

It was hilarious to watch Whitney choke on *that*.

Bud's right about our need to work hard every practice. Swift Current finished in the middle of the pack last year, so playing them will be a great opportunity to see where we stand in AAA. Amy starts in net today while Miranda starts tomorrow. Of course all of us are hoping Jodi will be on her game, as she has been so far.

"Do you think we're going to have many fans today?" Crystal asks. She has to speak loudly so we can hear her overtop of Carla's boom box.

"Probably more than we usually get," says Kathy. "Who knows?"

When I step out onto the ice for our warm-up, a hundred fans are assembled in the stands of Spectra Place.

"Definitely more than we got for our exhibition game," I say to Carla.

"Of course." She flashes a smile. "We're the big time now."

We're used to playing in the LMC, so the noise and space and spectators are intimidating.

We don't have an auspicious start. When Mr. Parker tries to play the tape of "O Canada," he has technical difficulties. Jennifer, Kathy, Randi, Jodi and I are waiting on the blue line, shifting from foot to foot. Eventually the ghetto blaster spits out three bars and a horrible grating sound.

"Excuse me, but my machine won't play this CD," Mr. Parker announces. "Is there someone who can get us started?"

"Go Jodi," Randi says.

Jodi looks at us uncertainly.

"Yeah, go!" Kathy says. "My dad's a brutal singer!"

Jodi skates over to the timekeeper's booth and exchanges her helmet for the microphone. The crowd is real quiet, and I get goose bumps, thinking about how lucky we are to have Jodi back on the ice.

But as I stare at the flags hanging at the end of the arena and Jodi's voice washes over us, I wish I'd gone to the bathroom one more time.

I'm just nervous, I tell myself. The urge will go away as

soon as the game starts.

It does.

Jodi scores two quick ones in the first period to put us up two zip. The Wildcats keep going glove side on Amy, and she keeps breaking their hearts.

"This league's going to be a cakewalk," Jennifer says to me on the bench.

"This game is far from over," I reply.

In the second period Swift Current takes a delay of game penalty, and Kathy scores on the power play. Later, Jodi puts one in, shorthanded. In the third, the Wildcats score two late goals, pull their goalie with a minute left, then watch in dismay as Whitney intercepts a pass and fires a shot into their empty net.

We coast to a 5–2 victory, thanks to Jodi's hat trick and Amy's stellar goaltending.

As I'm leaving the ice, I hear little people voices calling my name. I look up and see Breanne and Zack waving at me from the stands.

"Hey, Short Stuff!" I pull off my glove, reach over the glass, and smack her palm. "How you doin', Zack?"

He grins at me.

"I'm babysitting Zackary," Breanne informs me. "He's Coach Prentice's son."

"Grandson," I correct her.

"Where's Courtney?" Breanne asks.

"Ouch!" I exclaim in mock anger. "You don't care about me anymore?"

Breanne smiles shyly. "Yes, but where's *Courtney?*"

"I don't know. She and Gia are around here somewhere."

Kathy gives me a little shove. "Let's go!" she says.

"See you, Short Stuff! See you, Zack!" I call out.

Everyone is pumped in the dressing room. No finger pointing. No lip dragging. It's awesome.

"I don't know about you, but I'm looking forward to tomorrow," Jennifer says, hoisting her hockey bag onto her shoulder.

"Awesome way to start our season," Whitney responds. "2 and 0."

"Let's not get cocky," I warn her.

"Whatever," Whitney says. "Can't we just enjoy the moment?"

"Sure you can," I reply. "Just don't take this team lightly."

"Who said I'm taking them lightly?" Whitney looks around. "Did anyone hear me say that?"

"See you guys tomorrow," Jennifer says.

"Aren't you coming to my place?" Whitney asks.

"I can't. It's my grandparents' wedding anniversary," Jennifer says.

"You're kidding." Whitney turns back to Jennifer. "How're we supposed to *bond* if we're not all there?"

"I can't make it either," says Amy.

"Count me out too," Jodi says. "I have church."

Storm clouds roll in.

"I can't believe this," Whitney says.

"Man, if everybody keeps dropping out, the Rooks are gonna outnumber us," Kathy observes.

"Are you coming, Jessie?" Whitney asks.

"Somebody has to make sure lights are out by midnight," I reply. "Hopefully there's enough time to watch *Youngblood.*"

"For the hundredth time," Crystal groans.

I give some Rookies a ride out to Whitney's place. She lives a few kilometres north of Estevan. As soon as I pull in her lane, the Rooks start oohing and aahing. The house is huge, with a three-car garage, and a motor home parked in the driveway.

"Whitney must be rich," one of them says.

Mrs. Johnstone greets us at the door. "Hello, girls." She ushers us into the foyer and talks excitedly about our win, then leads us upstairs to the rec room over the garage.

"Wow!" a Rookie says. "A pool table!"

"Make yourselves comfortable," Mrs. Johnstone says. "Whitney'll be right up. I think she's straightening her hair. Doug and I are going out in an hour, but I think you'll have everything you need up here."

"Thanks, Mrs. Johnstone," I say.

She goes back downstairs.

"Get a load of the jukebox!" another Rookie says.

"I don't think we'll have time to watch *Youngblood* tonight," a third one says, making straight for the table full of pizza, snacks and pop.

I look at the food. "Go easy on the carbs and junk food, or you'll play lousy tomorrow. Proper nutrition is critical to success."

"Yeah, yeah," she replies, diving into a pizza box.

Whitney comes upstairs. She's decked out in makeup, jewelry and hair product – the whole nine yards.

"Pretty fancy, considering it's just us," I tell her.

Whitney pours herself a coke and plunks down beside me on the couch. "I'm the one scoring a hat trick tomorrow," she says.

"I hope you do." I reach over the back of the couch and extend my glass. "More ice, Rook."

The rest of the girls filter in by eight o'clock. We're so busy playing pool and air hockey we hardly notice when Whitney's dad comes upstairs to say goodbye.

"Nothing better than a hen party, right, ladies?" Mr. Johnstone asks. He places a tanned hand on my shoulder and squeezes. "Great game today, Cap'n Jessie."

"Thanks."

"You ladies have fun," Mr. Johnstone points a finger at Kathy and winks. "But not too much fun."

After he's gone, Carla says, "I could show *him* some fun."

"Yuck," Whitney says.

Much to Crystal's consternation, Kathy slips *Youngblood* into the DVD player.

"When are we going to dress up the Rooks?" Crystal demands. "I brought bags of stuff from the Salvation Army!"

"We're got loads of time," Kathy says.

The Rookies park themselves on the floor while the senior players recline all over the furniture. When we're halfway through the movie, a set of headlights swings into the yard.

"Whitney, are you expecting somebody?" I ask.

She doesn't respond, and the room is too dark to see her reaction.

"Maybe Amy decided to come after all," Kathy says.

Miranda yawns and stretches. "I hope not. I've seen enough of the Great White Hope to last me until tomorrow."

A Rookie runs to the window and looks out. "There're two trucks out there!"

Kathy pauses the DVD player. A vehicle outside revs, rattles and coughs – a vaguely familiar sound. Doors creak open and slam shut, interspersed with male voices and laughter.

"Looks like we's gonna have a few roosters in our henhouse," Miranda says.

# chapter
## twenty

**S**omebody turns on the lights, blinding us all.

"Are they Bruins?" one of the Rookies asks, rubbing her eyes.

"The Bruins are on a northern road swing. Everybody knows that," Carla says.

I squint over at Whitney. "You invited *guys?*"

"I invited football players," Whitney says.

"Yowza!" Randi says.

"How's that supposed to facilitate team bonding?" I ask.

"Who cares what *you* think...Captain Anal?" Whitney gets up and goes downstairs.

"Captain Anal?" I look around at the rest of the girls. "What's *that* supposed to mean?"

"She means you suck the fun out of everything," Kathy says.

"I don't," I say.

"Oh yes you do," Randi says.

I turn to Crystal. "Be honest, am I anal?"

Crystal nods and bites her bottom lip.

"How about – *psychotic?*" a Rookie volunteers.

"Who asked *you?*" Kathy growls.

The Rookies all sit there, wide-eyed, while the vets gather round and start barraging me with everything I've done to make their lives miserable for the past week. Apparently the list is pretty long.

Then Whitney comes back up with five guys in tow, each of them carrying a twenty-four-pack of beer.

The last one is Liam MacArthur. He low-fives Amy as he walks by.

"Obviously you're not injured anymore," I say.

He looks at me, surprised. "It was just a sprain, Hockey Girl. I didn't know you cared."

Kathy crows as she cracks open a beer.

"I thought we weren't drinking tonight," I say.

"Lighten up, McIntyre." Whitney takes a can from one of the guys. "It's just beer. I told them not to bring any hard stuff."

"Beer or not, this still breaks Bud's rule about drinking on a game weekend," I say.

"So you're going to narc on us?" Whitney demands, sipping her beer. "I should've known."

I stand up and wipe my hands on my thighs. "I'm going home. Anybody coming with me?"

The Rookies look at one another.

One of the guys drapes an arm around my neck. "You should relax. Have a couple of beers. See what happens."

"No thanks." I pull away and move towards the stairs. "Last chance, Rooks."

The Rookies start gathering their things.

Kathy squawks like a chicken.

"You're wrecking the party," Whitney says.

"No, Whitney, *you're* wrecking the party." I reach for my jacket which is lying on the sectional.

A brown hand grasps it first.

"Look, I'm sorry." Liam holds on, forcing me to yank helplessly on the sleeve like a dog at the end of a leash. "If I'd known you were going to react like this, I wouldn't have come."

"Right." I take a deep breath, remembering my promise to Amy to be nicer to him. "Now please let go."

"Can't we talk about this for a minute?" he pleads, releasing my jacket.

"No. I mean − no thank you." I'm trying to look very adult and self-assured. It doesn't help that my right sleeve is turned inside out, and my hand won't go in all the way. I start flailing like an idiot.

"Let me help you with that," he says.

I see the leers the rest of the guys are giving me. Some things never change.

I rip off my jacket and start down the stairs with the Rookies right behind me. When I realize I left the rest of my gear upstairs and stop, they pile into me, sending me flying.

I bounce down the stairs.

Carpet.

Ceiling.

Carpet.

Ceiling.

Carpet.

I end up in a heap at the bottom, head throbbing, staring up at a sea of terrified Rookies. For some reason, there are twice as many of them. That's when Carla and Kathy take over and push everybody back.

"Give her some air!" Kathy says.

Larissa manages to slip through. She kneels down and peers concernedly into my face. "How many fingers?" she says, holding up a blurry hand.

Somebody starts demanding my mother's maiden name. Somebody else insists I start counting backwards from one hundred. Kathy's threatening to kick Rookie asses all the way back to Estevan.

"I'm okay," I say groggily. "Let me up."

"I don't think she should move yet," Liam says, pushing past Kathy. "She probably banged her head."

"Does anything hurt, Jessie?" Larissa asks.

"My cheek." I explore the tackiness with my fingertips.

"Nobody's ever died from rug burn," Whitney says.

After a couple of minutes Liam and Larissa pull me up and help me walk to the living room, where they make me lie down on the couch.

"Should I call 9–1–1?" Carla asks from the doorway.

"I don't think so," Larissa says, "but she should see a doctor."

"Your dad's a doctor," I tell her.

"Good for you." She peers into my eyes. "Do you feel nauseated?"

"I don't think so."

"She's okay then," one of the guys says. "Let's go drink beer."

"She's definitely not driving home," Larissa says.

"You're overreacting," Whitney says. "She's obviously not hurt."

"I'll take her to emergency," Liam says.

"I'm not going," I say.

"I'll call my dad to meet you there," Larissa says. She puts two fingers against my throat and uses the clock app on her phone to take my pulse.

"Where did you learn to do that?" I ask.

She winks at me. "You have a vehicle?" she asks Liam.

"Yes, ma'am."

"I'll bring Jessie's car home tomorrow," Kathy says.

"Quit talking about me!" I sit up on my elbows. "I'm fine!"

"Do you want me to call your parents?" Larissa asks.

"No!"

"Jessie should go to the hospital," Kathy says. "And Liam should take her, right Rooks?"

The Rookies bob their heads in agreement, just like those little toy dogs some idiots put on their dashboards. It makes me dizzy.

Liam leans over and slides his hands under my waist and thighs.

"No way," I tell him. "I walked in here by myself, and I'm leaving the same way."

"Does that mean you're going to let me drive you to emergency?" he asks.

"Yes."

He removes his arms and straightens. "Let's go then."

I get up slowly. My head does feel better. No nausea. No dizziness. No blurred vision. But my cheek stings like a bitch.

"If your dad's not at emergency, I'm going home," I tell Larissa.

"He'll be there," Larissa promises. "Have you got your purse? You'll need your health card."

"Thanks, Mom," I say.

One of the guys shouts from the top of the stairs. "Straight home, MacArthur!"

# *chapter*
## *twenty-one*

I don't talk to Liam during the ten-minute drive to Estevan although he keeps up a steady stream of conversation. He turns west just outside the city limits and takes the back road to the hospital.

"I'm sorry, but my truck stalls at red lights and stop signs," he apologizes. "I try to avoid them."

He starts to pull up to the emergency entrance, but I point to the visitors' lot. When I try to open the truck door, I can't move the handle.

"It only opens from the outside," he explains. He gets out and runs around to my side. My head is feeling better as we cross the parking lot, moving towards the main entrance, but I think I have some pulled muscles in my back.

Inside, I give the receptionist my health card and the info she needs to type up a pink form. I don't recognize anybody in the waiting room. Just the same, I position myself in my chair so my cheek is facing the wall. I can't pretend to check my phone because I had to turn it off as soon as we entered the hospital. Liam and I sit there in awkward silence.

"You can go back to Whitney's if you want," I tell him after a while.

"I'll wait until Dr. Bilkhu's checked you over. You'll need a ride home."

"My dad can come get me."

"Sure." He leans forward, placing his elbows on his knees. "Do you want me to go outside and call him for you?"

Imagine how excited Dad'll be about *that*.

"No, I'll wait until after I see Dr. Bilkhu." I touch my cheek for the hundredth time. "How bad is my face?"

He places his fingers on my chin and gently turns my head so he can see the burn. "It'll heal," he says.

I turn my face away, and he pulls his hand back.

"Is there anybody else you want to call?" he asks. "Your boyfriend maybe?"

"No. I mean, not now."

We sit in silence for a long time. We pretend to look at magazines. We watch the clock. I try not to think about giving a blood sample.

He sits back and stretches his legs in front of him, crossing his boots at the ankles. "Can I tell you something?" he says at last.

"No."

"I get along with most people," he continues, undeterred. "You are a glaring exception."

Why didn't I phone my dad when I had a chance? Then I wouldn't be sitting here having this conversation.

Liam takes a deep breath and lets it out slowly. "Amy thinks you're awesome. She says you've gone out of your way to make her feel welcome on the team."

"I like Amy," I say.

"Can't we be friends too?" he asks. "I don't know what I did to piss you off, but I'd start over if you'd let me."

"Why do you want to be my friend anyway?" I ask.

He smiles. "Remember that time in Grade Eleven when Mr. Lazar had us do math presentations?"

I nod.

"Most of them were yawners. I don't even remember what I did, but yours was on that Greek guy..."

"Pythagoras," I say helpfully.

"The very one." He smiles. "The girls in that class were determined *not* to show how smart they were, and there *you* were, getting all breathless and dreamy about $a^2 + b^2 = c^2$."

"I wasn't!"

"Oh yes, you were." He pauses and heaves a heavy sigh. "And that was the moment I knew."

"Knew what?"

"That I was smitten."

I blush, making my cheek burn even more.

"Jessica McIntyre!" the admitting nurse calls from the doorway.

The words strike terror into my heart. "Come inside with me!" I beg.

He laughs.

"I'm serious!"

"You're afraid of Dr. Bilkhu?"

"No, I'm afraid of those people who take blood samples." I smile at the nurse, who's frowning at me, clearly impatient to get my show on the road. "Please come with me!"

"Only if you're nice," he says.

"I promise." I get up and move towards the entrance to the emergency ward.

"Now, I get it," he says, following me. "You're on medication for a split personality."

A few minutes later Dr. Bilkhu is clucking around me like a mother hen, manipulating my neck and shoulders, dabbing antiseptic on my rug burn, and asking a lot of questions. It's natural for him to be concerned. Larissa's at the party I just left, and he doesn't want *her* to be his next patient. I give him an abbreviated version of the events leading up to my arrival, leaving out the part about the five guys and the twenty-four-packs of beer.

He cocks his head as I describe Liam's role as paramedic.

"So how did *you* come to be at this slumber party?" he asks Liam.

Liam looks at me.

"I invited him," I reply. "He's my...friend."

"That's right." Liam displays his gap-tooth.

Dr. Bilkhu smiles knowingly. "Ah."

"Not like that," I quickly add.

Dr. Bilkhu takes a closer look at my pupils. "No hockey for you tomorrow, Princess."

"But I'm okay, aren't I?"

"Best not to take any risks within twenty-four hours." He smiles and pats my hand. "I'll be watching tomorrow."

As we leave the hospital, I realize we never called my parents, which means Liam has to give me a ride home. On the way, he tells me about his older brother Russell, who has Down's syndrome.

"As long as I can remember, he's been there for me," Liam says, pulling into my driveway. "It feels strange to not have him around the house, but he likes his roomies at the group home."

"What does he look like?" I ask.

Liam describes him briefly.

"Yeah, I've seen him at Sarcan," I say. "I'll say hi to him the next time I'm there."

"He'd like that," Liam says.

I know I should be getting out of his truck, but for some reason, I don't want to. "I'm sorry I've been rude to you." It feels good to roll out that apology. "I was angry at myself – if you want to know the truth."

"For what?" he asks.

"For jumping to conclusions at the talent show. And that day at Sarcan, I didn't know about Russell."

"Ah," he says, in a perfect imitation of Dr. Bilkhu.

I laugh. "What will you do now? Will you go back to Whitney's?"

He shakes his head.

We don't say anything for a while. But it doesn't feel awkward, this quiet. It feels okay.

"Tell me about high school rodeo," I ask him.

The world he describes for me is very different from my experience. In the arena, individuals compete tooth and nail, then bail each other out when equipment breaks or a horse pulls up lame. Liam has dabbled in all the events, with the exception of bull riding, but lately he's concentrated on training cutting horses.

"I'd like you to come out to my place," he says. "I'll introduce you to my favourite girl."

"One of your horses?"

"You'll see." He pauses. "What do you say? No strings attached. Just a friendly visit."

"Maybe. Sometime." To distract him, I ask about football.

Liam tells me he's a wide receiver. The camaraderie, the locker-room pranks, the chirping, the roller coaster of highs and lows of football is more familiar territory, although the lingo is overwhelming.

"But how do you keep track of all those plays?" I ask him. "Our team can barely learn two systems!"

"Football players have to be smart," he says.

"Do you want to keep playing after you graduate?" I ask.

"Thanks for the vote of confidence, but I don't have a hope in hell. No, I want to get into veterinary science one of these days."

"Good for you," I say. "I wish I knew what I want to do."

"You'll figure it out eventually," he says.

"I hope so."

It's quiet again.

"Does this mean we're friends now?" he asks.

"I guess." I reach for the door handle and fumble with it.

"So I can talk to you at school and you won't bite my head off?"

"Yes, but please – no more signs at my hockey games. Don't give people ideas, okay?"

He looks at me uncertainly and then laughs. "Sure thing, Hockey Girl." He holds out his hand. "Give me your phone."

I pull it out of my pocket. "What do you want it for?"

He turns it on, finds my contact list, and punches in a phone number. "Just in case you need me sometime," he says. "That's what friends are for, right?" He holds out the phone, and our fingertips touch briefly.

"Right," I reef on the handle again, then look at him helplessly.

"Allow me," Liam says, getting out.

A few minutes later I stand in my doorway watching his truck sputter and cough as it backs out of my driveway, and part of me wishes we could keep on talking. Wishes I could call his number and tell him to come back.

What would Evan say about that, my little voice says.

# chapter twenty-two

efore Game Two against Swift Current, the girls are smart enough not to talk about the party, the guys, or the beer, but they are clearly hung over. When I tell Bud about my accident, he brushes it off, but Sue looks suspicious.

"So what was going on at Whitney's last night?" she asks.

"Just a post-game meeting," I reply.

I hate lying, and I'm also lousy at it. Not a great combination.

I retire to the stands to watch the game with Amber. Ten minutes into the first period, it's abundantly clear the Wildcats are going to clutch and grab Jodi Palmer into oblivion and pepper Miranda with shots. She gives up two soft goals.

Teneil, the usual bearer of bad news, slides into a seat behind me. "So – you fell off your pedestal," she whispers in my ear.

"My what?" I don't give her the satisfaction of turning around.

She leans ahead and examines my cheek for a long moment. "Oh yeah, it's true."

"What is it I'm supposed to have done?" I ask.

"Got drunk at Whitney Johnstone's and fell down the stairs."

Amber's big blue eyes get bigger. "Jessie, you didn't!"

"Well, I did fall down the stairs. I told you that already."

Teneil leans closer. "I heard you were in no shape to drive, so Liam MacArthur took you to emergency. Dr. Bilkhu had to pump your stomach because you had alcohol poisoning."

"Is that all?" I ask.

She narrows one eye, clearly pissed that I'm not rising to the bait. "Sue benched you and stripped your C. You're probably going to get cut."

I consider how she'll be circulating through the lobby during intermission, spreading rumours and resurrecting the ugly ghosts of my past. Bud and Sue will hear about it, and then we're all in shit. Some captain. I never should have let Whitney plan that sleepover.

I stare at the ice, willing Teneil to leave. When she doesn't, I start humming "Hernando's Hideaway." Courtney skated to the song a few years ago, and it's the most annoying one I know.

*That* gets rid of her.

Amber places a cool palm on my forehead. "I worry about you. I think this whole AAA thing is driving you crazy."

"You could be right about that."

I pull out my phone, which has been beeping in my pocket for the last hour. Without looking, I know that the texts will be Evan's, but I'm not in the mood to read or respond to them.

An air horn sounds, announcing a Wildcat goal. The Swift Current fans on the other side of the arena cheer while their team celebrates on the ice. I hold up my hand and pretend to squish the heads of the Wildcats between my thumb and forefinger.

"Jessie, you're scaring me," Amber says.

"Sorry."

"You never told me you got benched." She wiggles closer and puts her arm through mine.

"I didn't. Dr. Bilkhu told me not to play, and I'm not. End of story."

"Are you sure?"

It *so* isn't the end.

When the period's over, I slip down to our dressing room. It's not a happy place. Everyone's fine while the coaches are there, but as soon as the door shuts behind them, the bitching and blaming begins. I always thought Carla wouldn't stand for that kind of talk, but she and Amy just sit in the corner and whisper while the rest of the team tanks.

"Nobody's actually trying out there," Kathy says.

"You're saying I'm not trying?" Jodi demands. *"Try getting open so I have someone to pass to!"*

I've never heard Jodi talk like this.

As for me, I'm stinging from the "Captain Anal" remarks. I can sit here and say nothing – if that's what they *really* want.

No skin off my ass.

I sit with Amber for the rest of the game, watching the Wildcats hook and hang on Jodi every time she steps on the ice. They know if they shut her down, they shut *us* down. One of them crosschecks her into the boards late in the third. There's no reason for it. They've already got the game in hand.

"That's checking from behind," Amber says.

"Hit her right in the numbers," I reply. "Good thing she had her head up."

But the ref doesn't call a thing. Kathy skates right at him, arguing. Then Jodi goes after him herself. He skates away, but Jodi keeps chasing him.

"What's she doing?" Amber asks.

The ref ends up giving Jodi two minutes for unsportsmanlike. Then she skates over to the Swift Current bench and starts screaming at their coach.

"Somebody needs to rein her in," I say.

Carla puts a hand on Jodi's shoulder and tries to reason with her. Jodi turns and flings an arm out, knocking Carla off balance, no small feat considering the difference in their size.

"Can you get two for roughing your *own* teammate?" Amber wonders.

The linesman escorts Jodi to the penalty box. On the way in, she bangs her stick on the boards and breaks it.

We lose 7–2. Furthermore, the Wildcats outshoot us 48–14, and that hurts just as bad as the score.

Bud doesn't tie into us after the game. He gives us a pep talk, tells us we'll get back to some basics in practice, promises to help us do better next time. Jodi apologizes to Carla and the rest of the team for her behaviour.

Sue sits there and dissects each of us with that piercing gaze of hers.

Only a matter of time before she figures it out.

*T*hat same night while I'm cuddled up on the couch with my calculus notes, I get a text from Jodi.

U home?

Yep.

Comin' over.

"Who did you say brought you home last night?" Mom asks from the dining room.

"I didn't say," I reply, willing the phone to ring or the dishwasher to spring a leak.

"So who was it? One of the girls?" Mom asks.

"Uh huh."

"Which one?"

"Why does it matter?"

"Because I want to thank her for taking you to emergency and getting you home safe and sound. It was the right thing to do."

Mom always knows the right thing to do.

I wish that knowledge would rub off on *me*.

"It wasn't one of the girls, Mom."

She comes out of the dining room.

"It was a guy."

"Are you involved with him?"

I think about the drive back to my place, the time we spent in his truck, talking and laughing.

"I don't know," I tell her.

"Does Evan know you feel this way?" She sits down at the end of the couch.

"No."

"Shouldn't you tell him?"

My heart sinks. "I can't, Mom. Not now. He says I'm all he has."

Mom pulls my feet onto her lap, warming my cold toes

with her hands. "Jessie, you're too young for this."

That gets me going. "You *wanted* me to go out with him!"

Mom shakes her head gently. "You're misunderstanding me. I just meant you're too young to be involved with someone who's so serious about you." She pauses and clears her throat. "I've had some heart to hearts with him – when you're not home."

"You have? What does he say?"

The doorbell rings.

We stare at each other for a second.

"That's probably Jodi," I say, standing up.

As soon as I open the door, I know something's wrong. Jodi's got a shopping bag in her hands, and I can tell what's inside.

Her Oiler jerseys.

"You didn't take long to get here," I say.

"I came from the church. I was talking to Pastor Matt," she replies.

"Do you at least want to come inside?"

She steps past me, and I close the door.

Mom waves at Jodi and slips back into the dining room. "I'll give you girls some space."

Jodi sets the bag beside the closet. "I'll get straight to the point."

"Okay."

She purses her lips, tucks her dark hair behind her ears. "AAA isn't what I thought it would be. I thought I'd be surrounded by girls who are serious about hockey, and I thought I could overlook the fact many of them don't put Jesus first."

"Jodi ..."

She puts up her hand abruptly. "I knew I could count on you to say and do what's right for the team and for us as individuals. That's why I voted for you as captain."

I am blown away. Jodi voted for *me?*

Her next words snuff out my joy. "But that was a mistake. You're not the person I thought you were." Her eyes search my face. "You're a lot like the girl I *used* to be. And this team is heading in a dangerous direction. I'm not getting dragged down again."

"Jodi, it's not what you think. Let me explain."

"It's too late for that." She takes a step backwards. "See you around."

She opens the door and shuts it behind her.

I stand there and stare at it for the longest time, wondering: how did I get here? If I could just figure out where I tripped, maybe I could make things right. But I can't.

And just when I think things couldn't possibly get worse. They do.

Oh, they do.

# chapter
## twenty-three

**S**hit hits the fan during dryland. I know something's wrong when Sue and Bud *both* show up at the Leisure Centre. We're doing circuit training when they walk in.

Sue marches straight over to me. "Team meeting in Room A in the library in ten minutes. Get your players there. Make sure you get hold of anybody who *isn't* here." She starts to walk away, then looks back at me. "No need to call Jodi, is there?"

"No, there isn't."

I harbour a faint hope the meeting is about Jodi quitting and the adjustments we'll have to make to compensate for her loss. But it's very faint.

The only girl missing from dryland – besides Jodi – is a Rookie who pulled her groin on Sunday. I text her and tell to get her butt over here ASAP. She doesn't have a ride, so Miranda volunteers to pick her up.

"Don't be long," I tell Miranda as she changes into her street shoes.

As we walk down the hall towards the library, music is booming through the walls of the multi-purpose room.

"Gunvor," Kathy says.

We look through the glass in the double doors. Gunvor, the Leisure Centre's premier fitness instructor, is putting the Bruins through their paces. Her workouts are legendary.

"Poor guys," Carla says. "She'll kill them for sure."

"Well, Sue's going to kill us," Kathy says.

Once we're in the library, we assemble around the tables arranged in the centre of the meeting room. No one talks. We just stare at one another like we're playing high-stakes poker instead of waiting for the hammer to fall.

I've no doubt it's coming down hard.

Then Bud and Sue arrive. They stand in the doorway like a pair of bouncers. Their faces are grim.

We're done, I think. And we hardly got started. We'll never know if Amy's got what it takes to get us through a whole season because our coaches are going to pull the plug.

When Miranda and the Rookie finally arrive, Bud and Sue step in the room. Sue slams the door behind her. She speaks first. In two years, I've never heard or seen her like this.

"Why is it we have to learn things about our *own* team from an outside source? Do you think we enjoy finding out our captain – a girl we trusted, a girl we respected – had the *audacity* to bring booze to a team party on a game weekend? And *lie* to us about how she sustained an injury to her face?"

Said face is flaming scarlet. Every girl in the room is staring at me, and I inhale their fear. If Sue finds out they were all drinking at the party, what will she do?

"Who told you?" I croak.

"Does it matter?" she demands. "The whole *city* knows about it."

Bud steps closer, and his disappointment washes over me. "Did it go to your head...being captain?" he asks.

What's the right thing to do now, I wonder.

You know, my little voice says.

"I guess it did," I reply. "I'm sorry."

"You're sorry." There's no pleasure in Sue's tone. "Do you have anything else to say to your teammates?"

"I let you all down," I tell them. "I set a bad example."

"Who else was drinking at that party?" Bud asks.

Shit.

It takes a few minutes, but Kathy puts up her hand, then Carla, then Whitney, then everyone else. Everyone except Jennifer and Amy.

"We weren't there," Amy says, pointing at Jennifer.

Bud leans against the wall and crosses his arms. "Jodi phoned me last night and told me she was quitting. She said she didn't realize how much of a commitment AAA would be. She said it was impacting her grades and other aspects of her life." He pauses. "Do you think she was influenced by what happened at that party?"

"Yes, she was. She told me so," I say, but telling the truth is no relief.

"Terrific," Sue says.

"Is there anything else we need to know?" Bud asks.

"We don't want to hear more crap later," Sue says. "We want it all – here and now."

We stare at the floor. One of the Rookies starts crying.

"That's it," I say. "Do whatever you need to do. We deserve it."

"Go home, and tell your parents exactly what you did," Bud says.

"And keep your mouth shut when you go to school. Our dirty laundry is nobody's business," Sue adds.

We file past them one by one. I'm last, and I'm hoping they won't hold me back for further reprisal. Mercifully, they don't.

Amy waits for me outside the library. "What in the hell happened at that party?" she asks.

"I don't want to talk about it." I brush by her.

What I want to do is go home and talk to Mom. There's no way I'm lying to *her* the way I lied to my coaches today.

I go to the locker room, grab my street clothes, and stuff them in my backpack. When I straighten up, Kathy's there. Most of the others are there too, but they keep their distance.

"I can't believe you threw yourself under the bus like that," Kathy says. "I owe you. We all owe you."

"Why did you fess up to the drinking?" I demand. "If you'd kept your mouths shut, they'd just punish *me*. They wouldn't quit on us. You do realize they're going to quit, don't you?"

"They would have found out, Jessie," Kathy says. "We couldn't keep lying to them."

"Then how come nobody told them *I* didn't bring the booze? Was that too much trouble?"

"I didn't think," Kathy says. "The whole thing took me by surprise. I'm sorry."

"Are you?" I dig in my backpack for my phone. "Or did you think this was a great way to get me stripped of the C?"

"Big Mac, I'd never do that."

They all start apologizing then. I can't stand it anymore, and I call Mom to shut them out.

"What's up?" Mom asks.

"Do you need me to pick up Courtney from volleyball? I'm done dryland already."

"Sure." She sounds surprised. "You didn't hurt yourself, did you?"

I swallow a sob before answering. "No, I'll tell you about it later."

"Okay, see you soon."

I hang up.

Kathy's still there. "What kind of a person do you think I am?" she asks.

I have no words left. I turn my body so I don't touch her or any of the others on my way out.

# *chapter*
## *twenty-four*

I heard Sue's quitting," Teneil says.

How in the hell did she know to look for me in this corner of the library?

"Please go away," I tell her. "This is none of your business."

"Why? Because I got *cut?*"

"Get over it already," I say. "You've got lots of positive things in your life. Why don't you focus on them for a change?"

She turns on her heel and walks away. I close my history textbook, fold my arms on top of it, and lay my head on my arms.

"Nice one," a male voice says behind me.

"It didn't feel very nice."

Liam slides into a chair across the table from me. "So how are things going? Amy says it's pretty bad."

"Bud cancelled our practices this week." I squeeze my

eyes to hold back the tears. "Luckily we don't have games this weekend, or he'd probably forfeit. I don't know if we have practice next week or if we'll go to North Battleford." I take a breath. "I think Bud and Sue are going to quit."

"Look, *I* know you weren't drunk that night. I can talk to them."

"They already know the whole team was drinking," I tell him. "What they think about me isn't going to make any difference."

"Did you tell your parents?"

"I told them the truth — if that's what you mean."

"And they believed you?"

"Well, there was a time when they wouldn't have." I smile at the thought. "It took some convincing to stop them from calling Sue and Bud themselves. That's all I need. Parents defending their kid. You know how *that* looks."

"So now what?" He leans forward and puts his elbows on the table.

"Sit and wait, I guess."

He looks from side to side, and then says quietly, "In the meantime, you could come out to my place. Have you ever ridden a registered quarter horse?"

"This isn't a good time, Liam."

"Funny you should mention time," he says. "I won't have her much longer, and I'd really like you to see her."

"I'm sorry. My life is just too complicated right now."

My phone beeps. A text from Evan.

Miss you, he says.

Speaking of complications.

"I have to get going." I stand and gather my books. "How did you find me anyway?"

"Amy told me." Liam says. "Coming to my football game tomorrow?"

"Probably not," I say. "The last thing I need is people linking our names. Not after what happened at Whitney's."

"Why are you so worried about what people think?" he asks. "You didn't do anything wrong. Isn't that enough?"

"I really have to go. See you around." I walk away without looking back.

Jodi and I have drifted apart in the last two years. Different interests. Different values. But she's important to me, and her opinion of me matters. She won't respond to my texts, so I try to call her at home on Thursday night. Her mom tells me she's at church. Apparently she and Michelle have started up a Bible study group for tweenies.

"I wish I knew why she quit hockey," Mrs. Palmer says. "Do you know, Jessie?"

How am I supposed to answer *that* question?

"I'm not sure," I tell her. "I think it had something to do

with school."

"There's no doubt it's more difficult for her since the accident," Mrs. Palmer says. "We're lucky to have her with us. The hockey was a stretch."

I hop in Sunny and drive over to Jodi's church and wait for her outside. While I'm sitting there, I get a text from Evan. There's been lots of them lately — and at odd times too. Times when he's usually in a lab or at practice. It worries me he's not more focused on school and basketball. His league is starting soon.

Call me, he says.

Jodi should be out any minute. I don't want to miss her.

In an hour. Promise, I text back.

I wish I knew what Sue and Bud are thinking. I'll find out at the pow wow at the rink on Monday night. Apparently representatives from Estevan Minor Hockey will be there too.

Talk about airing out our dirty laundry.

Cars swing in and out of the parking lot as kids dribble out of the church. Then Jodi and Michelle appear. Jodi's got her guitar case.

I roll down my window. "Hey!"

They both look in my direction.

"Jodi, can I talk to you for a minute?"

Jodi extricates herself from Michelle, who watches while Jodi approaches my car.

"What's up?" Jodi asks.

"I'd like to clear up some stuff. Maybe we could go somewhere and grab a pop."

She looks at her phone. "I have to give Michelle a ride home."

"Will you at least let me explain?" I ask. "I'm disappointed you didn't come to me before jumping to conclusions about that party."

"I didn't jump to conclusions," she says. "I got my facts from somebody who was there."

"Who?"

"Whitney."

"Jodi, you barely know her! Why didn't you ask *me* what happened? I thought we were friends."

"Jessie, until you put God first in your life, we will never be close," she says. "But you should know I quit hockey for other reasons. I want to apply to Education, and hockey interferes with my grades. I thought I could make it work, but I can't."

"But you're so talented. You're the best of all of us. Don't you *want* to play hockey after high school?"

"Jessie, aren't you listening? I *can't* do school and hockey. Not like you can." She sighs. "Besides, you saw how I acted this weekend."

"You mean when you scored a hat trick?"

"No, when I *freaked* on everybody." She shudders. "Aggression is a symptom of my brain injury. If I can't control myself, I need to stay out of the combat zone."

I can't argue with her.

"Good luck with your hockey, Jessie Mac, wherever it takes you."

It's the first time she's called me that in a long time.

"Thanks."

I watch as she and Michelle get into her car. I wave as they drive past, and Jodi waves back.

That's that.

A girl called for you," Mom says when I get home. She's sitting at the kitchen table, assembling a photo album. "I wrote down the number on the notepad beside the phone."

I pick up the notepad and stare at it. "I don't recognize the number. Did she leave a message?"

"She was in a hurry," Mom says. "Why don't you find out who it is?"

"I don't feel like it right now."

"Things didn't go well with Jodi, did they?" Mom asks.

I shake my head.

"Do you want to talk about it?"

"No." I wipe my eyes and take another look at the phone number. "Is that a Regina prefix?"

"Looks like it," Mom says.

I pick up the phone and dial. It rings four times before someone answers.

"It's Jessie McIntyre, returning your call," I explain, feeling foolish. "I don't know who I'm speaking to."

"It's Brittany," the voice says.

I mentally review the Brittanys I know. The list is remarkably short.

"Brittni – as in Brittni Wade," she says. "We played hockey together two years ago. I just saw you at a Rider game in August."

"Oh, right." I don't have the faintest notion why *she* would be calling me. "How are you?"

"Great," she says. "Jamie and I are getting married on New Year's Eve."

"I remember you telling me that."

"I was wondering if you'd like to be in the wedding party."

"You want me to come to your wedding?" I ask.

"I want you to be a bridesmaid."

It's another one of those knock-me-over-with-a-feather moments. I sit down on the kitchen tile.

"It won't be a big expense. I'm telling all the girls to buy black cocktail dresses, something that suits them. Nothing slutty. The guys are wearing black tuxes. Jamie and I will be wearing white of course."

"What about Cory?"

There's a brief pause.

"I told you about Cory and my ex-boyfriend, didn't I?" Brittni adds, "Are you going to do it or not?"

She makes me feel like I'm on a list of potential brides-maids. If I say no, she'll phone the name beneath mine. I don't know much about weddings, but finding bridesmaids shouldn't be like recruiting players for a three-on-three tour-nament.

"Why me?" I ask.

"You were a great teammate, Jessie," she says. "I could always trust you to be honest."

It's the nicest thing she's ever said to me. Maybe the only nice thing.

"I'd like a few more details. Are you getting married in Estevan?"

"Are you kidding? I live in Regina. That's where all my friends are."

Not *all* your friends – apparently.

She tells me more about her plans for the wedding and reception.

When she's done, I ask, "Can I get back to you on Monday?"

"Sure," she says. "Thanks for thinking about it. It means

a lot."

"Talk to you soon." I put the phone back in its cradle.

"Who was that?" Mom asks.

"Brittni Wade."

Her brows tie themselves in a knot as she tries to put a face to the name. It's fun watching them unravel when she figures it out. *"Brittni?"*

"Uh huh." I sit down at the table and pick up one of the photos. It's a shot of Courtney and me at the Forestry Farm in Saskatoon. I'm about eight, and Courtney is probably two. Man, she was a cute kid. Those were the days when she followed me everywhere, imitated my every word and gesture. Sometimes I'd wake up at night, and she'd be curled up beside me like a kitten. Nowadays if I say one wrong thing, her claws come out.

"Remember Courtney *before* she hit puberty?" I ask Mom. "She was just your average spoiled-rotten kid."

"We never spoiled her," Mom says. "And don't change the subject. I want to hear more about Brittni. Was she inviting you to her wedding?"

"She wants me to be a bridesmaid."

"But you were never friends. As I recall, you didn't even like her."

I pick up another photograph. "She had some good moments, like the night of Jodi's accident. Then again, she had some really bad ones."

"Exactly." Mom takes the photograph from my hand and places it in the frame she uses for cropping.

"I'm curious. I think I'll tell her yes." I pick up a photograph of me with a side ponytail and promptly tear it in half.

"Jessie!"

"Mom, there's no way that picture's going in."

Mom scowls at me and crops another photo. "Curious about what?"

"What Brittni will want to do to my hair, for one thing." I pull back my bangs. "And we probably won't have a team, so we won't be getting an invite to the Mac's after Christmas. No point in pencilling *that* on my schedule."

Mom's eyes get droopy. "I hope you're wrong about that."

Courtney wanders into the kitchen, holding her phone. I never see her without it. She goes straight to the fridge and pours herself a glass of milk. She stands and drinks, texting with her free hand.

"Girls like Brittni have very expensive tastes," Mom points out. "That bridesmaid's dress isn't going to come cheap."

I explain to her about the dresses.

"That sounds very practical," Mom says. "But maybe you should find out who else is in the wedding party. It won't be much fun if you don't know anybody." She pauses and thinks.

"Would you take Evan?"

December suddenly seems a long ways away.

"Who are you talking about?" Courtney asks, leaning against the counter.

"Why don't you come sit down?" Mom pushes a chair away from the table. "Jessie will tell you all about it."

"No thanks." Courtney doesn't look up from her phone.

"Courtney, Mrs. Gedak wondered if you'd babysit Breanne tomorrow since there's no school," Mom says.

"Gia and me are gonna hang out," Courtney says.

"Maybe you could hang out later," Mom says.

"I guess." Courtney continues texting.

"Would you be able to go over there around eight thirty?"

"Yeah." Courtney wanders out of the kitchen.

"I thought that phone was for emergencies," I say.

Mom starts digging through photographs in a recipe card box. "Unlimited texting is cheap, Jessie. It's not a big deal."

"She's wearing you down."

"She is not," Mom says.

"Whatever." I lean my chair back. "Do you think Sue and Bud will quit?"

"Can I give you some advice?" Mom asks.

"As if I could stop you."

Mom selects a photo from the box and picks up her

utility knife. "You better do something now. Before that meeting with Minor Hocky."

"I agree. The question is…what?"

"You're the captain. You figure it out," Mom says. "Meanwhile, I'll get ready for Thanksgiving. Good thing your grandma's bringing the cabbage rolls and your favourite cookies."

"Awesome."

My phone plinks. It's Evan.

Why haven't you called me?

"Got to go." I grab the cordless phone again. "Evan's headed to Victoria tomorrow with the Dinos. Time for a pep talk."

"Say hi to him for me," Mom says. "And Jessie?"

Something in her tone makes me stop in my tracks.

"Be honest with him. Okay? If you're not as serious as he is, he needs to know."

"I'll tell him – when the time's right," I promise. "But this isn't the time. He has a big weekend ahead of him, and midterms coming up. I'll tell him. After."

"Don't wait too long," Mom says.

# chapter
## twenty-five

**Y**ou want us to write letters to our coaches *and* Estevan Minor Hockey?" Kathy asks. "How's that going to help?"

It's Friday morning. I've rallied the Oilers to an emergency meeting-before-the-Monday-meeting in my basement. Larissa and a Rookie are the only ones missing.

"It won't hurt," I say.

Jennifer asks, "What should I write in my letter, seeing as how I wasn't there? What should *I* apologize for?"

"Can we deal with your letter later?" I tell her.

"I'll need some help writing mine," one of the Rookies says. "I have horrible spelling."

"Have you heard of spell check?" Carla asks.

"I'm beyond spell check," the Rookie says. "I can't even spell Christmas."

"I can spell Hanukkah," another one says.

"Shut up!" Kathy says. "You're driving me crazy!"

The Rookies look at their feet, cowed.

"I'm a good speller, and a good writer," one of the Rookies says, the one who was Carla's D partner against Swift Current. "I'll explain what happened, eat crow, and we Rookies will sign it. How's that?"

"Good idea," I tell her. "What's your name again?"

"Dayna," she says, smiling.

"Dayna, you've got potential," I tell her.

"And also bedhead," Carla points out. "Didn't you even try to make yourself presentable this morning?"

"Jessie said it was an emergency," Dayna explains. "I came straight over."

"Yeah, the pajama pants were a dead giveaway," Kathy says.

I tuck my feet under my own pajama pants.

"I think you should tell the truth," Kathy says to me. "It would make a huge difference with Sue."

"Oh no, it wouldn't," I reply.

"Sue loves you," Crystal says.

Everyone stares at Crystal.

"I didn't mean like *that*," she says.

"I don't know about everyone else, but I'm getting sick of your martyr routine, Jessie," Whitney says.

"Martyr routine?" I reply. "I thought I was anal?" It's on the tip of my tongue to let it all out, tell everyone what Whitney's been up to.

That'll only make things worse, my little voice says.

"Cool your jets, both of you," Carla says. "Kathy's right. The truth from you wouldn't hurt, Jessie."

"What I'd like to know," Kathy says, "is how this rumour about Jessie ever got started in the first place. It had to come from somebody who was at the party." She looks at Miranda. "Teneil's been blabbing about it at school all week."

"Teneil and me don't even hang out. She's not much fun these days." Miranda says. "And I didn't tell her anything."

"Then who did?" Kathy asks.

"This isn't the time for a witch hunt," I say. "We need to concentrate on getting Sue and Bud back."

"And Jodi," Crystal says.

"Has anybody seen Jodi lately?" Randi asks. "Any chance she'll change her mind?"

I tell them about my conversation with her outside the church, leaving out the part about Whitney. We've already lost our best forward. The last thing we need is for the girls to boot Whitney off the team.

"I can see why Jodi's quitting," Kathy says. "But it still sucks."

"It's better than her getting another concussion," Carla says. "And the way she was playing, it was only a matter of time before that happened."

After the girls leave, I spend the rest of the morning

catching up on homework and housecleaning the main floor. At noon I call Courtney to see how things are going and make sure she gets Breanne fed. The kid's the pickiest and slowest eater I know.

Then I park myself in front of the computer in the kitchen and start thinking about my letter. Why am I being so stubborn, I ask myself. Why don't I just tell the truth?

Because you're afraid Sue won't believe you, my little voice says.

It's funny Crystal says Sue loves me because I sure never get that impression. Most of the time she treats me like I'm a position, not a person.

Maybe I won't tell the truth, I decide. Maybe I'll just talk about our team and hockey and what it means to me. Maybe that'll be enough.

I start typing, and I don't second-guess a single word. I just let it all hang out. My hopes. My dreams. My teammates. My learning curve as a D-man. Everything I ever thought and loved about the game. I'll go back and revise later, I keep telling myself. It'll be too sappy otherwise. I'm halfway through page six, and bawling like a baby when the doorbell rings.

"Shit!" I tear a tissue out of the box and blow my nose.

Now somebody's knocking on the door. When I open it, the ground shifts under my bare feet.

Evan.

# chapter
## twenty-six

**W**hat are you doing here?!" I ask, dabbing my eyes.

He stares at me. "What happened to your face?"

"Rug burn. No big deal. I'll tell you about it after you tell me why you're not on your way to Victoria."

He walks through the door and puts his arms around me and pulls me close. "It's okay," he whispers in my ear. "I'm home for good."

Two thoughts strike me instantaneously:

1) He's quitting.

2) He's quitting because of me.

The words keep rebounding in my head. They have a hollow sound, like a basketball bouncing in an empty gymnasium where a boy is perfecting his dribbling. Putting in hours and hours of practice, honing the skills to attract university scouts.

See you soon, he told me, over and over again. Even though I knew I wouldn't see him for weeks.

Because that's the way you wanted it, the little voice says.

"What did you do?" I can barely get the words out.

He removes his arms, then cups my face in his hands, and drags it upwards, so I can see the happiness in his tired eyes. "I quit," he says.

"You quit basketball?" I ask.

"I quit everything," he says.

"School too?"

"Yes."

This isn't happening, I tell myself. It's not. It's a bad dream. Or I'm not really here. I'm somewhere else. Anywhere else.

"Come sit down." I grab his hand. "We need to talk about this."

He pulls me back and kisses me, long and hard, in a very un-Evan like way. It scares me. I don't mean *he* scares me. I could never be scared of Evan. But the power of his emotion is frightening, and so is the knowledge that I control it.

When he finally lets me go, I take him to the kitchen, pour him a glass of cold water, and sit across from him, holding his hand across the table.

But what I'd like to do is pound my head on that table. Pound it until there's nothing left of stupid, selfish, impulsive

Jessica Maree McIntyre.

I listen while he tells me about his gradual awakening. His dawning realization that what he really wants from life is to be a youth pastor. He's going to enroll at Bible college in Saskatoon next fall.

"So when you go to university we'll at least be in the same city," he explains. "You are planning to go to U of S, aren't you? Your mom thinks you are."

"There's a good chance I will."

"I'm not cut out for medical school," Evan says. "It took me a long time to realize that."

Oh no, it didn't, my little voice says. It only took two months of Jessie Mac's Road Show to convince you.

"Evan, this is pretty sudden."

"I know," he says. "I didn't mean to make it sound like you don't have any other options for next year. If you decide you want to go to university someplace else, I can find a different ministerial program. The only thing that matters is that you and I will be together."

He's been under too much pressure, I tell myself. It isn't just me. It's all those science labs. The coach who doesn't get him. His parents pinning all their hopes and dreams on him. His determination to get the best grades, so he can get scholarships to pay for medical school. I am part of it, but I'm not all of it.

Nice try, my little voice says.

He yawns, shakes his head, and beckons, urging me to sit in his lap. "Let's talk about you for a while," he says.

That's definitely something I don't want to do. Not yet.

"How about a cookie? They're not homemade, but they're pretty good." I open a cupboard and remove a package with trembling hands. "What did your parents say when you told them?"

"I haven't told them yet." Evan's brow gets wrinkly. "I drove straight to your place from Calgary."

"When did you leave?" I put some cookies on a plate.

"Four this morning. I was supposed to be get on a plane for Victoria, but I ended up driving here, instead of meeting the team at the university. Isn't that strange?"

I set the plate in front of him. "Evan, you need to talk to your parents."

"I'd rather talk to you." He pats his lap again. "Please come here."

"No. You need to call your parents. And while you're doing that, I'll go put on some jeans." I point to the phone on the computer desk. "I'll be right back."

I hurry upstairs, stumbling on the second last step because my legs are so weak. What am I going to *do?*

What you should have done a long time ago, my voice says. They all tried to tell you, didn't they?

In my room, I kick off my pajama pants and dig under the clutter for a pair of jeans. Mom folds my clean laundry and brings it to my room like a burnt offering, but she refuses to put it away.

"I'm not going to try to figure out what's clean and what's dirty," she always says. "That's up to you."

Well, I know what's dirty.

My soul is, and I am going to hell.

I kill time in the upstairs bathroom, washing my face, cleaning my teeth, freeing my hair from its pony, and brushing it out. Occasionally I lean into the hallway, listening for Evan's voice on the phone, but I don't hear a thing.

Maybe that's a good sign. Maybe he's listening to his parents' advice. Maybe it isn't too late for him to put his life back together.

When I return to the kitchen, Evan's still sitting at the table, dangling the phone by the antenna. The cookies are untouched.

"Did you call them?" I ask.

He nods. "I talked to my dad."

"What did he say?"

"I'm going to meet him and Mom right away," he says. "Dad doesn't want to talk about this in front of Breanne, so we're going to Houston's. I'd like you to come along. Would you mind?"

"I can't."

"Maybe you could come later."

"No." I suck in a deep breath. "Evan, I'm not serious about you. Not like you are about me. I'm not even sure I like you *that* way."

He doesn't say anything for the longest time. I wonder if he heard me.

"I never should have said I wanted to go out with you," I say. "I was wrong. I *wanted* to like you more, but I…"

"Stop it," he says. "Just stop it, okay?"

He's staring out the kitchen window. It's a sunny fall day. The leaves are clinging to the trees, but only for a little longer.

He bows his head and exhales. "I've been a fool."

I want to tell him he isn't. I'm the fool.

Shut up, my little voice says. Let him talk.

"All this time I thought you felt the same way. But you don't. When you didn't return my calls, I made excuses for you."

"I'm sorry." My eyes and my nose are running, and I'd reach for a tissue if I could.

His next words are so quiet I scarcely hear them. "I told you not to do it."

"I know." I sit down across from him and reach for his hand, but he pulls it under the table. "I'm so sorry, Evan."

The phone jangles, startling both of us. He gives it to me.

It's Mom.

"Oh good. You're home." She sounds like she's out of breath. "Have you heard from Evan? His mom got a call from his coach. Evan never showed up at the airport this morning, and nobody knows where he is. His roommate says his car is gone but..."

"He's here," I tell her, as gently as I can. "He's okay. He just talked to his dad."

"Oh." Mom sounds confused, and I don't blame her.

"I have to hang up now, Mom."

"Call me later," she says.

I set the phone down. "I don't know what to tell you. I wish I could make things better, but I can't. I didn't know you'd feel this strongly about me."

"You had to know, Jessie," he says. "How could you *not* know?"

"Okay, I knew, but I thought I could make myself feel the same way."

I try to remember why I wanted to go out with him in the first place. Was it really because of a *song?*

He stands, pushing the chair back and cracking the vertebrae in his long neck.

"Maybe if you hadn't been so far away, it would have been different," I tell him.

"I'm here now," he says wryly. "Is that making a difference?"

"Is it too late for you to go back?" I ask.

His face darkens.

Wrong question.

"Oh, that makes sense," he says. "I have three midterms next week I'm not prepared for. Yesterday after practice I wrote an email to the athletic director telling him exactly what I think of my coach."

"You didn't."

"Oh yes I did."

I decide not to push him. Maybe his parents can help him work something out. Maybe I could write *another* letter – to his coach. To the university.

You do that, my little voice says.

"Do you want a sandwich?" I ask.

"I'm not hungry," he says. "I don't feel like much of any-thing right now."

The way he says it makes me wonder if he's talking about himself.

"I have to go." He moves out of the kitchen, heading for the front door.

My guts start churning again as I follow him outside. The wind is cool, and I wrap my arms around myself. He walks to his car and opens the driver's door.

"Evan, I'm so sorry!" I call out, shivering.

He climbs in and drives away.

**E**van's dad drops by a few hours later to burn me in effigy. He alternatively sits, stands and paces, and I let him rant, too emotionally drained to say a word.

At the moment he's pacing. "Do you have the slightest idea how much you've hurt him?" he demands.

There's nothing of the mild-mannered pastor I know. Rev. Gedak's an Old Testament prophet, raining down the wrath of the Almighty. And I deserve every minute of it.

"Yes."

"How could you be so thoughtless? Did you enjoy leading him on for the past two months?"

I'd like to ask him if *he* feels at all responsible for Evan's meltdown, but I know better than to provoke him.

I hear the muffled sound of the garage door opening.

"That'll be my mom," I say.

Rev. Gedak sits down and puts his head in his hands. "He worked so hard to get that scholarship," he mutters. "It was all for nothing."

"Maybe it isn't too late for him to go back," I suggest. "Could you call his coach or the university and see?"

"You're missing the point," Rev. Gedak says bitterly. "He doesn't *want* to go back. Even now."

Mom and Mrs. Gedak enter through the kitchen. Mom's as white as a sheet. "How's it going?" she asks.

"How do you think it's going?" Rev. Gedak stands and begins pacing again. "Your daughter has ruined my son's life!"

"Don't you raise your voice in this house," Mom says. "Has he been yelling at you, Jessie?"

"She deserves far worse!" he shouts.

I blink rapidly to hold back the tears.

Mrs. Gedak moves towards her husband. "Honey, you're making the situation worse. And your blood pressure will be going through the roof. Let Diane handle it."

"That's the problem. She doesn't handle it!" He jabs his finger at me from across the room. "She lets this girl run *wild!* You think I haven't heard the stories about that *party?* This town isn't big enough for you to hide in, Missy!"

Oh great.

Mom folds her arms. "I'm asking you to leave."

"Let's go home," Mrs. Gedak pleads, tugging on her husband's hand. "Evan needs you."

The reverend's shoulders drop, and the anger drains from his face. The resemblance between father and son kicks me right in the stomach.

Why can't I feel about Evan the way he feels about me?

Felt about me.

He's so good, and I'm going to hell.

As if reading my mind, Rev. Gedak says, "We should ask for God's intervention."

My phone starts playing Gary Glitter, and we all look at my purse.

"Maybe that's Him now," I say.

Rev. Gedak glares at me.

"Or maybe Evan." I know damn well it isn't because his number plays Creed, but I'm looking for any excuse to leave the room. I dig out my phone and check the screen.

Liam MacArthur.

Better than nothing.

"I have to take this," I say, gliding out of the room.

"Jessie," Mom says.

"I'll just be a minute!" I sit down at the kitchen table, right where Evan sat a few hours ago. "Hey, Liam."

"Hey, Jessie," he says. "I was wondering what you're up to this afternoon. Want to come out to my place?"

"I can't," I say quietly. "I'm sorry."

"That's okay. Can I call you later?"

I wish I could let him do that. He's so easy to talk to, and right now, I could use a friend.

So one day you can make him feel like shit too, my little voice says.

"Not tonight," I tell him. "See you at school." I disconnect.

I sit there for as long as I dare, staring at my phone.

When I go back into the living room, no one has moved. It doesn't even look like they've said anything. Rev. Gedak's lips are moving in prayer.

Mrs. Gedak turns lifeless eyes on me. "Jessie, I just want you to know how disappointed I am. I never dreamed you were this shallow."

Ouch.

She stands up. "We'll be going now. I think it would be wise for you to avoid all contact with Evan. He's very confused and hurt and fragile, thanks to you."

After the Gedaks are gone, Mom wraps her arms around me. "Don't be too hard on yourself. I have a feeling he would have quit school even if you hadn't been dating."

She's shorter than I am, so I rest my cheek on top of her head. "That's the problem, Mom. I don't think we ever *were.*"

# chapter
## twenty-seven

L et's talk turkey," Kathy says. "My dad made ours in one of those deep fryers in the backyard. Nearly set himself on fire. Good thing he was wearing insulated coveralls."

"My mom forgot to take the bag out of the neck again," says Crystal. "It was so gross, I wouldn't eat the dressing."

The girls keep yacking until I think I'll go insane. The fate of our team hangs in the balance. Sue and Bud are meeting with our parents and the Estevan Minor Hockey executive right now.

The only player who says nothing is Whitney.

And that's as it should be, I think. Her bad decisions and big mouth got us into this mess.

"How's Evan doing?" Kathy asks, sliding closer to me on the bench.

"I haven't talked to him or his parents since Friday."

"It was pretty bad, huh?"

"Yep."

"I told you so," Kathy says with infuriating smugness.

The dressing room door opens, and Miranda's mom and stepdad walk in. The parent meeting must be over.

Soon we'll know if we've still got a team.

After what you did to Evan, should you be thinking about hockey at all, my little voice asks.

The rest of our parents file in. It gets crowded soon, and we have to squeeze together to fit on the benches. Kathy moves over, so Mom can sit beside me. Mr. Parker, whose eyebrows are singed and forearm is bandaged, sits with Kathy. Dr. Bilkhu sits with Larissa. Mrs. Jordan slips an arm around Crystal's shoulders. The Johnstones sit with Whitney of course. Mrs. Johnstone's eye makeup looks smudgy.

Definitely not tattooed on, I decide.

"It'll all be over soon, ladies," Mr. Johnstone says. "Only a little while now." He looks over at the Rookie sitting next to him. "How are you doing?" he asks.

"Fine." The Rookie looks petrified.

"Your coaches are very disappointed in the decisions you ladies made last weekend, but there's a chance they're willing to overlook them. Those letters you wrote had quite an impact. Whose idea was it to write the letters?"

"Jessie's," the Rookie offers.

Mr. Johnstone smiles warmly at me. "Good for you, Jessie.

A brilliant strategy."

"I wasn't trying to be strategic. I was being sincere."

"Of course," he says. "Sincerity does the trick every time."

The Minor Hockey executive enters and lines up near the door, since there's no place for them to sit.

We sit there in the hollow quiet for what seems an eternity. I check my phone. Ten minutes. Did Sue and Bud decide to go home without delivering a verdict?

The door opens, and Sue appears. She looks even grimmer than usual.

"Bud had to go home," she says. "There's an emergency at his daughter's house. Nothing serious. A problem with the septic system, I believe."

We're done like dinner. He was the good cop.

"I want to thank all the parents for coming. I know some of you drove quite a ways, and we appreciate it." She folds her arms and moves to the centre of the room.

Closed body language, I think. Bad. Very bad.

"What we have here is a trust issue," Sue continues. "Bud and I thought we could *trust* you girls, and apparently we can't. We can't trust you at home, so we can't trust you on the road. You can understand why we have reservations about going forward with this team. Bud's health situation isn't ideal, and my career is demanding. To put it bluntly, we don't have the time or stomach for this."

One of the Rookies sobs.

"Most of you wrote letters to apologize for your behaviour. One individual did not apologize, and that individual is a glaring exception." Sue turns and looks directly at me. "Why did you do it, Jessie?"

"Tell her," Kathy says under her breath. "Tell her now."

"I didn't bring the booze, and I didn't invite the guys." I nearly choke on the words. "I didn't drink either."

"I know you didn't, Jessie," Sue says. "I meant, why didn't you tell us the truth in the first place?"

"I don't know." I wipe at the corner of my eye. "It seemed like a good idea at the time."

"Well, it's a good thing the rest of your teammates, and their parents, felt differently." Sue shifts her eyes from me to Larissa's dad. "Dr. Bilkhu assured me you hadn't been drinking when he saw you in emergency that night."

I heave a big, ragged sigh.

"It's all my fault," Whitney says. "I invited the boys. I told them to bring the beer."

"Pretty late for *that* confession," my mom says.

Whitney's face crumples.

"Weren't you there last week when I asked for all the information?" Sue demands.

Whitney sobs. "I was scared everyone would hate me."

We already hate you, I'd like to say.

"I'm sorry," Whitney says. "I'm really, really sorry."

"Last weekend I had a conversation with your team sponsors," Sue says. "I asked them if they wanted to withdraw their support. After taking a few days to consider, they said they would support the team if we did. Estevan Minor Hockey responded in the same fashion." Sue shakes her head. "I also contacted the AAA League and the SHA. They all said it's up to Bud and me. Now Bud's gone home, and before he left, he said, 'It's up to you, Sue. You know these girls better than I do. Do what you think is best.'" Sue shakes her head and laughs. "Men are cowards, don't you think?"

Sue never laughs. She wouldn't laugh if she were pulling the plug.

I look over at Kathy. She winks.

"What kind of team can I expect if I *do* decide to go forward?" Sue asks.

That's when everyone starts spilling their guts, making outlandish promises like we'll always keep the dressing room orderly and bake muffins for every road trip and never eat junk food on game weekends or complain about having to pick up the pucks or bitch about our ice time or playing third line. Sue lets us go on for a few minutes.

"All right," she says. "We don't have much time to get ready for North Battleford. Prepare for Death by Dryland tomorrow. I've hired Gunvor."

# chapter twenty-eight

**D**id you watch Sports Centre last night?" Kathy asks as we line up at the cafeteria salad bar.

"Missed it." I pick up a bowl.

She grabs one too and moves to the other side. "They did a segment on potential picks for the World Juniors. Guess who they talked about?"

"No idea."

"Aren't you interested?"

"I'd *like* to be interested," I tell her, "but all I think about these days is calculus. Now that we know there's such a thing as Death by Dryland, I'm wondering if there's also Death by Derivatives."

"I'm talking about Mark Taylor," Kathy says. "As in Mark 'I'm Going to the Show' Taylor. Mr. Hitman. The Big Defensive Threat."

"They mentioned Mark on TSN?"

Kathy pops a crouton in her mouth, which earns her a

dirty look from one of the cafeteria ladies. "What?" she asks.

"Mark's the second highest scoring defenceman in the WHL. He'll be playing in the Subway Series against the Russians. He deserves a mention." I load up on cherry tomatoes and sunflower seeds.

Kathy adds three dollops of ranch dressing and flings the spoon in the container. "Funny you'd care about his stats."

"Funny you'd care that I care," I retort. "For a change of pace, why don't we talk about hunting season for a while?"

Kathy piles on the bacon bits. "That's all Brett talks about. And here I thought the ref talk was bad enough! And if he's not actually pushing bush or talking about it, he's busy making sausage. I don't even remember the last time..." She pauses. "You're not listening to a word I'm saying. Are you thinking about Mark?"

"No," I lie. "I was thinking about Courtney."

"How's Little Sis doing?" Kathy asks.

"She's got Mom and Dad wound around her little finger, that's what."

"Whoa, family drama," Kathy says, "the best kind."

On the way to our usual table, I tell her about the way Courtney's been acting since she started hanging out with Gia.

"She can't think for herself. She spends every second with Gia, and when she's not with her, she's texting her."

"Excuse me," Kathy interrupts. "Did you say *texting?*"

"Uh huh."

She stares at me in fascination. "Explain to Auntie Kathy how that happens. You didn't get a phone until you were fifteen."

"Curfews are different. Rules about makeup and clothes and hairstyles are different. Everything's different." I pause to take a bite of my salad.

"Keep going," Kathy says. "I love it when somebody's parents lose it."

"They say, 'She was miserable for two years. Now she's has a friend at school. Can we hold that against her?'" I stab a chunk of lettuce with my fork. "They're giving her a puppy for her birthday."

Kathy sits up straight. "I love puppies."

"Focus, Parker." I wave my fork. "I'm looking into a crystal ball. I see Mom and Dad trying to get Courtney to feed the dog and walk the dog. I see the dog crapping in my room. I see *me* cleaning it up."

"Are your parents still letting her play hockey?" Kathy asks.

"She refuses to figure skate, and we have to keep her busy somehow. I just hope she doesn't embarrass herself, and me, at bantam practice." I pick at my salad. "I have a feeling it's going to be brutal. You're going to come, right?"

"Oh yeah," Kathy says. "I want to see this for myself."

**W**ill you quit following me around, telling me what to do?" Courtney explodes. "I'm not the only one who needs help!"

Yes, but they're not holding their hockey sticks like pitchforks, I'd like to say. Instead, I take a deep breath and back off. "Sure thing. You call me when you need me."

Should be timed perfectly with hell freezing over.

I skate over to one of Courtney's teammates, who's trying to master the art of stickhandling a puck around her hockey gloves. I watch her for a while, then put a hand on her shoulder.

"Your stick's too short," I tell her.

"But my dad says it's good enough. "

"Your dad's wrong."

Her face lights up. "I told him the same thing," she says.

I show her how tall her stick should be, demonstrating with my own.

I help another girl with her grip, and then watch Kathy, who's working on slapshots with some of the more skilled players, like Gia.

Skilled, yes, but I'm glad I won't have to deal with her in the dressing room next year. I'll be long gone.

Afterwards, I wait in the rink lobby for Courtney to finish getting undressed. There's not much time between her practice and mine. Kathy's already headed over to Spectra Place. I try to avoid talking to the bantam parents, but one of the dads sneaks up on me.

"What do you think of the team?" he asks.

I load him up with clichés.

Then he starts telling me about his daughter's plans for getting an NCAA scholarship and using that as a stepping stone to the Canadian National Team.

Every little girl's dream. Shared by every little girl's daddy.

Courtney and Gia finally come along. Courtney dumps my equipment at my feet. No thanks for letting her use my stuff. No kiss my ass. No nothing.

"Thanks for helping, Jessie. See you, Court," Gia says before she walks away.

I pick up my equipment. "You improved a lot from the beginning to the end of practice. If you keep working hard on shooting and stickhandling, you might get a point this year."

Courtney snorts and mutters something under her breath.

"You've had a mad on the whole practice. What's the problem?" I ask.

"Why can't you leave me alone?"

"I care about you. I don't want you to make the same mistakes I made."

"That's just it!" Courtney explodes. "You don't make mistakes! Do you know how hard it is growing up in *your* shadow?" Her tone becomes increasingly sarcastic. "Perfect Jessie McIntyre. Hockey star. Model student. I hate it!"

"Do you want me to stop coming to your practices?"

She wipes an eye with her finger. "Gia wants you and Kathy to come all the time."

"What do you want?" I persist.

"I don't know," she says. "I'd be easier if Kathy helped me."

My phone plinks. "You better go. Dad's waiting for you, and I have to get to *my* practice."

She turns and walks towards the exit.

"You're welcome!" I shout at her back.

# chapter
## twenty-nine

**O**n Friday after school we leave for North Battleford. Mr. Johnstone had originally booked a charter bus, but he cancelled it after the rookie party fiasco.

So it's up to us to find a way to North Battleford – a six-hour drive, not including pee breaks. Our games are scheduled for Saturday and Sunday afternoon. Amy and I hop in with Kathy and Mr. Parker.

It takes a while for Mr. Parker to get our equipment and Amy's goalie pads stacked in the back of his SUV. Red-faced and puffing, he eventually opens the driver door and fumbles around in the console.

"I need a cigarette." He digs one from a package. "Hope you don't mind waiting a few minutes longer."

"As long as you don't mind me chewing." Amy spits some brown juice into the pop can in her hand.

"How can you do that?" I ask her. "It's gross."

She shrugs.

"Have you tried to quit?" Kathy asks from the front seat.
Amy shakes her head.

"I heard the best way is to eat Milkbones," Kathy says.
"They kill your craving for nicotine."

"Yuck. I think I'd rather chew." I look at Mr. Parker outside, waving his cigarette around while he talks on his cellphone. "Everybody's got their addiction, I suppose."

"What's yours?" Amy asks.

"Making bad decisions."

"Why do you say that?" Amy says. "You play great D."

"Thanks," I reply, "but I was talking about life, not sports."

"Correct me if I'm wrong, but weren't you all three outs in one inning in softball last season?" Kathy reminds me.

"Is that possible?" Amy asks.

"It is if Jessie strikes out twice, gets put in as a pinch runner, and gets picked off at first base."

"Thanks for remembering." I dig my phone out and pretend to check my messages.

"So how do you like your new D partner?" Amy asks. "The two of you looked all right in practice."

Amy's referring to Dayna. Bud's decided to pair me with her, instead of Jennifer.

"And how about that power play unit, huh?" Kathy asks. "Did you ever think you'd be QB1, Jessie?"

"No." The thought makes me a little queasy. Quarterbacking the power play is something I've dreamed of, but reality is something else.

"It's gonna be a great weekend," Kathy says. "I'm feeling a W. Two of them in fact."

The North Battleford Sharks have a very talented centre who skates circles around us. When the puck is on Number 4's stick, none of us can take it away from her.

On the other hand, anyone watching our first game would think Dayna and I are Dumb and Dumber. One time I'm behind the net getting the puck, and Dayna arrives a second later. I look at her, and she looks at me, and it's like, "If you're back here, and I'm back here, who's watching Number 4?"

We end up losing the puck, and the Sharks' star player scores on us again. Later on a PK, I try to clear the puck, but end up scooping it right into her stomach. It falls at her feet, and she rips a shot at Amy, scoring low blocker.

You're welcome, Number 4.

On power plays, I suck at setting up behind our net. I'm having trouble predicting the right moment to start up the ice. The Sharks keep plugging up my passing lanes.

I end up minus three on Saturday afternoon.

The Oilers – minus Jodi – are incapable of getting the

puck past the Sharks' netminder. We lose 4–0.

The goose egg haunts us in Game 2 on Sunday afternoon. We lose by a narrower margin of 2–0.

But a loss is a loss. The failure to score even once on the weekend means there's virtually nothing to celebrate.

Bud tells us not to worry. "You girls are playing good defence," he says. "The goals will take care of themselves."

"Maybe if Sue had been along, things would have been different," Kathy says on the ride home.

"Maybe," I concede.

But I know we're all thinking the loss of Jodi hurt as much as Sue's absence.

What if we never score another goal?

It's nearly midnight when Mr. Parker drops me off at home. All I want to do is take my equipment downstairs to air out and go straight to bed. The house is dark, which suits me fine.

Everybody must be in bed already.

I use the garage entrance, which leads to the small entryway adjoining our kitchen. A strange smell greets me as I open the back door. When I flip on the light, I notice sections of newspaper scattered everywhere.

"What the heck?"

The doorway to the kitchen is barricaded with a baby gate, and there's a small dog kennel in the corner. I bend down and peer inside. Two black eyes, beneath fluffy white bangs, peer back at me.

"Hello, little fella." I fumble with the latch on the kennel. As soon as I open the door a white ball with black ears spills out and bounds onto my lap.

"Who are you?" I pick up the puppy and hold his squirming body against my chest. "Whoever you are, you're cute."

He licks my face.

The kitchen light turns on, and I see Mom standing there in her robe. "I thought I heard a car," she says. "What do you think of him?"

"He's adorable, except for his breath." I turn my head away as a pink tongue tries to explore my ear. "When did he arrive?"

"Your dad picked him up from a breeder in Regina on Saturday. He's a Coton-de-Tulear."

"A what?"

"Just call him Rufus."

"Sure thing, Rufus. You're beautiful, did you know that? Beautiful." I hold him closer. "He's a pretty fine birthday present. I hope Courtney appreciates him."

"She's gaga over him," Mom says.

"Good thing – because he's such a big boy, isn't he?"

"So how was North Battleford?" Mom leans against the doorway.

"A disaster. Without Jodi, we're terrible."

"Did both goalies play?"

"Actually Amy played both games. Apparently she's not coming next weekend, so Miranda will start." Reluctantly I put Rufus back into his kennel and close the door. "I'm not looking forward to it."

Mom holds her fingers to her mouth to conceal a yawn. "The season's barely underway. You girls will get better."

"That's the whole problem. I don't know if we can."

"If you don't believe in your team, who's going to?" Mom asks.

She may not know much about hockey, but every once in a while, she sets me straight.

She shuts off the light, and Rufus starts whimpering.

I hesitate in the doorway. His black nose is poking through the bars of the kennel door. "He could sleep with me tonight."

"No, he can't." Mom gives me a gentle push. "If he smells weakness, we're dead in the water."

# *chapter* *thirty*

**R**ufus becomes the centre of our universe. Mom comes home at lunch to keep him company. Dad falls asleep in front of the TV with the puppy tucked under his arm. On days when Courtney has volleyball, I slide home after school for a little Quality Rufus Time before hockey practice or dryland.

But it's Courtney who spends the most time with him, taking him for walks, measuring out his dog food, playing with him for hours on end. Mom and Dad's master plan seems to be working like a charm. Move over Gia. Make room for Rufus.

Courtney's hockey team has more luck on the ice than mine. Our double-header in Prince Albert has nearly the same result as the one in North Battleford. We don't score a single point, and Miranda gives up fourteen goals, six in one game and eight in the next. Morale on the Estevan McGillicky Oilers is at an all-time low.

After the second game, Bud says to me, "I'm counting on you to kick start this team, Jessie."

"What do you want me to do?" I reply, frustrated. "If I step up on offence, who's going to cover the blue line?"

"Have some faith in your teammates," Bud says. "Jump into the play. Shake things up. Quit playing like you're afraid."

Courtney's team travels to Weyburn and beats their bantam team 4–3. Courtney is walking on air all week, regaling us with stories of the dressing room, the Dairy Queen, Gia and the road trip home in the Beastie Bus.

Frankly, the success of her team is sickening. But it has at least one positive result. Dad takes Courtney shopping for new equipment. No more strapping on soggy elbow pads.

On Halloween I get a cold blast from my not too distant past. I have to pick up Mom after dryland that day because the Explorer's getting a wheel alignment.

Evan is the first person I see when I walk through the door of the law office. He's talking to the receptionist.

I can't pretend I don't see him because we instantly make eye contact.

"Hello, Jessie." His voice is devoid of expression.

"Hello." I feel like a fool. "How are you?"

"How do you think I am?" he counters.

This is going to be ugly.

"You didn't try to go back, did you?" I ask.

"No." He takes a sip from the water bottle he's holding.

"Are you going to Bible college next fall?"

The receptionist's head is swiveling back and forth between the two of us.

"I have no idea what I want to do," Evan says.

"I'm sorry to hear that. I'm sorry about everything."

"Good for you," he says.

"I never meant for this to happen. I never knew you'd be so serious," I try to explain. "We weren't even going out for that long. Don't you think it's strange that you threw it all away – just because of me? Maybe there were other stresses in your life. Maybe you should see a doctor or something."

He lets me ramble, his eyes judging me. "Are you saying I need a psychiatrist?"

"No, I'm not."

"You're the one who could use some help," he says, screwing the lid back on the plastic bottle. "I'm done talking about this."

Mrs. Gedak and Breanne come down the hall right then. Breanne takes one look at me and starts crying. Mrs. Gedak doesn't say a word. She grabs Breanne's hand and pushes past me.

Evan turns and follows them both out of the office.

Oh yeah, going to hell for sure.

On the ride home I don't tell Mom about it. I'm too embarrassed. I know things can't be very good between her and Mrs. Gedak at work. It's all my fault.

I spend Halloween night giving out candy to little kids while Courtney goes trick or treating with Gia. Dad bought Rufus a Zorro costume, and we manage to keep it on him for an hour. Bud brings by Zack and his other two grandchildren.

They are so sweet.

On the other hand, my little sister comes home two hours past her curfew, and Mom and Dad tie into her. Rufus and I hide in my room, where I cave on nutrition and consume a dozen mini chocolate bars.

When I go to bed, I stare at Liam's phone number and wrestle down the urge to call him. I gaze at the ceiling for a long time, wondering when my high school years will magically metamorphose into the best time of my life.

*T*he first week in November we have a home-and-home series with Melville Prairie Fire. We'll host them on Thursday night, then travel to Melville on Saturday for an afternoon match-up. Bud has been working us hard in practice, but it's obvious we could use a sport psychologist.

Evan's right. I do need help. We've totally lost our confidence, and a few of the Rookies are already talking about playing for other teams next year. Not that I blame them.

Our team is attending the Notre Dame Showcase at the beginning of December. Some of the top Midget teams in

Canada will be there, including the Pursuit of Excellence from Kelowna and Balmoral from Winnipeg. If we can't score a goal in our league, how will we fare against teams of *that* caliber?

As I walk into Spectra Place on Thursday, my equipment bag feels like a lead weight. Where is the joy, I think to myself, when there's such a slight chance we're going to win another game this year.

I keep to myself during the pregame stuff, turning a deaf ear to the banter in the dressing room. I justify my behaviour in the name of mental preparation. But I'm not focused on the upcoming game, as much as I'm replaying moments from previous games. Times when I was zigging when I should have been zagging. Taking risks when I should have been conservative. Being cautious when I should have jumped into the play.

Sue enters long before she normally does and hovers on the fringe of the dressing room routine. Eventually she catches my eye and jerks her head in the direction of the door.

A summons.

I follow her into the hallway.

"Leave your game face at home?" she asks.

That gets my back up right away. "I don't know what you mean," I tell her.

"It's only a popularity contest until you *get* the C, Jessie," she says. "After that, it's lead by example every second, on or off the ice."

"They voted in the wrong girl."

"The hell they did." Sue assures me. "Bud and I are counting on you. Don't you give up on this team."

"But how are we going to win if we can't put the puck in the net?" I wipe away the tear welling in the corner of my eye. "I can't stand losing like that here."

"Are you forgetting everything we talked about the last three practices? Two – one – two. An aggressive forecheck to force turnovers. We're a fast team, Jessie, and we have outstanding goaltending. This year isn't over yet."

L iam and some of his football friends are waiting in the stands when we jump on the ice for our warm-up. They've painted themselves orange, and they're wearing hardhats that light up. They've brought all kinds of noise-makers – cowbells and pots and pans and an air horn hooked up to an air compressor. I can still hear the noise they're making overtop the Motley Crue Mr. Parker is playing in the sound booth.

Bud's paired me with Dayna again, which works for me. She's always asking what she needs to do to be better.

"You and I are going to work our asses off," I tell her as we head out for our first shift. "If we aren't bagged by the end of this game, we've let our teammates down."

She nods.

The first period is a huge improvement on our performance of the last two weekends. Neither team scores, but we tie Prairie Fire on shots, seven a piece. We spend most of the period battling in the neutral zone, but we do get one great scoring opportunity with seconds left in the period.

Kathy gets the puck in deep. She's on the boards behind the net, getting manhandled by Number 6. One of the Rookies is parked in the high slot, fighting to stay open. Kathy flips the puck out to her on her backhand, and the Rookie chops it down in midair and throws it at the wide open net. It bangs the crossbar and bounces away just as the buzzer sounds to end the period.

Number 6 deliberately gives the Rookie the shoulder as she skates past, sending her flying. Kathy lunges at the Melville player, but the linesman grabs her and dances her out of reach.

"Just *try* to pull that shit again!" Kathy screams at Number 6. She calls her a bunch of names too.

Despite my efforts to lobby the ref, Kathy gets an unsportsmanlike, so we're doomed to spend the first two minutes of the next period short-handed.

"Like we needed that," Carla murmurs as we're heading for the dressing room.

"Let it go," I say. "Nothing we can do about it now."

Between periods Bud gives us his analysis of Prairie Fire's forecheck, then hands the floor to Sue, who reviews our PK. For the first time in a long time, it feels like a real hockey game.

When we come back out, Liam and his motley crew have moved their act to the seats above the Prairie Fire bench. The banging is so loud it hurts my ears, and the Melville fans look thoroughly annoyed.

Before Kathy heads across the ice to the penalty box, she chirps at the Prairie Fire bench.

"What did she say?" Dayna asks me.

"I think it was, 'Don't touch the Rooks.'"

Our PK is perfect. Melville doesn't get a single shot on net, and we gain momentum every time we ice the puck. I ring one around the glass with seconds left, and Kathy picks it up on the fly as she barrels out of the penalty box. She blows past a Prairie Fire defenceman and bears down on their goalie, who comes out of her crease to cut off the angle. Kathy dekes left, then toe drags around her and pokes the puck through the daylight between the goalie's left skate and the post. The puck barely squirts over the line, but the red light glows. Carried by the momentum of her rush, Kathy slams shoulder first into the corner, then bounces back to her feet, miraculously unhurt, only to be tackled by Randi and Carla.

We are deafened by Liam's air horn, which announces the

goal long before Mr. Parker does.

Kathy's goal turns out to be the only one of the game — for either team. As we shake hands with our scowling opponents, it's hard to keep the grin off my face.

When I reach the Melville coach, he squeezes my fingers firmly and says, "Great game, Captain. Bus legs got us today. We'll be ready for you Saturday."

The boys in orange are hoarse from screaming as we step off the ice. They lean over the glass and smack our heads as we parade by.

"Way to go, Oilers!" Liam shouts.

It's hard to take him seriously when he's wearing a sombrero, a black handlebar moustache, and orange paint for a shirt.

That's the last thing you want to do...take him seriously, my little voice says.

I try to walk past without making eye contact, but he calls my name and points to a guy standing next to him.

"Jessie, this is my brother Russell!" he calls.

Russell's not quite as tall as Liam. Instead of being painted orange, he's wearing an Edmonton Oilers jersey and World War I flying ace headgear and goggles.

"Nice to meet you!" I call back.

"Go Estevan!" Russell jangles a cowbell over his head.

"I have to go!" I wave and walk away.

Mr. Johnstone manages to slide into the dressing room in the wake of our coaches. He's grinning from ear to ear. He seeks out Kathy immediately. "That goal was a beauty!" Then he singles out each of us for praise until Mrs. Jordan ushers him back through the door.

The coaches give us about thirty seconds to bask in the glory of our greatness before they start delivering Saturday's game plan. When they're done, I take a cue from Mr. Johnstone and make a point of telling each Rookie what she did right.

"We can't take Saturday's game lightly," I say to Dayna. "They'll be ready for us."

"We'll be ready for them too," Dayna says.

iam and Russell and my family are waiting for me in the lobby.

"You've got quite the cheering section." Dad nods his head in Liam's direction. "You know these boys?"

"Sort of." I smile and wave at Liam and Russell, hoping that will appease them.

Mom gives me a significant look, but she doesn't say anything.

"Great game," Dad says. "Easily your best sixty minutes this year."

"Thanks." Out of the corner of my eye, I can see Liam's

making his way over.

Oh please.

At least he's wearing a jacket now.

"Jessie, can I talk to you for a minute?" he asks.

I have no choice but to turn and face him. "What's up?"

"I'm having a party out at my place on Saturday. I was hoping you'd come. Most of the other girls said they would."

I feel the jaws of a trap pinching me. "I'm not sure what time we'll get back from Melville. If it's not too late, then maybe we could."

"Great," he says. "Oh, and Russell has something he'd like to ask you."

"Will you sign my jersey?" Russell asks, holding out a Sharpie. His jersey is covered with autographs.

"I'd be honoured." On his right shoulder, I carefully write my initials above a Number 13.

"Liam likes you," Russell says.

If I wasn't blushing before, I am now.

"Jessie knows that, Captain Obvious." Liam laughs. "See you Saturday night, Hockey Girl. And good luck in Melville."

"Nice fellas?" Dad asks, watching them leave.

"Too nice," I reply.

# chapter
## thirty-one

**W**e end up sweeping Melville, winning the second game 3–2 in overtime. Miranda's in net for this one, and she plays over her head.

"You are an inspiration," Bud tells her.

"I don't know about you guys," Carla says, "but my favourite Ebberts' moment was when she deflected a shot and hit that guy right in the nuggets."

She times the remark perfectly with Randi taking a sip out of her water bottle. Randi's spray reaches halfway across the dressing room, and Kathy has to pound her between the shoulder blades to help her cough up the liquid that went down the wrong way.

We're all cracking up. I nearly pee my pants, recalling the expression on "that guy's" face, as he sat there with a lap full of chicken nuggets.

We're back in Estevan by nine o'clock. After a quick shower, I pick up Amber, Kathy and Dayna and head a few kilometres west of town for the victory party at Liam's place. Apparently he's got a heated arena, where he's hosted some epic football parties in the past.

"It's an awesome locale, even if Liam's dad is the party Nazi." Kathy says. "And you have to give Liam's mom your car keys when you get there."

"You're kidding me," I say. "I don't drink. I'm not giving up my keys."

You might need to make a quick getaway, my little voice says.

"Take the next left," Kathy says.

A familiar half-ton is parked at the lane entrance, with two Labs milling in the truck box. A big man climbs out and wanders into the middle of the road, blocking our path. I stop, put Sunny in park, and roll down the window. The man shines a flashlight in my face.

"Name?" he barks.

"Jessie McIntyre," I reply, squinting. "And this is Kathy Parker, Amber Kowalski and Dayna Something."

The flashlight swings around, inspecting each of the occupants. I get a closer look at the man who must be Liam's dad. He's got craggy, pockmarked features and Liam's bushy brows, which make him resemble a bird of prey.

"Head over to the house," he says at last. "Knock on the door and give your keys to Connie."

"Actually, I won't need to do that," I tell him. "You see I don't..."

"Just go with it," Kathy says. "Thanks, Mr. MacArthur!"

He steps back from Sunny and gestures impatiently at the vehicle behind us.

"What does Liam's dad do for a living?" I ask Kathy.

"Works rigs," Kathy says.

"Ohhhh." Everyone says at once.

"I bet nobody messes with him," Amber says.

The two labs bound out of the truck box and escort us to the house, barking excitedly, tails wagging, and tongues lolling.

"I don't like big dogs," Dayna says.

The smaller lab greets me when I open my door. She's practically wriggling out of her skin.

"Some guard dog!" I laugh.

Liam's mom, who has long red hair and Liam's quirky gap-toothed smile, is friendly too. She shakes hands with each of us as we introduce ourselves. Her grip is firmer than I would have expected from a woman, and her hand feels calloused and rough. She tags my car keys and hangs them on a pegboard behind the door.

"You girls come here if you need to pee," Mrs. MacArthur says. "The boys can use the great outdoors. The world is their bathroom."

"I know, and it sucks," Amber says.

"Have a good time," she says. "But be careful around those football players. Don't get fooled by any sweet talk."

The dogs are gone when we come out of the house. The ground between it and the arena is a wasteland of frozen mud and ice patches and horse turds. The cold night air is pungent with barn smell.

"I hope we get to see Liam's horses," Dayna says. "I really like horses."

"You don't like big dogs, but you like horses," Kathy says. "Does that make sense?"

There're already a couple dozen people at the party. Most of them are my teammates and football players. The quonset is lit with floodlights and a few strands of Christmas bulbs. It has a soft dirt floor, but there's plywood laid out for dancing and an assortment of picnic tables and benches for seating. Some big heaters are blowing warm air not far from a bar made of planks and barrels, where Amy and a few football players are gathered. Liam's serving them in his shirt sleeves.

"Is this a rave?" Amber asks.

"Hardly," Kathy says.

We join the rest of our team, congregated close to the heaters, and exchange enthusiastic hugs and high fives.

"We're on a roll now!" Miranda announces, smacking my outstretched palm.

"Want a coke, Jessie?" Dayna asks.

"Sure." I hang back while Liam bartends for my carpool. When they return, they're hanging on Amber, laughing.

"What's so funny?" I ask while Dayna hands me a can of Coke.

"Amber's got a new nickname," Kathy wheezes. "Liam called her Betty Boop."

"I don't know why." Amber frowns.

"He also wants to know if you'd like to see his horses. He said he'd take us over to the barn," Dayna says.

"All of us?" I ask.

Kathy sips her drink. "I don't think he cares who comes along – so long as *you* do."

I'm glad it's too dark for her to see my face.

Dayna, Kathy, Amber and I follow Liam to the barn. It's a long, rambling building east of the quonset. Liam unbars a large sliding door and heaves it open, stepping aside to let us walk past. The barn is warmer than the quonset and better lit. There're four large stalls on either side and several narrow ones. The usual horsey sounds greet us: hooves, snorts and large molars grinding hay.

A pretty sorrel head is looking at us from the first stall.

"This is Rusty," Liam says, reaching up to scratch the horse's ears. "She's my ticket. Six-year-old quarter horse. Her registered name is Lady Freckles Lena."

"This is your favourite girl," I say.

Liam stares at me so intently I drop my gaze.

We all take turns rubbing the white stripe on Rusty's nose, patting her red coat, and generally sucking up. Liam disappears into the tack room and returns with an apple and a small knife. He cuts off a section for each of us, so we can feed her a treat.

"She's beautiful," Dayna says as Rusty takes the chunk of apple from her outstretched palm. "Why is she your ticket?"

"I'm training her to compete at Agribition," Liam says.

He briefly outlines the contest, which has three separate events: reining, cutting and fence work. The competition is followed by an auction. Proceeds from Rusty's sale will help pay for Liam's university education.

"What do you hope to get for her?" Kathy asks.

"What I hope for and what I'll get are two entirely different things," Liam says. "Horse prices have tanked lately."

"That's a big risk, isn't it?" I ask.

"Anything worthwhile is risky." Liam rubs Rusty behind the ears.

"Won't you be sad to sell her?" Dayna asks.

"Oh yeah," Liam says, as Rusty shoves Liam with her nose, pushing him back.

"I think she's saying she'll miss you too," Amber says.

"Going to Agribition is a big deal," Kathy observes. "People come from all over Canada and the US to compete."

"That's the general idea," he says. "Hopefully there'll be a rancher who wants a great little cow horse like Rusty."

He takes us to the other stalls and introduces us to a three-year-old colt nicknamed Sherman and an old gelding named Buster.

Liam nods. "Buster was Dad's horse back in the day. Dad doesn't ride anymore because of his knees. But he was quite a cowboy when he was in his prime. He did it all – saddle bronc, bull riding, calf roping. But his best event was steer wrestling."

"Those poor steers wouldn't stand a chance," Kathy says.

Liam slides the door shut behind us as we leave the barn.

"Thanks for letting us see your horses," Amber says.

"My pleasure," he says.

I try to plant myself in the middle of the girls on the way back to the quonset, but Liam calls out to me, "Jessie, hold on a sec."

I can't see the girls' expressions as they walk past, but Kathy flicks me on my ear. "Be nice!" she hisses.

Once they're gone, Liam asks, "So how's it going with Whitney?"

"We don't talk."

"She ever fess up to starting that rumour?"

"No, and it doesn't matter. She's learned the value of keeping her mouth shut." I take a few steps towards the arena entrance.

"Are you mad at me?" he asks.

"No."

"Are you sure?"

"Yes. Can I go back to the party now?"

"You *are* mad at me."

"I'm not."

"You're been avoiding me for weeks. Most of the time, you won't even look at me."

"I'm dealing with stuff."

"We're right back to where we were before Whitney's party," he says. "I thought we were making progress."

"Progress?" I laugh. "Where are we supposed to be *going?*"

"Wherever you'll let me take you," he says quietly.

His honesty is unnerving.

"Liam, I just got out of a relationship. I can't do that again."

He shifts his weight to his other foot, considering. "Just what are you saving yourself for?"

"Aren't you being a little personal?"

"I'm not talking about sex," Liam says. "It's obvious you're not *that* kind of girl. That's probably why you started dating Billy Graham. So you wouldn't have to worry about sex."

I'm blushing now. "Who in the hell have you been talking to?"

"Think about it, Jessie. A long distance relationship with a guy who's saving himself for his wedding night. What could be safer?"

"What happened with me and Evan is none of your business!"

"Can we talk about us then?"

"There is no *us.*"

My eyes have adjusted to the dark, and I can see his face more clearly. He's frozen in place, eyes intent.

"If you won't go out with me," he says, "don't go out with anybody else. Okay?" He grabs my hand and squeezes it gently. His palm feels hard, like his mother's.

"Look, it's not you that's the problem." I try to take my hand back, but he locks his fingers firmly around mine. "It's me."

He steps closer. "How about I kiss you? That should convince me it's not going to work."

"You're only interested in me because I'm *not* interested in you," I tell him. "If you kiss me, you won't find me nearly as fascinating."

He brings his face close to mine. "Close enough to *yes,*" he says.

His lips are soft and gentle, but when the kiss deepens, I pull away. He leans in again, but I step back. My blood is rushing to places, and my pulse is racing.

"No more," I whisper, freeing my hand.

He clears his throat. "So much for that theory."

"I'm going back inside," I squeak out. "The girls'll be wondering where I am."

You're ridiculous, my little voice says.

"Please don't go yet," Liam says. "I want to ask you something." It comes out in a rush. "I want you to be my escort for grad."

Oh no.

"Liam, I can't. The truth is...there's this other guy, and I still like him."

My stupid words just hang in the air between us, surprising me as much as him.

He folds his arms across his chest. "I guess that's that." He exhales slowly. "I won't be bothering you anymore."

He goes in the arena, leaving me in the dark.

# chapter
## thirty-two

O ne thing I will say for alcohol. Sometimes it paves the road to reconciliation.

I'm not sure what went on at Liam's party because I left five minutes after my conversation with him ended. But Monday morning at our usual table in the courtyard, Miranda and Amy are sitting hip to hip, talking and laughing.

"They're BFF's now," Kathy informs me. "You should have seen them at the party. They talked goalie shit until one in the morning."

"Awesome," I tell her. "A little less drama in the dressing room wouldn't hurt us."

"Good thing Brett came over after he got off work," Kathy says pointedly, "or we wouldn't have had a ride."

"Sorry."

"What happened with Liam anyway?" Kathy persists. "You stayed back to talk to him after we looked at the horses."

"Nothing," I reply.

She raises a blonde eyebrow. "Then why'd you take off like somebody shoved a firecracker up your ass?"

"Don't go there," I say.

"Up your ass?" she replies. "No problem."

"Did you know Liam named his dogs Little Ann and Old Dan, after the dogs in *Where the Red Fern Grows?*" Amber asks.

"Awww," everyone says.

"I loved that book," Amber says.

"Liam is so cool," Dayna says. "He's our best fan."

"Yeah, he is," Kathy says. "Isn't that right, Jessie?"

Mercifully the buzzer sounds for first class, and I seize the excuse to get the hell out of Dodge.

Kathy's right behind me though.

"Mac, you are gonna tell me what happened at that party if it's the last thing you do," she says.

I stop so suddenly she runs into me, knocking my books to the floor.

"What the hell, Parker."

"What the hell yourself."

As we gather up my stuff, we narrowly avoid being trampled by the other students. When the hallway's quiet, I tell her what happened. I nearly choke on the words, but I tell her everything. For once I don't care if I'm late for class, and neither does Kathy.

"You're crazy, McIntyre," Kathy says. "Deep down, you think you're saving yourself for Mark, is that right?"

"I don't know," I say. "Do you think there's a chance I'll get to see him when we play Saskatoon? The Hitmen are playing there that weekend."

"Who cares? The final buzzer sounded on Mark a long time ago. Meanwhile back at the ranch, Liam's the real deal. Just ask Amy."

"I'm an idiot." I blink back the tears. "And I don't know how to fix this."

"You don't have to fix it," Kathy says. "Just quit screwing up."

*T*he week passes quickly enough. I see Liam a few times in the hallway and the cafeteria, but now he's avoiding *me.*

Should that surprise you, my little voice asks.

If only there were a couple more hours in the day. There's barely enough time for hockey and the gym, studying for unit exams in calculus and biology, finishing up an essay on *Hamlet,* and helping out with Courtney's practice on Tuesday and her game against Moose Jaw on Thursday night. Gia's dad wants me to run the defence.

It's kind of fun. The girls want to play better, and at least I don't have to deal with Courtney. She does much better with Kathy or Gia's dad giving her pointers on how to play left wing. One time in the Moose Jaw game, she ends up on a 2 and 0 with Gia, and it looks like she's going to go offside.

"Oh shit," I moan.

Just before she hits the blue line, she slows and lets Gia blow by, setting up behind her. When Gia fakes a shot and lets the puck drop back between her skates, Courtney winds up to fire on net but fans on the shot.

She bangs her stick when she comes to the bench and curses under her breath.

"Hey, Number 16," I say, taking a chance. "That was heads-up, even if you didn't get a shot away."

Her head swivels in my direction, and for a second I think she's going to swear at me too. Then she nods in acknowledgment and turns her eyes back to the ice.

"That's my baby sister," I tell one of the defenceman.

"So you keep telling us," the girl replies.

**O**n Friday after school my mom drives me to Saskatoon for our double-header with the Stars.

Miranda gets the nod for our Saturday afternoon game, and she plays decent, but we're no match for Saskatoon's two top lines. She gives up five goals on thirty-three shots. Whitney manages to score late in the third, so at least there's no goose egg.

When I come out of the dressing room, Holly's leaning

on a set of crutches, talking to my mom and Kathy.

"What happened?" I ask.

"Damn ankle sprain," Holly says. "It keeps coming back to haunt me. We've got a tournament out East at New Year's, and I want to be healthy enough to go."

"Well, it's nice of you to come watch us," I tell her. "You're going to Mark's game tonight, right?"

Tonight, on the other side of the city, the Calgary Hitmen will be playing the Blades, and I won't be able to go.

Why *should* you, my little voice asks. It only lasted a few months, and it's been over for two years. You don't even know him anymore, and he doesn't know you.

Holly nods. "Are you coming? I know there's some news Mark would like to share with you."

"I can't. Bud's arranged for us to watch the U of S women's game tonight from a luxury box."

Bud told us, just before our game. He was so pleased I didn't have the heart to tell him I'd rather be at the Blades game.

Sometimes it bites to be captain.

"How's Mark's dad doing?" Mom asks Holly.

She fills us in on all the details of Mr. Taylor's treatments. Most of it's way over my head, but I'm glad to know he's responding well.

"That's great," I tell her.

"Okay, since you're not coming tonight, I'll share *Mark's*

news." Holly beams. "He thinks he's getting an invite to the World Junior camp in December."

I'm having a tough time equating Holly with the girl who, a few months ago, wanted me to talk Mark *out* of playing Major Junior. "Does he really think he'd make the team?"

"There's only three guys returning from last year," Holly says.

"Wow." I think about the ramification of this news. Mark has never been drafted, but not every player makes it to the NHL through the traditional route. The World Junior tournament has launched the careers of many unscouted athletes.

Holly looks at her phone. "I better go. I want to get in a few hours of studying before the game. What time do you play tomorrow?"

"Two."

"I'll try to come, but I can't make any promises," she says. "I have two midterms and a lab exam next week." She gives me a quick hug, made awkward by the crutches. "See you!"

Kathy runs ahead to hold the door open for her while Mom whispers in my ear, "How are you feeling?"

"Okay."

"You're finally letting go of him?"

"I'm trying to."

"Good for you," she says. "Let's get something to eat."

**P**uck drop is at seven. I spend most of the first period watching the Huskie rookies, gauging their skill level and their ice time. One rookie defenceman is on a power play unit and does some PK.

Good to know.

It's pretty cool watching the game from a luxury box, which has the best view in the rink. No exit signs or posts to block our vision.

The Huskies are playing their archrivals, the Regina Cougars, which means the stands are nearly full. Apparently in Regina last night, the Huskies won 4–3 in a shoot out.

"Out of nine shots, five girls hit the post and one hit a crossbar," Kathy says. "Wish I could have been there to see that."

I ask our vets to sit with Rookies who are playing similar positions. "Tell them to watch the little and big things these university players do. We'll talk about it at our next practice."

When I'm not answering Dayna's questions about defence, I get Larissa to check the Blades game on her iPhone. The score's been deadlocked 2–2 since the end of the first period. By the time the Huskies have treated the Cougars to a 6–1 drubbing, the WHL game is just beginning the final period of play.

"Could we go some place like Boston Pizza and watch the Blades' game?" I ask Mom.

"I doubt it will be televised," Mom says.

"Maybe we can catch the highlights on Global," Kathy says.

It takes ages to get everybody organized and headed in the same direction. Then we have to wait for a table when we get to the restaurant.

"Do you know if the Blades won tonight?" I ask our waiter as soon as we're seated.

"Sure did," he says. "In overtime."

Mark won't be happy about that. I check my phone and see I've got voice mail.

"How come I never heard it ring?" I say out loud.

"What's that?" Kathy asks.

"Nothing." I punch in my password.

As soon as I hear Holly's voice, I know something's wrong.

"His *knee.*" Her voice is breaking.

At that very moment, Global shows the game highlights. One piece of footage is of a Blades player laying a hit on a Calgary defenceman, just as he is executing a sharp right pivot. They show it over and over again. Forwards. Backwards. Fast motion. Slow motion.

But every time, two variables remain the same.

The Calgary defenceman is definitely Mark.

And that knee is definitely not going to a World Junior camp in December.

# chapter
## thirty-three

I t sucks. Totally," Kathy says in the dressing room before our game on Sunday.

It took me a long time to get to sleep last night. Every time I drifted off that footage kept replaying in my head. I know next to nothing about the anatomy of a knee, but even I know that's a season-ending, potentially career-ending injury. It makes me feel sick to think his torn ACL might never hold a pivot again, even after surgery.

What about Mark's dad? What about all the hopes and dreams he's had for his son? How will this setback affect Frank? *Sucks* isn't a word that even comes close. I want to call them both, but I have no idea what to say. Mark's got a good head on his shoulders, I tell myself. He'll get his engineering degree like he always planned. He'll move on.

With Holly, my little voice reminds me.

I take extra care putting on my equipment. I feel fragile. Any minute something could happen. A girl could give me a little nudge next to the boards and I could end up para-lyzed – or worse. The fingers tying my skates are actually trembling.

Snap out of it, my little voice says. A city bus could have hit you yesterday. Your mom could roll the Explorer on the way home. Tragedy can happen any time. Any place. Would you rather live in a plastic bubble?

I think about something Jodi said to me after her acci-dent. *It would have been my last game – and I didn't even play it.*

Well, I'm playing today.

In hockey there are so many variables. Twelve players on the ice at any given moment. Every one of them the key performers in her own little universe.

Countless variations.

My boyfriend broke up with me.

My dad says I suck.

Why did I have to have my period *today?*

Then there's officiating.

A call – or a no call – can destroy a team's momentum in a second.

Too many variables.

In our second game against Saskatoon, all the planets roll and lock into perfect alignment. The fickle deities of ice hockey, suspended high above the play in their invisible luxury boxes, pluck the crucial weight from our golden plate and watch us rise.

Okay, hockey gods be damned.

Amy has a *lot* to do with it.

I have doubts about where I'll be playing one year from now. But there's no question about Amy Fox. She is destined for bigger things.

Then again, there's nobody like Bud to help put stuff in perspective.

"Do the math, girls," Bud says. "Saskatoon scored five power plays goals yesterday. Five on five you beat them one zip. Stay out of the box, execute the PK properly when you don't, and play like you played yesterday. Show them you belong in this league."

We hit the ice running in the first period. We take it to the Stars on our very first shift, crashing the net and tallying four shots before their goalie finally freezes the puck. The momentum of the first line buoys the second. Three minutes pass and the Stars still haven't moved the puck past their blue line. While we've got them tied up, our third line switches in, player by player.

Totally textbook.

Sue juggles the D too, throwing Carla and me back out.

One of the Stars crosschecks Larissa in front of the crease, and the ref raises her arm. Amy races for the bench while

Randi barrels into the high slot as the sixth attacker. She hammers her stick, calling for the puck, and I saucer it over to her. Tape to tape.

She shoots. Low glove side. Buries it.

You'd think we'd won the Stanley Cup final instead of scoring the first goal against the second ranked team in our league, the team that won the Mac's last December.

I'm on Randi's heels as we sweep by our shrieking bench. Sue nearly clotheslines me, yanking on my jersey and tugging me close. "Line up as a left winger!" she shouts in my ear. "Randi's lining up on left D. Kathy's going to win that draw back to Randi. Give and go with Randi and she goes wide!"

I know Sue well enough not to question why.

When the linesman drops the puck, Kathy executes perfectly. As Number 10 steps around me to cut Randi off, Randi snaps me the puck, and I flip it back. The Stars right D catches an edge trying to back pedal, and Randi blows by her. We're three on one. The Stars' left D flops down to take away the back door pass, but Randi rifles the puck to me.

I wait. Wait for the goalie to move. Pull the trigger – going five hole.

Red light.

I don't know which makes us happier – the fact we scored *again* – or the fact we accomplished one of Sue's plays.

And Sue, the coach who rarely smiles, is grinning like a

lion that's just swallowed the lion tamer, whip and all.

Bud squeezes my shoulder as I line up on the bench. "Great job, Cap," he murmurs in my ear. "No mercy now. Keep your foot on the gas."

**A**fter a gritty 3–0 win, Randi, Amy and I are named game stars.

"Bet that hurts," Randi says as she watches the *real* Stars file back to their dressing room.

"We did them a favour," Amy says. "It isn't any fun if they win all the time."

"Can't wait to play the Hounds," Kathy says.

Carla laughs. "Don't kid yourself. Notre Dame will chew us up and spit us out."

"Maybe they will and maybe they won't," Kathy says, pulling out a Bud-ism. "That's why we play the game."

Later in the dressing room, I check my phone. There's a text from Holly, saying that Mark's headed back to Calgary for surgery.

Tell him I feel bad for him, I text back.

Sure will, she replies.

I look up to see Whitney staring at me. I bet she hasn't said a dozen words to me since the Rookie party fiasco. Of course, that's more than I've said to her.

Maybe you could let her off the hook, my voice says.

"Good game, Johnstone," I say. "This afternoon you played both ends of the ice."

"Don't I normally?" she replies coldly.

"Are you giving your captain the sauce...after she gives *you* a compliment?" Kathy asks.

Whitney ducks her head and mumbles something.

"I thought not," Kathy says.

# chapter thirty-four

**W**e got an invite to the Mac's," Bud announces before practice on Tuesday.

We're gathered around him on the ice.

"You're kidding." Randi shifts her position so she's leaning on the opposite knee.

Kathy is speechless.

"Sue wanted to give you the news herself, but she got tied up at work. How many of you left the week open between Christmas and New Years?"

What was I thinking...telling Brittni I'd be a bridesmaid? I shake off my gloves and tighten a skate lace, gathering my thoughts.

"Only the top four teams in our league get an invite," Carla says, "and we're definitely *not* in the top four. In fact, we're in sixth place."

"Yep," Bud says.

"So how come we get to go?" Larissa asks.

"I'm guessing it's because Sue knows the right people," Amy says.

"That's right," Mr. Johnstone says from inside the players' box, where Bud always tells him to stay until he's done talking to us. "So hopefully none of you ladies have made plans for Christmas holidays."

"I have," I say.

Bud looks at me. "What's up, Jessie?"

"I'm a bridesmaid at a wedding on New Year's Eve."

"Since when?" Kathy asks, discovering her voice at last.

"I've known about it for a while," I say.

"Whose wedding?" Kathy asks.

I finish tying my lace. "It's not important."

*"Whose* wedding?" Kathy persists.

"Brittni Wade."

*"Brittni Wade!"* Randi exclaims, throwing herself on the ice, like she's passed out from the shock.

Everyone laughs, even the Rookies, who don't know Brittni at all.

"You're out of your mind, McIntyre! "Kathy says. "Out – of – your – freakin' – mind!"

"When did you even *see* Brittni Wade?" Miranda asks.

"I told you I saw her when we were at the Rider game last August." I start working on my other skate. "Can we talk about somebody *else's* holiday plans?"

Randi raises her head from her prone position. "You saw her at a Rider game, and she asked you to be a *bridesmaid?* Just like that?"

"It was a while later," I explain. "She called me."

"And you said *yes?*"

"As a matter of fact, I did."

"Got your bridesmaid's dress yet?" Kathy asks. "I'll bet it's super gaudy."

"Then you'd be wrong. We're supposed to pick out the quintessential little black dress."

Everyone stares at me, mouths open.

"It actually makes a lot of sense," I tell them. "Very understated."

"Well, it looks like Big Mac won't be going to the Mac's," Bud says. "And that's a disappointment. You can't get out of this wedding, Jessie?"

"I can try," I tell him. "I'd rather go to Calgary, that's for sure."

It turns out Miranda's the only other one who'll be away. She's going to Mexico with her family.

"That's too bad, Miranda," Bud says, keeping his face expressionless. "We'll miss you in Calgary."

"If I'd known we were getting an invite, I wouldn't be going to Mexico," Miranda says.

I feel the same way. Going to Brittni's wedding doesn't

hold the appeal of going to a major tournament in Calgary, especially since it'll be my only chance to go.

"Maybe it's not too late for Brittni to find someone else to stand up for her," I say to Kathy.

"Can I be there when you run it by her?" Kathy asks. "I'd sure like to hear what she says about *that.*"

**A**ll Wednesday I feel like I'm coming down with something. I duck out a half hour early from dryland and hardly eat any supper.

I go to my room and lie down on my bed and stare at my cellphone. Time to bite the bullet. I find Brittni on my contact list.

She's not home, but Jamie is.

"So how are the wedding plans coming?" I ask him.

"I don't understand any of it," Jamie says. "Good thing all I have to do is show up in a white tuxedo."

"Are you going on a honeymoon?"

"We can't afford it."

"Maybe you could go to Vegas," I suggest. "My parents are going for their twentieth wedding anniversary, and they got a great deal."

"Brittni's not twenty-one yet," Jamie says. "Maybe next year." He sounds depressed.

"Who's standing up for you?" I ask, trying to cheer him

up. What guy doesn't like talking about his buds?

"Funny you should ask," he says. "We were going with five attendants, but now I've added Mark, so Brittni has to find another bridesmaid."

My heart jumps. Suddenly I don't feel sick. "Do you mean Mark Taylor?"

"Yeah. Here's Brittni now. I'll get her for you." Jamie sets down the phone.

Mark will be all alone, my little voice says. Didn't Holly say she had a tournament in Ontario at New Year's? Now what are you going to do?

I hear Jamie and Brittni talking before she picks up the phone. She sounds angry.

"Hi Jessie," she snaps. "I've just had a run-in with my florist. Looks like I'll be finding a new one. What's up?"

My desire to back out has evaporated.

"Um – not much. Just checking on your plans."

"Did Jamie tell you about Mark?"

"Yes."

She softens. "Too bad about his knee and everything, but it worked out for Jamie. He wanted Mark to be a part of our big day. He phoned him last night, and Mark said he'd do it, so at least *something's* gone right this week. Mark's pretty bummed out. Have you talked to him lately?"

"Not since it happened."

"He was pleased to know *you're* in the wedding party," Brittni says.

My heart leaps again. "He was?"

"You and Mark have some history," she says. "Want to tell me about it?"

"That's all over," I say quickly. Brittni is definitely not someone I'd confide in. "Tell me about how the plans are coming."

She has a lot to tell me. Apparently the florist isn't the only one to get the axe. But I'm not listening.

Mark.

"So are you bringing an escort?" Brittni asks at last. "I'd like to know – for the seating plan."

"I won't be bringing anyone," I assure her.

You don't need to now, my little voice says.

"Got your shoes?"

"Yes."

"Remember, I'm buying the jewelry. I ordered it at a discounted rate through the salon."

"That's great."

"Something wrong, Jessie?" she asks. "You sound like you're sick."

"I'm just tired."

"How's your hockey season going?" she asks.

"Not bad. We're almost at .500. Four wins and six losses."

"Who do you play next?"

"We go to Regina tomorrow." I consider asking her if she wants to come watch, but I know better.

"Look, Jessie, I have to go." She sounds distracted. "Take care of yourself."

"You too."

She hangs up.

I set down the phone and stare at the ceiling.

"Why didn't you tell her about the Mac's?" I ask out loud.

You know why, my little voice says.

# *chapter*
## *thirty-five*

I go to school in the morning, even though I've got a pounding headache and I'm all stuffed up. In homeroom, I'm shaking like crazy and running a fever. Mr. Gervais takes one look at me and buzzes the school secretary, telling her to call my mom. He escorts me to the office himself.

Mom walks in fifteen minutes later.

"What about Sunny?" I ask.

"We can pick it up later. Right now, I'm getting you home and into bed."

"But I have a game tonight!"

"No hockey for you," Mom says.

"You should get her tested for mono," the school secretary says.

"The *kissing* disease?" Mom asks.

"I've seen a lot of it around here." The secretary peers at me over her reading glasses. "Believe me. I know mono when I see it."

That scares the hell out of me. We've talked about mono in health class. All the way home I'm checking my neck for swollen glands and my abdomen for bloating.

Where would I have gotten mono? I haven't...

Lightning bolt.

Oh yes, you have, my little voice says.

Well, then Liam better have it too. If I had a voodoo doll, I'd make sure of it.

I go straight to bed and sleep until after suppertime, with Rufus curled up beside me. He's the only one happy with this turn of events.

The Oilers beat the Rebels 4–3 in OT that night. I get a thousand texts from the girls while they're on their way home from Regina.

Missing hockey sucks. Being sick sucks.

I stay home from school on Friday. My head is pounding, and my nose is stuffy, but the fever's under control. Courtney comes home at noon and makes me a bowl of chicken noodle soup. Sometimes she manages *not* to be a pain in the ass.

After she leaves I have a hot bath. As soon as I get out of the tub, I notice the spots on my stomach and legs.

"What the hell?" I towel myself off.

My fears about mono are coming to fruition.

Later in the afternoon, right around the time the spots

start itching, Dad comes home early from work and takes me to Dr. Bilkhu. Sitting in the waiting room at the doctor's office, I feel like I have a big M painted on my forehead.

Damn you, Liam MacArthur.

Dr. Bilkhu checks my ears, nose, throat, and stomach, checks my lungs, and makes a few notes in my folder.

"Do I have mono?" I ask him sorrowfully.

He spins around in his chair. "Have you ever had chicken pox?"

"When I was a baby." I stare at him. "Mom said I only had a few spots. I can't get it again, can I?"

He nods. "If you had it very young, and didn't have many symptoms." He turns back to his desk and writes more notes. "Take ibuprofen for the headache and an antihistamine at bedtime to help with the itch."

"What about during the daytime?"

"Calamine lotion. Lots of it. And no hockey until I see you again, Princess."

The Oilers lose 5–1 to the Rebels on Saturday afternoon while Courtney's team hangs a licking on Fort Qu'Appelle at the LMC. My sister trumpets about the Xtreme's 7–1 victory downstairs while I lie in bed with my pillow covering my ears.

I do not share her joy.

I'm too miserable. I'm covered from head to toe in red welts. Even the bottoms of my feet itch. There are blisters inside my ears and between my fingers. I've draped a sheet over my dresser mirror, so I don't have to look at myself. No way am I going to school until *all* the spots are gone.

"You have to look at the bright side," Kathy says when she phones me on Sunday.

"There *is* no bright side," I tell her.

"What if this happened just before Brittni's wedding?" Kathy asks.

"Point taken," I concede. "But missing the wedding wouldn't be that big a deal. I'd rather go to the Mac's with you girls."

"Funny you should say that." Kathy sounds edgy. "I thought you were backing out."

"I couldn't," I tell her. "I'd already committed."

"You have a bigger commitment to your team," Kathy says. "Here we are, finally hitting our stride, and you're getting all flakey on us."

"I'm not flakey," I assure her. "I'm itchy. Should I send you a picture?"

"Spare me."

After she hangs up, I drop the phone on the bed, startling Rufus. "I really would rather go to the Mac's," I tell him, ruffling his head.

I turn up the volume on my iPod to shut out the voice.

I faithfully follow Dr. Bilkhu's instructions, especially for the spots on my face, and they start to heal. Thanks to daily homework delivery, courtesy of Amber, I manage to keep caught up in my classes.

By Thursday afternoon I'm presentable enough to go back to school. There's a nasty scab on my temple, but my hair pretty much covers it. Long sleeves and a scarf do the trick for my arms and neck.

Mom insists on driving me even though I tell her I'm okay to drive myself.

"I don't want you overdoing your first day back," she says as she pulls into the parking lot behind the Comp. "And no hockey practice tonight."

"I know. We have a bye weekend anyway. Dr. Bilkhu says I can go to practice next week. He's pretty sure I'll be good to go for the Notre Dame tournament."

"When's the first game?"

"A week from today. Then there's a game on Friday and two on Saturday."

"Sounds like too much too soon," Mom says.

"I'll be fine by then. Quit worrying." I open my door.

"What time should I pick you up after school?"

"I'll get one of the girls to give me a ride." I climb out of the Explorer and reach for my backpack. "See you later."

The back entrance is great for avoiding people. I manage to slide through the afternoon without attracting too much attention. In history, I'm actually ahead of the class. In calculus, wonder of wonders, I'm rocking the derivatives.

At the end of the day, while I'm waiting for Amy in the main foyer, I see Liam's football buddies, but I don't see Liam. I'd like to ask them where he is. Ever since the party at his place, I've wanted to apologize to him...although I'm not sure where I'd begin. Self-conscious about the marks on my face, I turn my head and let the guys go by.

Amy shows up a few minutes later.

"Hey!" she says. "Welcome back to the Land of the Living."

"Thanks." I shoulder my backpack. "Sure I won't make you late for practice?"

"No worries. I've got time to drop you off *and* pick up Subway."

We step out into a cutting November wind. The light is already changing as Planet Estevan hurtles towards the shortest day of the year.

"If it weren't for hockey, I'd hate winter." I'm puffing from the effort of keeping up with her long strides.

"Yeah, it bites." She turns to look at me. "What are you doing tomorrow?"

"What do you think?" I jiggle my backpack. "I've been

missing for a week."

"Will one more day hurt?"

"What have you got in mind?" I ask.

"I'm heading to Agribition early tomorrow. My brothers are competing in the rodeo, and the whole fam's up there. I stayed back because of practice tonight." She gives me a little push that nearly knocks me over. "I could use a sidekick for the drive."

"Are you coming back tomorrow night?"

"No, but my auntie is, if you need a ride. Or you can bunk at the hotel with us." She pauses. "Just so you know, we all snore."

"I can't skip out after missing a whole week!"

"Get your mom to call the school and tell them you had a setback."

"I can't ask her to do that."

"No wonder Whitney calls you Captain Anal," she says. "McIntyre, when will you cut loose?"

*T*he next morning I'm sitting beside Amy when she heads north out of Estevan. It's six thirty, bitterly cold, and that November wind is roaring. The cold seeps into my guts as well, where a frozen lump of guilt resides.

"What did you tell your parents?" Amy asks, turning on the heater full blast.

"I left them a note."

"Whoa, Jessie." Amy picks up a pop can and spits a brown blob into it. "You're out of control."

*"You're* out of control. How can you *chew* so early in the morning?" I ask.

"It's not a matter of choice," she says. "I'm compelled by powerful forces."

"I heard it's worse than cigarettes. You're going to get mouth or throat cancer for sure. You should quit."

"And you should quit being a mother hen," she says. "Want to stop and grab something in Weyburn? I need a coffee."

I am about to remark on *that* habit as well, but I catch myself in time. I feel like a rat for slipping out of the house without telling my parents.

"You're seventeen," Amy says, as if reading my mind. "It's time to start thinking for yourself."

*"You're* the one doing all the thinking," I reply.

Amy laughs.

Just before Weyburn, Mom calls.

"What are you doing?" she demands.

"Like my note said – driving to Regina with Amy."

"But you just missed a week of school!"

"And I did a whole week of school while I was cooped up in my room. I need some fresh air." I look at Amy and tell a lie I know will appease Mom for the moment. "I'll be home by suppertime."

Amy scowls and starts to protest, but I shake my head.

Mom sighs loudly. "You're going to have a setback."

"I'll be fine, Mom."

"You've got warm clothes? And winter boots?"

"Yes."

"Call me at noon and let me know how you're doing."

"I will." I give Amy a wink. "Will you let the school know I couldn't make it in today? You don't have to lie. They'll assume I'm still sick."

There's a longer pause.

"I'll think about it," Mom says. "Don't forget to call me later."

I slip my phone back in my pocket.

"Whoa, Jessie," Amy says. "You are living on the wild side."

# *chapter*
## *thirty-six*

A
t Evraz Place, we pay our admission to the shivering attendant in the ticket booth and find a parking spot close to the Brandt Centre, where the rodeo events are held.

"What time do your brothers compete?" I ask, slipping on my mittens.

"The rodeo isn't until tonight," Amy says.

"So why are we here so damn early? It's not even nine o'clock!"

"There's another event I want to see." She opens the driver's door. "Hurry up!"

Once we're inside, I hear an announcer's voice and see a sprinkling of people in the stands. In the arena below a horse and rider are loping in a circle.

"What competition is this?" I ask.

"Watch," she says.

The horse makes a tighter circle, then does a figure eight,

and begins loping in a counter clockwise direction. After a few more circuits, the horse lopes to the opposite end of the arena, turns, stops, then takes off full tilt. He slides to a stop in a cloud of dust, haunches tucked beneath him.

"This is what Liam does," I whisper to Amy, suddenly excited. "He told me about this! That's the big stop, right?"

She nods once and cautions me to be quiet.

The horse begins spinning in a circle, using its hindquarters to pivot once, twice, stopping on a dime, then taking off to perform the same stop and pivot at the opposite end of the arena. One more "big stop" midway and the cow horse moves in reverse, backing up more than a dozen steps, its neck bowed, ears swiveled sideways in concentration.

"This is so cool!" I say.

"Next is cattle work," Amy explains. "The cow horse has to show that steer who's boss."

"What steer?"

A gate opens at the end of the arena, and a steer ambles out. The horse approaches it, ears pointed straight ahead. Amy points to the markers on the fence and explains briefly how the horse and rider need to maintain control of the animal. For the next few minutes, the horse and rider shadow the movements of the steer, racing, turning, dodging, always staying in its flight path. At the end of the demonstration, the announcer requests our applause, and the small audience scattered throughout the stands whistles and cheers.

"That was awesome." I lean over and speak right into Amy's ear. "Are we going to see Liam compete?"

"Do you want to?"

"Yes!"

Amy grins at me.

We move down into the stands and watch a few more competitors. Amy patiently answers my questions and explains the finer points of the reining portion of the event. I am on pins and needles waiting for Liam to appear.

"Quit fidgeting," Amy says. "You're making *me* nervous."

Finally Liam trots out on Rusty. Her forelegs are wrapped in white bandages below the knee, a bright contrast with her shiny red colour.

"Rusty's definitely got on her show coat today. Let's see if she's wearing *her* game face."

I hear a husky male voice down below scream, "Go Liam!"

"Betcha that's his dad," I say.

I don't listen for Amy's response because Rusty's already in motion, performing the same loping circuits, lead changes and figure eights as the previous horses. Her ears are in constant rotation, soaking up Liam's voice and the crowd reaction. Liam sits back easily in the saddle, rein hand floating above the horn.

"She is so pretty," I breathe, leaning forward and putting

my elbows on my knees. "It must be hard for him, knowing he's got to auction her off after this is over."

The last figure eight brings Rusty to the opposite end of the arena, where she explodes into a gallop, ears flat back, tail bannering behind her, performing the big stop with muscles popping. She switches gears and spins gracefully on her hindquarters.

"How does he get her to do that?" I ask.

"How do you know how hard to give a pass?" Amy asks. "You do it differently for every girl on the team. Practice."

A steer trots out.

I find myself hanging on the seat in front of me while Liam and Rusty shadow the animal. At one point I realize I'm actually leaning and moving my head in imitation of the mare's pivots. Even my untrained eyes can tell Liam's perform-ance working the steer isn't as good as the older riders, but Rusty puts in a game effort, tracking the animal's movements.

When time's up, Liam lopes Rusty out of the arena.

"How does Liam train for this?" I ask Amy.

"They have a small herd of cattle," Amy says. "He spends at least an hour in the saddle every day. The training is all about programming the horse so she responds automatically. It's muscle memory, just like in hockey." Amy's phone plays a twangy country song, and she stares at it, smiling.

"Who's texting?"

"Russell." Amy texts a reply and places her phone on her lap. "A few minutes ago you seemed pretty excited to see Liam."

I shake my head. "We're just friends. At least, I think we are."

"Come on, how can you resist him?" Amy teases. "Football player? Cowboy? Future Doctor Doolittle?"

I keep on shaking my head, but I can't wipe the grin off my face. "The last thing I need is another *guy* hanging around."

"Why not?" Amy asks.

I take the plunge and tell her about Evan. It takes a while, but Amy's a good listener.

"I already did a number on Evan. I'm not doing that again," I tell her.

"I think you're scared of Liam," Amy says, reaching in her back pocket for her tobacco tin.

"That's what Kathy says."

"There you go." Amy unscrews the cap. "We must be right."

I sit up straight and put my hands on my thighs. "Why don't we talk about your love life for a change?"

"Okay." Amy extracts a plug of tobacco. "You want to know who I like?"

"Yeah, I do."

She pulls open her lip and jams the tobacco in before inclining her head towards mine. "Well, first off – it's somebody on our team."

That shuts me up in a hurry.

"Don't worry. It's not you," Amy says. "And secondly, it's not anybody I'm going to tell. She's not like me."

We sit quietly, listening to the arena sounds.

"Thanks for confiding in me," I say after a while. "I won't tell anyone."

"I know you won't. That's why I told you."

"Does anybody else know?" I ask.

"Just Sue. She's good to talk to about stuff." Amy picks up her cup and spits.

This part of her confession makes me feel uncomfortable. Amy's known Sue for such a short time, and she already knows her better than I do.

Amy stands up. "Let's go find Liam."

We make our way down to the horse barn, where Liam is in a box stall with Rusty, giving her a well-deserved rub down.

"Lot of fuss for a few minutes," Liam's dad is saying as we approach.

"What about eight seconds?" Liam says over his left shoulder. "Or *less* than eight!"

"Zing!" Russell says, giving his dad a playful shove.

"Look who's here!" Liam's mom hugs Amy and squeezes my forearm. "I didn't expect to see you girls!"

"Your family was just here," Mr. MacArthur says to Amy. "You missed them by five minutes." He eyes me uncertainly.

"I'm Jessie," I say. "I was at a party at your quonset a few weeks ago. I know Liam from school."

Mrs. MacArthur starts directing the small talk at this point, and from the information and looks she and Mr. MacArthur are trading, I gather they know *exactly* who I am. It's a little unnerving to think I've been a topic of conversation in their household.

In sharp contrast to this friendly exchange is Liam's silence.

He's squatted in front of Rusty, rewrapping her front legs. While Amy and the MacArthurs make small talk, I put my hand under Rusty's nose, and she sniffs it. I rub the velvety skin between her nostrils while she explores my sleeve with her lips, then snorts, throwing a string of snot on my jacket.

Everyone but Liam laughs.

"No hockey today?" Russell grins at me.

"Not until Thursday."

"I want to come," Russell says. "Can we go, Liam?"

Liam mumbles something.

"It's in Milestone, Russell," I explain. "We don't play at home again until the week after."

"We'll be there," Russell grins. "Won't we, Liam?"

No response.

"That was an awesome performance, Liam," I say. "I'm glad I got to see it."

Liam shrugs, his back still turned.

"Do you think Rusty will get a good price at the auction?" I ask.

"We'll find out this afternoon," Mr. MacArthur says.

"I'd bid on her myself if I had the cash," says a female voice behind my right shoulder.

I turn around to see a very pretty blonde. She has curves in places I can only dream about, a beautiful mouth and soft brown eyes. Worst of all, she is one of those girls born to wear a cowboy hat.

"You folks thinking about getting something to eat?" she asks.

"Sure thing." Liam's dad drapes an arm around the girl's shoulders and leans his head toward hers, dwarfing her. "I missed breakfast this morning. Been thinking about a stack of pancakes and a pound of crisp bacon for *hours.*"

"Me too." She flashes her pearlies at Russell. "Comin,' Hot Stuff?"

"Sure am!' he says.

Her eyes swing right over me and Amy and rest on Liam's mom. "What about you, Connie?"

"I'll hang out here for a bit," Mrs. MacArthur says. "Maybe you girls would like to go."

"I'm not hungry," I say. "And we have to find Amy's family, right Amy?"

"They were going to check out the exotic livestock," Mr. MacArthur says.

Liam stands up and leaves the stall. "I'm ready for something to eat," he says. "Thanks for coming, Amy. I'll see you later." Liam walks away with the others, without a backward glance.

Why would he look back, my little voice reasons. You saw the way the blonde was looking at *him*.

"Liam said one time he wanted you to come out to our place and go riding," Mrs. MacArthur says. "Do you think you might like to do that?"

"I don't have time," I tell her, running my hand along Rusty's neck. "I'm pretty busy with school and hockey and stuff."

"You kids," Mrs. MacArthur says. "Liam's the same way. Thank goodness football season is short. If he isn't with Rusty, he's over at Anne's clinic."

"Clinic?" I ask.

"Liam works for a vet," Mrs. MacArthur says. "He wants to be a vet one day."

"Yeah, he told me that," I say, giving Rusty a final pat. "Good luck with the sale."

"See you later, Connie," Amy says.

"See you."

As we walk away, I feel something gnawing at my stomach. It's a familiar sensation. It means I've screwed things up royally. Again.

"You sure pissed *him* off somewhere along the way," Amy says.

A bubble of regret rises in my throat. I nearly choke on it.

"Let's go look at those exotic animals," Amy says gently. "Nothing cheers me up like an ostrich. Aren't they the goofiest things?"

I paste a smile on my face. "Who needs cheering up?"

Amy smacks me on the back. "Atta girl!"

After the evening rodeo, I hitch a ride home with Amy's aunt, who has to work the next day. As hard as I try *not* to, I sleep most of the way home. We don't get back to Estevan until well after midnight, but Rufus waits up for me.

I open the door to his kennel, and he emerges, wiggling and peeing on the newspaper, thrilled to be released from his prison.

"How's my big boy?" I pick him up and tuck him under my arm.

Together we explore the contents of the fridge and find a package of yogurt. After I remove the top, I let Rufus lick the underside of the plastic wrap. I set him down and go into the living room, where Mom's sleeping on the couch with a paperback propped on her chest. I sit in Dad's recliner while Rufus hops up on the couch next to Mom, knocking her book onto the floor and waking her.

"Hey! How did you..." She looks over at me and starts, lying back with her hand on her chest. "You scared me!"

"Sorry." I dip my spoon in the yogurt and savour the cool, creamy texture on my tongue. "How was your day?"

"I'm far more interested in *yours.*" Mom rubs her eyes and pushes Rufus' nose aside when he tries to lick her face.

"Lots of horses and cows. I'm talking hundreds."

"Did you learn anything?"

"Loads. Amy knows *everything.* Her family does it all – cattle showing, sales, rodeo – you name it. One of her dad's heifers got reserve champion, and after the show, some guy from Ontario wanted to buy her."

"Well, somebody *should* buy her if she won."

I point my spoon at her. "Actually, reserve champion means she came in second. Grand champion is first."

"I guess you did learn something." Mom sets her book on the coffee table, then pulls Rufus onto her chest and strokes his ears. "Would you like to explain your behaviour today?" She's looking into Rufus' eyes, but I know it's me she's talking to.

I scrape the bottom of the container for the last spoonful

of yogurt. "Can I tell you some other stuff first?"

Mom stifles a yawn. "How much stuff?"

I unload. By the time I'm finished, she's sitting straight up, wide awake.

"So what happened at the auction?" she asks.

"A rancher from Camrose bought Rusty. Good price too. But the whole thing made me feel sad, even though I know I should be happy for Liam and his family."

"You know what I think?" Mom asks. "I think you've beaten yourself up long enough over Evan. And what happened with Liam isn't your fault either. You're a good girl, Jessie, and you have a big heart."

"You're my mother. You have to say that."

She stands up and tucks Rufus under her arm. "It's impossible to get through life without hurting people. You can try to avoid it, but it happens, in spite of your best intentions. Learn from it, and move on."

"I'll try."

"Now, on another front, I didn't tell Courtney what you did today. I don't need her thinking she's got a free pass for skipping school, so don't *you* tell her either." She moves towards the stairs then pauses. "Do you think it's all right for her to stay at Pam's while your dad and I are in Vegas?"

"Of course. Pam's a sweet kid."

"I'm glad Courtney's stayed friends with her," she says.

"Are you going to bed soon?"

"Pretty soon. I'm going to sit here for a while."

She walks back to me and deposits Rufus in my lap. "Here's company." She bends over and kisses my forehead. "I meant what I said earlier. Let yourself off the hook."

"Thanks, Mom."

# chapter thirty-seven

Our first game of the Notre Dame Showcase won't be a walk in the park. The Balmoral Hall Blazers from Winnipeg play in the JWHL, a league comprised of ten teams from across Canada and the United States.

"I keep telling myself the best part of this weekend is seeing Tara and Shauna again," I say to Kathy as we step onto the ice for our warm-up. "I hope it's not the *only* part I'll want to remember."

Somebody tackles me from behind and pulls my jersey over my head, rendering me blind and helpless – but not deaf. Kathy's splitting a gut, laughing.

"Team captain, my ass!" Tara murmurs in my ear.

I'm laughing too by the time my jersey is sorted out again, and Tara is grinning at me from behind her cage. I haven't seen her for over a year although we've kept in touch.

"How are things in AAA?" Tara asks.

"Definitely decent, for a first go-round," Kathy says, "but we haven't played Notre Dame yet."

"Neither have we," says Tara. "Guess that's what the weekend's all about, huh?" She stares pointedly at the opposite end of the arena, where university scouts are rumoured to be milling about in the lobby. "That – and them."

"Don't remind me," Kathy says.

"You girls going to the Mac's tournament?" Tara asks.

"Most of us are," Kathy says, giving me a significant look. "Jessie here's got another commitment."

Tara raises a dark eyebrow.

"I'm a bridesmaid at a wedding," I explain.

We make some small talk, catching up. Tara's headed to Brown University in Providence next fall. I ask her about her Uncle Frank, Mark's dad.

Her shoulders droop. "His last report wasn't good," she says. "There're some spots on his lungs."

"That's terrible," I say.

"Cancer's the worst," Kathy says.

"It's really hard on Mark," Tara says. "I don't know how he does it."

"Well, he's got Holly to help him through it," Kathy points out.

"Yeah, she's awesome," Tara says.

I notice Bud and Sue watching us from high in the

stands. "We better get warmed up. Talk to you after the game?"

Tara smiles. "Maybe we can catch up when I go deep in *your* corner."

"I'll be ready," I say.

Tara nods and skates back to her end.

Game on.

**A**my's in net for this one. Balmoral's top two lines forecheck the hell out of us, and we spend most of the first period battling to get out of our end. Kathy takes a penalty for roughing, and early in the PK, Carla gets one for hooking. Brutal call. The Balmoral winger was clearly hanging on Carla's stick.

Bud sends Jennifer, Whitney and me out for the five on three. We get trapped in our end with no relief for over a minute. I block one of Tara's shots with my ankle, but there's no time to acknowledge the pain. Lungs burning, I finally manage to dump the puck down the ice and limp for the bench.

Crystal's mom is all over me, but I wave her off.

"I'm fine," I tell her.

Dayna, Randi and one of the Rookies kill the rest of the two-man disadvantage, which gives us a big boost. Randi ices the puck just as Kathy gets out of the box, and Kathy dives in after it with two Blazer D-men on her tail. The Balmoral goalie beats Kathy to the puck but fans when she tries to clear it. Kathy poke checks and fires on the empty net.

Scores.

Balmoral retaliates with two unanswered goals, both of them Tara's. On her second marker, Tara comes in hard at me, and I try to force her wide. She puts a move on me and gets a shot away, scoring low blocker.

"She always was a sniper," I tell Amy, tapping her pads.

Amy clears the snow out of her crease and bangs the posts with her stick, already shutting the door on Tara's goal.

Balmoral scores a power play goal in the second, and Whitney responds with one of her own with seconds left, making the score 3–2.

"At least the score's close," Dayna says while we're making our way back to the dressing room.

"The scouts are important, not the score," Randi says. "They're watching what you can do with the puck — and what you do when you *don't* have the puck."

"Enough about the scouts," I tell her. "Keep your head in the game."

The Blazer coach gives his third and fourth lines more playing time in the third, allowing us to generate some offence. Randi has one more great scoring opportunity, but the Balmoral goalie deflects her slapshot. The Blazers transition quickly to offence when the rebound pops past Carla, creating a 3 on 1 with Tara head manning the puck. Jennifer positions herself to prevent a pass, so Tara takes the puck in deep and slings it to her right winger, who's breaking for the net.

Amy reaches for the save, but there's too much net.

We go down 4–2.

As we shake hands after the game, the Balmoral coach says to me, "Great shut down defence."

"Thanks," I tell him.

As I skate over to talk to Tara, I can't wipe the grin off my face. The other girls who knew her from the Xtreme join us too. When the gate opens for the zamboni, we exchange hugs and clear the ice.

Back in the dressing room, Bud's round belly is bursting with pride. "You girls played a solid game – in all three zones. You tied them in shots in the third, with just one breakdown. No need to hang your heads."

"I hope we play as well against the Hounds tomorrow," I say.

"Don't we all," Bud says. "Get some shut-eye, and eat smart, or that big ice at Notre Dame will *eat* you up."

The next morning when Amy hobbles into homeroom, I know we're in trouble.

"You pulled a groin on that last goal," I say.

She rolls her eyes. "How'd you guess?"

"You won't be playing tonight against the Hounds," I say, more to myself than to her. "At least it's not a league game."

"Yeah, it's only a tournament with university scouts," Amy says dryly. "Loads of them. Didn't you see all the binders and clipboards yesterday?"

On my way to second period, I run into Jodi in the stairwell. I see her at school nearly every day, but it's like we're two different people now.

"Heard you had a good game last night," Jodi says. "Congratulations."

"Thanks." I step aside to let some students pass.

"Lots of scouts there?" she asks.

I nod.

"Don't let it get to you," she says. "You're going to play *somewhere* next year."

"What makes you so sure?" I ask.

"Because you're better than you think you are," she says.

Her compliment chokes me up a little. "So what about you? Do you still want to get into Education?"

She shakes her head. "I'm applying for a music program in Toronto."

"Oh," I reply, surprised.

While she tells me about it, I remember what her mother said to me about the nature of her brain injury. The impulsivity. The inability to concentrate.

"Sounds like an awesome opportunity," I tell her when she's done.

"Have you seen Evan lately?" she asks.

"No." I lie. I can hardly tell her I hide whenever I catch a glimpse of him downtown or at the mall or in Canadian Tire.

"It took him a while to get over you," she says. "But he seems happier now. Did you know we're going out?"

"No, I didn't."

What if she changes her mind about him, just like she changed her mind about hockey and school and who knows how many other things?

I suddenly realize the stairwell and the main foyer are vacant, except for us. "We'd better get to class."

She smiles. "God bless you, Jessie. I still pray for you."

As I watch her descend the stairs, I say a little prayer for her too.

# chapter
## thirty-eight

I hate this place," Randi says, as my dad pulls up in front of the Duncan MacNeill Arena in Wilcox. "You know what it makes me think of?"

"I'm afraid to ask," Dad says, opening his door.

"Pain," Randi says. "Lots and lots of pain."

"Sore arms," Kathy says.

"Sore calves," I say.

"Do they take the Hounds in a little room before every game and show them how to slash people where it hurts most?" Randi speculates.

"It's called the dressing room," I say.

Dad opens the rear hatch and starts unloading our equipment. The frigid December air wafts over us.

"Well, I'm mad, and I'm not taking it any more," Kathy says. "If I go down with a slash to the box, I'm taking somebody with me, and it's not going to be pretty."

Behind us, Dad clears his throat.

"Sorry, Mr. McIntyre," Kathy says. "I was forgetting myself."

"Just try *not* to get suspended," I tell her. "Who'll protect the Rooks if you're watching from the stands?"

"Yeah," Dayna says.

"No danger of anyone getting suspended if you all remain *inside* the vehicle," Dad says.

"Parker, move your ass," Randi says. "No time like the present and all that."

"Pip. Pip," Dayna says.

Inside the arena the first people I see are Bud and the U of S coach. They're standing at the top of the stairs, deep in conversation.

Whoa.

"Let's go!" Kathy smokes me with her hockey bag. "It's cold out here!"

*"Now* you're in a hurry?" I reply.

Down in the dressing room, the tunes are on, and most of the girls are assembled. The mood is remarkably relaxed, considering we're about to play a team on a thirty-five-game winning streak.

"Think the coaches will let us go to the pool tonight?" one of the Rookies asks. "I brought my water gun and some other stuff."

Maybe too relaxed.

"Depends on how well we play." I deposit my sticks by the door and squeeze into a spot between Carla and Jennifer. "Let's focus on the game."

"I brought mini-sticks," another one says. "We can play in the hallway if we can't go swimming."

"Anybody seen Shauna?" Kathy asks.

"I talked to her for a few minutes," Carla informs us. "Did you know she's playing at U of M next year? She wants to get into architecture."

This news makes me uncomfortable. How come these other girls know what they want to take, and I'm undecided?

"She also said we have the best coaches and goaltending in the league, and we're playing over our heads," Carla adds.

"Did you know Regina only scored *one* goal against Notre Dame last year?" Crystal asks. "And they beat some team 14–0 during playoffs."

Miranda looks stricken.

"Way to pump up our goaltender," Kathy says.

Before warm-up, Bud reminds us again about the "big ice" at Notre Dame.

"You need to make your passes," he says. "Move the puck, keep skating, and avoid mistakes."

"I don't always know when I'm making a mistake," says one of the Rookies.

"Don't worry," Kathy says. "I'll tell you."

When we head out to the ice, I try not to watch the Hounds too much. Talk about moving the puck. They have skills we can only dream about.

Dayna lines up behind me at the blue line for a defensive drill. "Are you as nervous as I am?"

I paste a smile on my face. "They all put their hockey pants on one leg at a time," I quip, trying to evoke a confidence I don't feel. "Let's stick to our game plan."

The game plan doesn't help us against Notre Dame. Sure, Randi does manage to score two minutes in, a greasy, garbage goal that only seems to wake up the Hounds and make them angry. Retaliation occurs on the scoreboard as they put three quick ones past Miranda, and in the corners where they take the lumber to us.

But we're the only ones who take penalties, two of them late in the period. Kathy gets one for two-handing a Hound in the shin, and just as her penance is done, Jennifer meets her on the way out of the box.

While we sit in the dressing room, listening to Bud break down the Hounds' forecheck, I try not to think about my throbbing wrists. I have to endure forty more minutes of this punishment?

We'll start the second shorthanded, so Bud reviews PK.

Not that it helps. When we head back out, Notre Dame scores with thirteen seconds run off the clock.

Correction. *I* score.

The puck goes in off the back of my leg although Shauna gets the credit for her shot from the point. I turn to Miranda, my mouth open to apologize.

"Go away," she says.

Notre Dame's Number 23 punches one of our Rookies in the head and takes a roughing minor.

Our first power play.

The Hounds' coach sends out her top four players, who tie us up in our own end for most of the one-man advantage and score shorthanded.

"Maybe we could play straight time," Dayna says as a number five appears under Home.

"Don't give up yet," I say. I make her retell me the game plan.

By the end of the second, it's 7–1. Worse yet, we only have three shots. The Notre Dame student body is merciless in their heckling as we lug our asses off the ice.

Bud dissects the Hounds' special teams for us, but I barely listen. I am too tired and too sore and too beaten.

"Suck it up," Sue hisses in my ear as I leave the dressing room. "You're supposed to lead this team, not drag it down."

I'd like to say I'm the one who lights a fire under

everyone's ass in the third.

But I'd be lying.

Two minutes into the period, Dayna lifts Number 22's stick just as the Notre Dame centreman is receiving a pass. Somehow she manages *not* to draw an interference call and, poking the puck ahead to Whitney, generates an odd man rush.

One of the Hound's D-men loses an edge and goes down.

Three on one.

Whitney drives to the net while Randi's wide open on the left wing. As the remaining D positions herself to remove the pass, Whitney flips the puck to Larissa, who shoots, low blocker. The goalie makes the save, but the rebound comes right out to Dayna, who is cheating in from the point. Roofs it.

This kid's a beauty.

Shrieking and flailing her arms, Dayna skates straight for the Notre Dame bench. Her enthusiasm is so contagious the Hounds start laughing.

Meanwhile I retrieve the puck from the linesman. "It's her first AAA goal. She'll want this."

The linesman nods.

The momentum of Dayna's goal carries us for five minutes, and we experience the thrill of outworking Notre Dame's top lines until I take a hooking penalty. They score on the power play, and the snowball starts to roll overtop of us, pinning us down.

In the end, it's 9–2 Notre Dame.

"Gritty game," Shauna tells me as she shakes my hand.

"Thanks."

In spite of all the positive things Bud tells us afterward, morale in the dressing room is low.

"Hey, we scored two goals," I point out. "That's more than lots of teams have done against the Hounds. We're not going home with our tails between our legs.

"Damn right," Randi says. "We're going to a *hotel.*"

We have two more games tomorrow, but it's already clear we can't advance to the semi-final round. Only one team from our pool will do that, and there's no chance it will be us.

I track down Shauna in the lobby. She has her hair cut very short and dyed jet black.

"Look at you," she says. "You've turned into quite the D-man."

"Thanks. You set the bar high," I reply.

She nods in acknowledgment. "Too bad Fox wasn't in net. She hurt?"

"Groin."

"Oh well, next time." She stares at the pointed toe of her boot. "Not long before we make the trip down to Spectra Place. What's it like playing there?"

"It totally feels like the big time."

"Looking forward to it." Shauna heaves a sigh. "I miss you girls."

"Believe me, we miss you too."

"You've filled in the gaps Tara and Kim and Jodi and I left. You didn't make it easy for us today."

"Excuse me?" I shake my head. "Did you *see* the scoreboard?"

"You didn't lie down and play dead," says Shauna. "And that little D-partner of yours is something else."

"I hear you're playing at U of M next year," I say.

Before Shauna can respond, someone taps me on the shoulder.

The U of S coach.

"Just wanted to let you know how much I enjoyed watching you today. Nice puck movement and decision-making. You've got a good head on your shoulders."

"Appreciate it," I say. "Maybe I should thank the Hounds for letting me keep it."

He laughs. "You coming to the Huskies' camp in April?"

"Planning to."

"Excellent news. Good luck in your games tomorrow." He walks away.

Shauna grins at me. "Looks like somebody else is playing university hockey next year."

# chapter thirty-nine

After going 0 and 4 in the Notre Dame Showcase, we are happy to host Prince Albert for a double-header the following weekend.

"Maybe we have a chance at beating dem Bears," Kathy says as I drive her home after dryland on Wednesday. "They'll be over-confident after kicking our asses last time."

"Let's hope so." I put my foot on the gas and wheel quickly into her driveway to avoid getting trapped in the freshly fallen snow.

"Whoa, Days of Thunder!" she says as we slide to a stop.

"I'm tired of getting stuck," I say. "Dad says he's putting snow tires on Sunny, but she doesn't have enough clearance. It bites."

"I'll tell you what bites," Kathy says. "I don't have a sniff of getting to Regina before Christmas to buy my grad dress. Can you imagine how bad the selection is going to be when I *do* go?"

"You were in Saskatoon twice," I remind her. "But you were too damn fussy."

"Good thing the escort department is looked after. What about you?"

"I'll look for a grad dress after Christmas. No time right now."

"I was referring to your grad escort." Kathy's tone reeks of agenda. "Do you have one?"

"Not yet."

Still hoping for Mark, my little voice says.

"What about Liam?" Kathy asks.

I shake my head.

"In that case, Brett has this friend."

"Is he a referee?"

"He's really nice."

"No way."

"He'll wear anything you want."

"Kathy."

"It'll be like a double date."

"Get out of my car. Right now." I point a finger at her.

"But why?" she pleads.

"A *blind* date with a *referee?* I'll never live it down!"

"Okay." Kathy opens her door. "But if you change your mind..."

"Out."

When I get home, Mom and Courtney are decorating the Christmas tree. It's a quaint domestic scene. The gas fireplace is on, the house smells like lasagna, and Rufus is munching on tinsel.

"Supper's on the counter," Mom says. "You'll have to nuke it."

I pick up Rufus and try to retrieve the slippery strings from his mouth. "I don't think we should leave this stuff lying around."

"Oh dear!" Mom looks up from the strands of lights she's untangling. "I lost track of him. Sorry!"

Rufus coughs, hacks, and burps as I extract the last slimy bits. I set him down and move quickly to pick up the card of tinsel before he can get to it. "Where's Dad?"

"Downstairs," Mom says.

I go into the kitchen, wash my hands, fill a plate with lasagna and salad, and take it back to the living room. Courtney's attaching lights to the bottom branches while Mom sorts through boxes of ornaments. Rufus is chewing on our treetop angel.

"What are you going to do with him while you're in Vegas?" I set down my plate and pry Rufus' mouth open to dig out the angel's head. "Is he going to Pam's too?"

"Apparently Pam's mother is allergic to dogs," says Mom.

"I thought Cotons were hypoallergenic."

"It doesn't have anything to do with hair," Courtney says. "Small dogs freak her out."

"There's a good kennel at..."

"He's not going to a kennel," Courtney insists. "Gia's dog went to a kennel once, and he got really sick. He nearly died."

"It's only for two nights. Maybe he can stay home," Mom says. "Courtney can stop by and see him a few times a day. Would you do that, Court?"

"Yes."

"Everything set for Brittni's wedding?" Mom asks.

"I'll head up there after lunch on the 30th. Everything's at the Seven Oaks. Brittni booked a block of rooms, and there's one under my name."

Mom says, "I guess that works."

"Are you coming on the bench for my game tomorrow night?" Courtney asks.

"Are you coming to watch me play PA on Saturday?" I counter.

She nods, and I nod back.

Life is good.

I eat my lasagna and watch them work on the tree while Rufus makes a general nuisance of himself. I call him, and he tries to hop up beside me, but the distance is too great with the chair tipped back. I lean forward and give him a lift. He watches me raise a forkful of lasagna to my mouth and licks his chops.

"Not a chance," I say.

"Apart from the wedding, Christmas holidays will be quiet for you, Jessie," Mom says.

"That's okay by me," I reply.

Since I'm not going to the Mac's, I'll be off for two weeks. I'm looking forward to sleeping in, watching DVD's with Courtney, snuggling with Rufus, and getting ready for final exams.

As much as I love the Oilers, I'm seeing way too much of them lately.

And not enough of Mark, my little voice says.

Never mind.

# chapter forty

I stand in front of the full-length mirror in my hotel room and stare at myself. I just spent an hour and a half in the salon where Brittni works.

"Who knew side ponytails would make a comeback?" I say to my reflection.

The three of us bridesmaids with long hair were shampooed, rolled and tucked under hair dryers. Brittni's team of stylists pulled our loose curls off to the side and inserted black feathers.

I have a French manicure and pedicure, my first ones ever. My legs and pits are freshly shaved, and Brittni's necklace and earrings perfectly accessorize the little, low-backed black dress. Unfortunately the sky-high silver heels, which felt so comfortable in the store, are already killing me.

The rehearsal went well last night, in spite of the fact one bridesmaid and two groomsmen were MIA. The missing bridesmaid was attending a different wedding, one groomsman was playing hockey in Brandon, and Mark's flight from Calgary was delayed by bad weather.

I heard Brittni say today he's here now. Somewhere in this hotel. Getting ready with Jamie and the rest of the guys.

You always knew you'd have one last crack at him, my little voice says. This is it, isn't it?

It isn't. It's Brittni's Big Day.

I check my phone. Think about deleting those angry texts from Kathy.

What kind of captain r u? Deserting yr team. I no Mark's there. Tara told me. R u crazy?

I shut off my phone and tuck it in my clutch, along with my hotel key and a pack of gum. I drape my bare shoulders with a filmy silver shawl. As I step into the hallway chlorine fills my nose.

I've heard your sense of smell is the one tied closest to memory.

We stayed here during the Regina tournament in my first year of hockey. Kathy and Jennifer and Larissa got in trouble with Steve for some pranks down at the pool, and we all got bag skated at the next practice. But it didn't matter because we got bag skated *together*.

Good times.

As I take the elevator down to the lobby, I think about the fun I've had playing with the Oilers. And before that, the

Rage. The Xtreme. There's been some bad stuff too, but all in all, it's been a great ride.

The elevator doors open.

I see a collection of guests in the lobby, including some of the bridesmaids. One's a hair stylist, another's a tattoo artist, and the matron of honour is a massage therapist. None of them have ever hefted a hockey stick, and only one of them has even been to Brittni's hometown. I must be proof Brittni had friends in Estevan.

It's been fun answering the "back in the day" questions about Brittni. I can't out and out tell them we were ecstatic when she stormed out of the dressing room for the last time. I just tell them the good stuff she did. Like the time she calmed Jennifer down after one of Mr. Scott's rants and took charge after Jodi had her accident.

I make my way towards the banquet hall Brittni and Jamie are using for the ceremony, supper and dance. Quite a few guests are assembled in the hallway.

I'm on high alert for Mark.

The matron of honour – I think her name's Loni – waves me over.

"You look great!" she says. "That's a terrific dress. Where did you get it?"

After I tell her about my outfit, she tells me about hers then introduces me to some of Brittni's other friends.

But I'm on reconnaissance the whole time. He's here somewhere.

"Jessie's hockey team is playing at a tournament in Calgary," Loni's telling everyone. "She missed the tournament to be here. Isn't that sweet?"

"How's your team doing?" somebody asks.

"They went 1 and 3 in the round robin, so they didn't make it out of their pool," I explain. From the blank looks I'm getting, it's clear the terminology is zooming right over their heads. "That means they'll get to go shopping," I add.

They all nod and smile.

"Jessie wants to play university hockey next year," Loni says proudly. "If she makes the team, she'll get to travel to Vancouver and Edmonton and Calgary for games."

"No shit," one says, the one who's been chewing her gum like a cow. "Too many books for me, even with the perks."

"Bet you'll party like a rock star," another one says.

"I have to make the team first, and after that there're probably a lot of rules about conduct," I assure her.

Everybody looks disappointed.

"But the men's football team will come to the games, all painted up, to cheer for us," I add.

"Cool." Gum Chewer blows a bubble and pops it.

The conversation drifts to the topic of the gift opening tomorrow. I wish I could be as excited as they are about electric grills, food processors, crystal tumblers and dinnerware.

That's when I see him.

He's leaning on a cane. The rented black tuxedo doesn't fit him quite right, but it doesn't matter. He's still the best-looking guy ever. His blond hair's longer than I've ever seen it, but it's neatly combed and tucked behind his ears. He's talking to the groomsman who plays for the Brandon Wheat Kings.

Probably speculating on the outcome of the Team Canada–Russia game tonight. Wishing they were parked in a sports bar somewhere with a pitcher of beer and a widescreen plasma TV. Or on the ice with Team Canada.

I try to remember the last time I saw Mark. It's been months.

Then we make eye contact.

He gives me a smile – a casual, oh-just-another-wedding-guest sort of smile – and turns back to his friend.

My heart sinks.

Then his head swivels back, and he mouths, "Jessie?"

I nod, heart flittering.

He makes his way over to me. It isn't easy for him, because of the cane and the crowd, so I meet him halfway.

"Wow," he says. "I've been looking for you ever since I got here, and you were standing there the whole time." His grey eyes are as beautiful as ever.

"Yes, I was." Scintillating conversation opener. "Is Holly

here?" I ask.

"She's at a tournament in Winnipeg," he says. "I'm headed there tomorrow night."

"Too bad she couldn't make it," I lie. "You probably don't get to see her much."

He smiles wryly and gestures at the cane. "Not much else to do – except go to class and the physiotherapist."

"I'm sorry about your knee," I tell him. "It's a rotten way to end your season."

"Yeah, it is."

Naturally he asks me all about our league play, and I give him the straight facts. A recent split with PA and two losses to Notre Dame have dropped us to seventh place. We talk about my plans for next year – or lack thereof. Sure, I've filled out the application forms and mailed them off – with commerce, engineering and arts and science as my three choices. But I really have no idea if I want to do any of those.

"Why don't you do a math degree?" he suggests. "You'll find out damn quick if it's the area for you."

We're talking so easily. It's like old times. Maybe better than old times. Whenever I see him, Holly's usually around, so it's hard to tell how we fit.

All too soon, Loni starts rounding up the wedding party to go to their stations. It's just ten minutes to show time.

"Talk to you later," I say.

"You can count on it," he says.

The guests pour into the banquet hall, half of which is set up with chairs and an archway wrapped in tulle and calla lilies. I deposit my clutch and shawl at my place at the head table and rejoin the other bridesmaids.

I am amazed at how downscale Brittni's wedding is. No elaborate and frivolous expenses or wasted time. By now, Brittni and Jamie have already had a barrage of wedding photos taken. After the wedding, there will be a brief photo shoot with the wedding party in the adjoining banquet room, followed by supper and speeches and a deejay and dance. The gift opening is at Brittni and Jamie's house tomorrow.

We bridesmaids wait patiently outside the banquet hall for Brittni's arrival. Classical music is playing softly in the background. The JP is serene, book tucked under his arm. The groom and his entourage are assembled, looking handsome but slightly uncomfortable in their formal wear. I predict those bow ties will be strapped around their foreheads by midnight.

Brittni doesn't come.

It better go ahead after all this. I wish I could check my phone for the time. I look at Jamie, standing with the other groomsmen, looking nervous. He'd be heartbroken if Brittni left him at the altar.

Then Mrs. Wade appears around a corner, wearing a red

sheath and heels, hair elaborately coiffed. She's holding Brittni's bouquet in front of her as if it's her own. Brittni's right behind her, holding hands with the three-year-old flower girl, Loni's daughter. I forget her name. It starts with an L too. In her other hand Brittni carries a basket of crimson rose petals. The flower girl has red blotches around her eyes, and she's wiping her nose with the back of her hand.

"See, Leticia? There's your mommy, right there," Brittni says.

I knew her name started with an L.

Loni bends over, picks up her daughter, and attacks the snot and tears with a tissue.

"She wanted to stay with me until we came down," Brittni explains. "Then she changed her mind. I don't know if she'll walk by herself."

As I am the first bridesmaid down the aisle after Leticia, it falls to me to salvage the rose petals.

"Leticia, will you let me carry you?" I suggest. "I have gum in my purse."

Magic words.

Leticia holds out her arms to me, and I take her from her mother.

"You hold the basket while I hold you," I say. "I'll tell you when to start scattering the petals."

Everyone beams at me. Clearly, I have saved the day.

Brittni gives Leticia the basket, and Mrs. Wade hands Brittni her bouquet. For the first time I really *look* at Brittni. She's dazzling.

"Are you ready, Honey?" Mrs. Wade says.

Brittni nods.

I look over Leticia's head to the place where Mark and the rest of the groomsmen are standing.

"Leticia, let's rock and roll," I say.

# *chapter*
## *forty-one*

'**ve** never seen Mark like this.

When we dated, we didn't go to many parties, and when we did, he didn't drink a drop if he was driving. Even if we tagged along with Shauna and her boyfriend Brian, Mark's limit was two beer.

So it's peculiar to watch him toss back double ryes, chased with water. Clearly there's something going on, and it doesn't take a rocket scientist to figure out what.

Team Canada beat the Russians earlier tonight. During the speeches, the best man razzed Jamie mercilessly about making his buddies miss the game. Mark didn't laugh at any of it. I could see his mood get darker by the minute as he sat, slumped in his chair. Good thing he wasn't making any toasts. Good thing the bridal party photo shoot was *before* supper.

I sat with him at the head table after the obligatory dances, and we've been sitting here ever since. He's been telling me about his hockey season, his conversations with the

World Junior coach and some NHL scouts and agents.

"I was close," he says, "but it's over."

"It doesn't have to be over," I tell him. "Lots of players come back after knee surgery. And you've got a year of major junior left."

"You don't understand," he says. "It doesn't matter any more." He takes a drink of his rye. "My dad."

"I heard," I tell him. "His cancer is back, isn't it?"

"He kept telling me he was feeling good, so I wouldn't worry. So I'd focus on hockey, and getting an invite to the December camp." He takes another drink. "But he's dying."

"Mark, I'm so sorry." I gently touch his clenched fist. His hand gradually relaxes, rolls over, wraps around mine. "When did you find out?"

"A week ago. I found Gary, crying. He told me the cancer's spread to what's left of Dad's pancreas and liver and his lungs." Mark squeezes my hand, but I don't think he knows he's doing it. "It's not fair."

"No, it isn't."

"There I was, thinking I could make a difference by playing hockey. How stupid was that?"

I don't know what to say, so I decide to listen instead. Maybe he needs silence more than he needs assurance.

Right then, the deejay cranks up the tunes, and I have to lean closer to Mark to hear anything. I catch about every third word. All can I do is sit and nod and smile and look sympathetic and hope he doesn't ask a question. One of the other groomsman brings him a pair of drinks, and I shake my head at him, but Mark picks one up and tips it back.

At this rate, he's going to be under the table before long.

The rest of the bridesmaids swarm me, urging me to dance with them.

"Maybe later!" I shout in Loni's ear.

Mark shifts back to the subject of his knee. Apparently he has a video of his surgery, which he can't bring himself to watch. The likelihood of a return to Major Junior next season is remote.

"Dad...pointless...wait...talk?" He looks at me expectantly.

I smile at him and nod, hoping *yes* is the right answer.

He stands, tugging the hand he's still holding, and picks up his cane.

Obviously we're going somewhere. I grab my clutch and my shawl and follow him out of the banquet hall, trying not to make eye contact with anyone.

Is there a reason I should feel guilty? We're not doing anything wrong.

The music and voices are left behind, and the air is lighter and cooler.

"Better, huh?" he says over his shoulder.

"Definitely." My ears are ringing.

He leads me to the lobby, which is deserted apart from the lady behind the registration desk. Mark lowers himself onto one of the couches by the fireplace and beckons me to join him.

My heart does a little flip.

You know where you want to sit, says my little voice. If you're not doing anything wrong, what's the big deal?

I sit down across from him and begin unbuckling the silver straps wound around my ankles.

"These shoes were not made for dancing," I say, depositing my heels on the coffee table between us.

Mark shrugs off his tuxedo jacket, lays it across the back of the couch, and rolls up his sleeves. He sits back and spreads his arms. "Now, enough about me. Let's hear about you."

We talk about *my* hockey for a change. I manage to stick to the good stuff and the funny stuff. It feels so amazing to have him to myself again and to make him laugh.

"I guess that's it," I say after a while, tucking my bare feet underneath me.

He narrows one eye. "So what about Evan?"

I do a masterful job of maintaining my expression. "We broke up."

"I know *that*." He raises one blond eyebrow. "I tried to talk to him about it, but he wouldn't say anything."

"I just – I mean, I didn't..." I pause and take a deep breath. "We weren't – connecting."

"That's not surprising, considering he was in Calgary, and you were in Estevan." He nods knowingly. "But he came back home to be near you."

I smile at him, hoping he'll drop the subject.

"And...?"

"And...I realized he was more serious about me than I was about him."

"Why weren't you as serious about him?"

I'm amazed he can persist in this line of questioning, considering how droopy his eyelids are.

"I just wasn't." I reach for my shoes. "Should we go back to the party?"

"Sit back," he slurs. "We just got here."

"You've had a lot to drink."

He leans towards me. "Do you think *she* would mind if you got me another one?" He gestures at the woman behind the reservations desk.

I look over his shoulder. "I think she would."

He slumps and closes his eyes.

"Maybe you should go up to your room and sleep this off," I suggest.

He nods.

"Give me your room key. I'll take you."

Sometimes you start down a road, with all the best intentions in the world, but if you're not careful – if you don't listen to your internal GPS – you can end up totally...

Lost.

# chapter
## forty-two

**M**ark leans against the wall while I insert the card into the slot.

Green light.

"There you go." I push the door open and putting my back against it, step to the side. "Do you think you'll be all right?"

As he hobbles by, he grabs my hand and pulls me into the room. The door closes behind us. He tugs me towards the desk and places his cane against it.

"Need help with something," he mumbles. He leans heavily on my right shoulder as he hops towards the end of the bed and plunks down. He laughs a little, then points at the chair. "Slide that over."

I set my stuff down on the desk and help him raise his foot onto the chair.

"Is that better?" I ask.

"Better." He pats the bed beside him. "Come and sit."

My heart jumps. It's been racing ever since he pulled me into the room. I always knew this would happen *sometime.*

He starts to say something, then stops and shakes his head.

I sit down beside him. "What is it?"

"I want to thank you," he says slowly. "You've always been there for me. No matter what. And I haven't been fair to you."

"You don't have to apologize."

He puts his arm around my shoulders. "You look beautiful. Did anybody tell you?"

I shake my head.

His hand slips to the nape of my neck, and he gently pulls me towards him. My body follows his impulse, but my little voice starts nattering immediately.

This isn't right, it says. He's drunk. He doesn't know what he's doing. He'll regret it tomorrow.

Maybe he will. But I won't.

Oh yes, you will, the voice says. You know you will.

Okay, but just give me *one* minute, so I can be sure.

I let him kiss me. His breath smells like rye, but I don't care. I tell myself I'm not betraying Holly if I don't kiss him back.

My thoughts shift to Liam – and how it felt when he kissed me.

Liam?

What does Liam have to do with anything?

I return the kiss while my fingers explore the top button

of Mark's shirt. He tugs at the zipper on the back of my dress. It gives way a little, but he's too clumsy to do more. I can help him, or I can tell him to stop.

You know what you should do, my voice says. If the roles were reversed, he'd *never* do this to you. How many more bad decisions do you plan to make this year?

I turn my face away from Mark's and peer at the red numbers on the clock radio sitting on the nightstand. It's already midnight.

"Happy New Year," I tell him.

"New year," he mumbles against my neck.

I feel his hands on my spine as he lies back on the bed and pulls me down on top of him.

No, my little voice says. This is wrong. You'll never be able to look yourself in the mirror tomorrow.

I deserve him, I think, fighting back. He was mine before he was Holly's.

That doesn't make this right, my voice says. And you know it.

Yes.

I push myself off Mark.

"I have to go."

He mumbles something and reaches for me, but I waylay his hands and crawl off the bed. His eyes are closed, and his breathing is deep and slow.

I suddenly feel very cold. My hands and feet are like ice. I want more than anything to go back to my room and put on warm clothes.

"I'm leaving now," I tell him. "Are you going to be all right?"

He mumbles again and rolls over onto his side, wincing. I manipulate his arms until he's lying in the recovery position, then move the chair to support his injured leg.

"Long live Captain Anal," I say out loud as I pick up my shawl, clutch and shoes.

A contented smile spreads across his face.

You've got no right to muck with his world, my voice says. He's got enough going on. If you're meant to be with him, he's the one who has to make it happen.

That's where you're wrong, I think. I'm not meant to be with him. Part of me feels sad, because I always dreamed we'd be together again one day, and it's hard letting go of a dream once and for all.

But I'm done waiting. And hoping. And praying. I'm done with all of it.

I close the door gently behind me.

# *chapter*
## *forty-three*

n the hallway, I lean against the door and open my
clutch, fumbling inside for the little envelope con-
taining my room card. My fingers encounter my
phone, and I remove it. It's been shut off since the
wedding ceremony. That was hours ago.

Shit.

I turn it on and start walking fast. The messages from
Courtney spill in.

Where r u? Call me now!

My hands are trembling as I choose her from my contacts
and speed dial. I feel colder than ever. She picks up on the
second ring.

"Why did you shut off your phone?" she shrieks.

"Never mind that. What's going on?"

"There's something wrong with Rufus!" She takes a
ragged breath. "He's really sick. He's jerking and frothing at
the mouth."

"Did he eat something he shouldn't have?"

"I don't know. Maybe."

"Where are you?" I ask. "Are you at home or at Pam's?"

"At home!" she shouts. "And I want you to come! Right now!"

"Courtney, I'm on my way, but Rufus probably needs a vet. Call one of the neighbours."

"No," she says emphatically.

I press the elevator button. "Courtney, why are you at the house? You're supposed to be at the All-Nighter."

"Never mind," she says.

"Where's Pam?" I ask.

"In the bathroom. Please come home," she begs.

"Courtney, I'm two hours away. At least."

"He's going to die!" Courtney wails.

"I'm going to send someone over who'll know what to do about Rufus. In the meantime, go next door and see if Mr. Millard is home."

There's a noise in the background, like a door opening, and the sound of voices and hip-hop music.

"Who else is there?"

"Gia and some of her friends."

"How many?"

"Just a few," she says.

"How many?"

"I don't know! Six or seven! It wasn't my idea," she says angrily. "It was Gia's."

The elevator doors open, just as the realization slams me right between the eyes.

Betrayal.

How stupid can a seventeen-year-old and two parents be?

I climb in and press the button for my floor. "Courtney, how could you?!"

She starts sobbing again.

Calm your shit, my little voice says. This isn't the time. Take control. Be the adult.

"I'm calling my friend, and I'm leaving right now. Tell everyone the party's over."

"Okay."

I quickly call Liam and try to explain the situation.

He doesn't make it easy for me.

"Maybe I'm busy," he says. "And here you are, barging into my New Year's Eve with demands on my time. Assuming I'm not doing anything."

"I'm not assuming," I tell him. "Please help us. You said I could call you if I needed you. Well, I need you *now.*"

He heaves a sigh. "All right. But those little freaks better clear out before I get there." I start to give him my address, but he says, "I remember where you live."

He hangs up.

The doors open, and I run down the hall to my room, where I change and grab the rest of my stuff. I avoid the girl at the reservations desk until after I go outside and start Sunny. She's frozen solid.

I won't lie about the ride home. Highway 33 isn't busy at night, even on New Year's Eve, so I speed as much as I dare. Now that I'm on my way, I debate whether I should call Mom and Dad.

What are you going to tell them, my little voice says.

I don't know anything. Would it be better to wait until I get home and see what's actually happening?

That's when I realize that in the excitement of Brittni's Big Day, I forgot to charge my phone. There's hardly any battery life left, and I don't have a car charger. I shut the phone off to save what power is left.

I hit fog at Francis and have to slow down to 90 km. As the towns crawl by, I sing along to the radio and my iPod, trying to make time fly. But it doesn't. I think about the party at our house and what might have gone on there. I think about turning my phone back on and calling the police. I think about kicking Gia's ass. I think about Mark, and wonder what *he'll* think about me in the morning. Will he even remember what happened?

The sensible part of me hopes he won't.

It's nearly three a.m. when I reach Estevan's city limits. I put on my earbud and call home. No answer. I call Liam but get his voice mail. I try Courtney's cell next. She picks up on the first ring.

"Where are you?" she sobs.

In the background there's a telephone ringing and deep male voices.

"Where are *you?*" I reply.

"The police station."

Too late to hope Mom and Dad don't know anything about this.

"Liam called the cops when he got to our place."

I take a second to process this piece of information. "Where's Rufus?" I ask.

"Liam took him to the vet clinic. I don't know what's happening over there." There's a brief pause. "What if Rufus is dead?" she cries. "I hate my life."

"I'll be there soon," I promise.

When I get to the station, a number of vehicles are parked on the street. I manage to squeeze Sunny into a snowy spot.

I meet Gia's mom on the stairs outside. Her eye makeup is runny, and her updo is in shambles. It's obvious her New Year has not gotten off to a great start. "This is the limit!" she is screaming at Gia, who is right behind her. "The limit, do you hear me?"

As I open the door, I meet Pam and her parents. Her mom pushes past me, not even acknowledging me. Pam quickly averts her eyes. There is the sharp, unmistakable smell of vomit on her clothing.

"Have you seen Courtney?" I ask Pam's dad.

"She's inside," he says.

"Can you tell me what happened?" I ask him.

"This isn't a good time," he says. "Can you call me tomorrow?"

Inside the station's small waiting area, a man and a woman are talking to a young constable behind the counter. Another girl from Courtney's hockey team is sitting in a chair, her head in her hands.

"We appreciate the way you handled this," the woman is saying. "I wish I could say the same for the McIntyres. What were they thinking, leaving their daughter alone like that?"

Part of me wants to try to explain. Part of me wants to tell her to shut up until she gets her facts straight.

The constable catches my eye. "Can I help you?" he asks.

"I'm Jessie McIntyre, Courtney's sister. Is she here?"

The man and woman turn around and glare at me.

"It's about time," the dad says.

The constable motions me towards the keyless access door, which he unlocks from his side and opens.

"She's being interviewed in that room." He gestures to the first one on the right. "You can go in."

Courtney is seated across from an older constable with a grey moustache. He's taking her statement.

As soon as she sees me, Courtney jumps up and hugs me. It's been a long time since she's done anything like that.

"I'm so glad you're here," she mumbles.

"Do Mom and Dad know?" I murmur in her ear.

She nods and buries her face in my shoulder. "They changed their flight. They'll be home at noon tomorrow. I mean today." She sits back down, wiping her nose. "This is my sister Jessie."

The officer steps out from behind his desk and extends his hand. "Hello, Jessie. I'm Constable Michaels."

"Hi." I shake his hand. "Is Courtney going to be charged?"

"She's eleven," the constable says. "We can't charge anyone under twelve. I spoke to your father on the phone earlier, and he gave me permission to interview Courtney. She knows her rights."

Courtney nods.

"Would you like me to get you a chair?" Constable Michaels asks. "It isn't very roomy in here, but I can accommodate you."

"I can stand, thanks."

"Courtney and I were just trying to establish whose idea it was to mix energy drinks and alcohol."

My knees buckle.

"Maybe you better get me a chair," I tell him.

# chapter
## forty-four

Later in the waiting area, I check my phone. I decide not to read or listen to my Mom's texts or voice mails. I don't want my phone to die before I try Liam again. This time he picks up.

"I was wondering when I'd hear from you." He sounds tired.

"Are you at the clinic?"

He yawns. "Just finishing. Where are you?"

"At the police station."

"I'll bet *that's* a gong show," he says.

"It wasn't as bad as I thought. They had the kids split up in different rooms to get their statements." I try to stifle a yawn. "How's Rufus?"

"He's good now. The doc gave him something." He yawns again. "Courtney was scared shitless when I got there. How's she doing?"

"Okay. She's in the bathroom, washing her face."

"And what about the other girl? The one who was puking her guts out?"

"Fine, I think."

"At least she didn't combine alcohol with an energy drink. Straight booze is bad enough for a little kid like that."

"Liam, why did you call the police?"

"I had to," he says. "They refused to leave, and they got really lippy. I was afraid I was going to kill that Gia kid." Another yawn. "I was just going to *pretend* to make the call, and then I thought – what the hell. They deserve it. The cops came right in the house. Said they had permission from the owner. Arrested the whole works and hauled their asses down to the station."

"My mom gave permission," I tell him. "Before she left for Vegas, she told the police they could go in our house if Courtney had a party."

"You're kidding."

"My mom works for a lawyer, Liam. If there's one thing she knows, it's the law."

"I know this is going to sound bad, but I'm glad it was Rufus, and not your little sister who got sick. I heard of a kid who had a heart attack from mixing that stuff."

I interrupt him, shuddering. "Liam, how bad is our house?"

"Not great. They stayed in the basement at least, and they

didn't wreck anything. Look, I'm going to curl up on the couch in the waiting room and get some sleep. You and Courtney should go home and get some sleep too. You're going to have a long day tomorrow."

"You're right about that."

He doesn't say anything for a moment. "By the way, you're welcome." He hangs up.

I stare at the phone in my hand. It's after four in the morning, and I'm too tired to beat off the guilt, fury and helplessness any more. And the fear most of all. The feeling of having just dodged a bullet. What if I hadn't pulled away from Mark when I did? What if I hadn't seen that Courtney had been calling?

Courtney comes through the access door. There are huge black circles under her eyes.

Constable Michaels leans over the counter. "Thanks for coming, Jessie." He looks at Courtney. "Your family loves you. Maybe you better start showing them you appreciate it."

Courtney nods and looks like she's going to start crying again.

The access door closes.

"Thanks again," I tell the constable.

"Let me know what happens with your dog," he says. "We had our hands full with the kids earlier, so we couldn't make an emergency trip to the vet. Remind your friend he needs to come in first thing tomorrow, so we can get his statement."

"I'll tell him."

We're only halfway through Grade Six, I think as we exit the building. What's next? I wait until we're both in the vehicle before I say anything. Sunny hasn't cooled down much, but I give her a chance to warm up.

"Here, put this on." I reach between the seats and grab a fleece blanket off the floor.

Courtney wraps it around herself, still shivering. "Do you know how Rufus is?"

I tell her about my conversation with Liam, wishing the lighting was a little better so I could see her face.

"That's a relief," she says when I'm done.

"Aren't you upset that one of your friends tried to kill your dog?" I demand.

"Nobody tried to kill Rufus," she says. "He just drank something he shouldn't have. That's all."

"That's *all?*"

"I'm sorry," she says quickly.

I turn the fan up a notch. The heater is blowing luke-warm at the moment. "Do you know how dangerous it was to mix those drinks?" I place my hands on the steering wheel and push back, stretching my arms.

"I didn't drink anything like that!" Courtney yells. "I'd

never do that! Not ever!"

"Explain to me how you and Pam and those other kids ended up back at our place when you were supposed to be at the All-Nighter?"

"We were at the All-Nighter. But we got bored."

"Great."

"Will you just listen?" she demands. "You want to know what happened, and I'm trying to tell you!"

I shut up and let her talk.

"Gia was at the Leisure Centre with some of the other girls, and she decided we should go someplace else. We planned to be back to the All-Nighter before it ended, when Pam's dad would pick us up. Nobody would ever know we left." She adjusts the blanket. "I thought we'd watch a movie or play Wii or something, but Gia got into our liquor cabinet, and everybody started drinking, and I couldn't stop them." She rubs one eye with her fist. "I wanted to call the cops, but I was too scared."

"You should have at least called Pam's parents."

"I wanted to. But Pam made me promise I wouldn't," Courtney says. "She didn't want them to see her puking."

"Yes, so much for pure, sweet Pam. You never should have let those girls come over to the house. You had to know that was a bad decision."

"I tried to talk Gia out of it."

"Bullshit," I say. "If Gia told you to throw yourself in front of a train, you'd do it."

"I would not," Courtney insists.

"Courtney, you need to start thinking for yourself."

"I do," she says. "Why won't you trust me? I don't even drink."

I scoff at her.

"You don't believe me," she says.

"Why should I?"

"Because I know I'm not old enough yet. I'm not ready."

I aim the defrost function at the windshield. "And you expect me to believe you *don't?* You tell me one person you know of that hangs out with a bunch of people like that and doesn't get dragged down with them."

"You don't drink," she says slowly. "And you hang out with people who do."

"That's different," I tell her. "I've seen first hand what alcohol can do. Look at what happened to Jodi. One bad decision changed her life."

"It's the same for me as it is for you," she says. "I have to be strong, so I don't give in." She pauses and looks out the side window. "That's why I knew I could call you. I knew you'd *want* to come home. And I knew you'd be able to *drive.* You always do the right thing."

Don't you wish she was right about that, my little voice asks.

"Courtney, you really don't know who decided to mix the energy drinks? That could have been Pam or Gia going to the hospital, instead of Rufus."

She shakes her head. "I was in the bathroom with Pam, holding her hair." She folds her arms across her chest and squeezes herself.

"That's what friends are for," I say wryly, putting Sunny in reverse and trying to back up. We hear the unmistakable sound of tires whirring.

"Get out and give us a push, will you, Sis?"

While she's positioning herself behind the car, I put the car in drive. It suddenly occurs to me that this is the best talk we've had in a long, long while. Maybe it's the only talk we've ever had like this.

My sister is no longer a child.

I'm seeing through a window of what it'll be like in the years to come.

I'm looking forward to it.

# chapter
## forty-five

A s soon as we get home, I send Courtney down to the basement to clean up while I call Mom and Dad.

It's nearly four thirty a.m., and I am bone tired. Too tired to give my parents details of the police station interview.

"Can we talk about it when you get home?" I ask Dad.

"You better believe we will," he says. "Get some sleep in the meantime, okay?"

After I hang up, I check the liquor cabinet in the living room. It's empty.

"That can't be good," I say out loud.

I grab some garbage bags and go downstairs to check on the basement. Nothing's broken at least. No holes in the walls. There're energy drinks scattered all over, and an empty bottle of scotch.

I've heard some real horror stories about house parties. Kids mixing booze and energy drinks and their parents' prescription drugs.

Maybe we got off easy.

"Where's the rest of the booze?" I ask Courtney, who's trying to scrub dog puke out of the carpet.

She points at the bottle. "That's all they could find."

"All?" I scan the room. "Where's the vodka? And rum? and rye?" I pick up the liquor bottle. "Your friends actually drank scotch? Are they *crazy?*"

Courtney sits back on her heels. "Mom and Dad will never let me out again." Her voice is quivering.

I feel another meltdown coming, but I'm too beat to care.

I start bagging cans. "Try some cold water and vinegar on that stain."

"Can't I do it in the morning?" she whines.

"No."

I open the windows to air out the room. I help her for a while, then decide it's time to go upstairs and catch a few zzzs.

"Make sure you vacuum," I tell her. "And don't forget to do the bathroom."

She starts crying.

Shades of the child I thought she'd left behind.

"I'm not cleaning up the mess your friends made," I tell her.

Even so, I help her with the bathroom.

It's six o'clock when I finally crawl into bed.

I get up at eleven and head for the vet clinic, leaving Courtney to sleep. Mom and Dad's plane won't get in until noon, and they have a two-hour drive after that. With any luck, Courtney won't have to face them until late this afternoon.

My eyes are red and sore, and my head is stuffed with cotton balls. It's that hung-over feeling without actually being hung-over. Not that I've been hung-over since the day after I drank a bucket of screwdrivers and lost Mark. Alcohol can really do a number on you sometimes.

When I get to the clinic, there's an SUV parked out front, but the main entrance is locked. I pound on the glass door and one of the windows until the vet lets me in.

"Is Liam here?" I ask, rubbing my cold hands.

"No," she says. "He left hours ago."

"Can Rufus come home?"

"We'll keep him here at least another twenty-four hours for observation. Do you want to see him?"

"Yes. Please."

"Wait here."

She disappears into the back. I stand in the lobby in my sock feet, surrounded by that wonderful blend of animal and antiseptic, and wonder if I dare go over to Liam's right now. I hate to wake him, but I need to know *his* version of last night's events. I also need to thank him.

I hear excited barking, but it doesn't sound like Rufus. A door slams and the vet reappears with Rufus parked under her arm. His eyes are listless, but he licks my hand when I hold it under his nose.

"His pupils are huge!" I rub his ears. "He's going to be okay, isn't he?"

"They're not as dilated as they were last night." She strokes Rufus' front paws with her free hand. "Liam thinks one of your sister's friends gave Rufus an energy drink because she thought it would be funny to get him hyperactive. That was a cruel and stupid thing to do."

I don't say anything.

"A small dog like this can't metabolize that much caffeine. He could easily have died."

Later, while I'm driving over to Liam's farm, I think about how close we came to losing our dog. I have to pull over for a minute and have a little cry. I know it's stupid. It's the first time I've cried like this in a long time, and I'm not even sure what I'm crying about.

Liam isn't sleeping when I get to his place. His mom says he's in the arena. She insists I put on an extra coat, and she even wraps a woolen scarf around my head. Old Dan and Little Ann, the two chocolate Labs, keep me company on the walk over to the arena, loping beside me, bumping my legs, sticking their heads under my hands. But when I open the side entrance to the arena, they barge ahead of me like kids on the last day of school.

Liam is working the grey colt, the one named Sherman, on pivots. The horse starts when the two dogs barrel over, but he doesn't shy. He faces them and puts his head down low, blowing out his breath in soft clouds.

Liam steps off the colt's back. He makes an abrupt gesture, and the dogs sit immediately, wriggling, while Sherman smells their heads.

"I know where to bring Rufus for obedience training." My voice sounds loud and hollow, like I'm speaking with a tin pail over my head. By now I'm a few metres away.

Liam turns his back and checks the cinch. He's wearing a fleece lined jean jacket, a toque, and soft yellow gloves.

"What are you doing here?" he asks.

"I just came to remind you to go to the police station. I also wanted to say thanks."

He pushes on Sherman's shoulder, forcing the colt to shift his weight, then bends over and takes the hoof between his knees, examining the sole.

I stand there like a fool. Little Ann comes over and rubs her nose against my thigh. Liam turns his head and lifting his upper lip, makes a sharp, sucking noise with his teeth. Little Ann folds back her ears in apology and lies down beside Old

Dan, placing her head on her paws.

"What — they're not supposed to talk to me either?"

Liam releases the hoof, then goes around to the other side and picks up Sherman's right.

I follow him, determined not to give up.

"What do you want from me?" Liam asks.

I sigh loudly. "I told you. I want to thank you for what you did for Courtney and for Rufus. You're a good friend."

Liam lets go and stands up, facing me for the first time. Even though the lighting is poor, I can see he's haggard.

"Am I?" he asks quietly.

I start to feel nervous. Like the next thing he's going to examine more closely is me.

"Yes."

"You only called me because I work for a vet. That's it."

"Why are you so angry at me?" I ask him.

"I don't like being used."

"I wasn't using you." I shove my hands in my pockets because they're starting to shake. "I'm not that kind of person."

"You're not?" He takes a step towards me. "Just where were you last night anyway?"

"I told you. I was in Regina at a wedding."

"Was that guy there? The one you still like?" he demands.

"Yes."

His face hardens. "Look. I've made no secret of the fact I like you, but it's not working. It hurts too much to get pushed away all the time."

"I'd really like to be friends," I tell him. "Maybe even more than friends. I'm ready this time. Honest."

"You don't sound ready," he says.

I think about the drinks I watched Mark put away, the way I let him unburden himself, and the shame washes over me. If Liam knew the whole story, what else would he say?

"I asked you once what you were saving yourself for." Liam slaps the reins lightly against the palm of his glove. "It wasn't what. It was who. I hope he was worth it."

"Liam, nothing happened!"

He starts leading Sherman towards the double doors at the back of the arena. "You do whatever you like. I've given up on you." He stops and delivers his last comment, back turned. "Don't call me the next time you have a crisis."

He leaves without saying goodbye.

The two dogs come up from behind and push their noses into my palms, begging for a caress. I kneel down and let Little Ann lick the salt away from the corners of my eyes.

"Damn him, anyway," I say to her.

You know he's right, says my little voice. That's why it hurts so much.

# *chapter*
## *forty-six*

**R**ufus comes home from the clinic after a few days. He's pretty much his old self, although he sleeps even more than usual for the first week.

Dad posts the vet bill on the fridge where Courtney can see it every time she goes for a snack.

"You're going to work that off," Dad tells her at supper one night. "You can start by cleaning the garage."

"Okay," Courtney says.

"Your dad and I are taking you out of hockey," Mom says.

Courtney immediately shifts gears. "Why?"

"You haven't done a good job of picking your friends," Dad says. "We think you should go back to figure skating."

"I don't want to figure skate," Courtney says.

"You used to love it," Mom says. "I talked to the club president, and she said..."

"I'm not going back," Courtney says. "I'll hang out with

whoever you want me to hang out with on the hockey team, but I'm *not* quitting!"

Mom and Dad exchange glances.

You devils, I want to say out loud. That's what you were waiting for.

"All right." Mom turns to me. "Who do *you* think Courtney should hang out with?"

"I'm not around the team that much," I say evasively. "I'm not a great judge of character."

"Take your time," Dad says. "Think about it, and get back to us."

All three of them are looking at me expectantly.

Super duper.

I slide back into the practice/dryland routine. I feel rejuvenated after the two-week break from hockey. Besides, throwing myself heart and soul into my sport keeps me from thinking about other stuff.

When I go back to school in January, I see Liam nearly everyday at school, but he treats me like a stranger. Worse than a stranger.

I should be used to it. First Mark. Then Evan. Now Liam.

Mark calls me the night before we host Weyburn. My pulse doesn't even jump at the sound of his voice.

I'm embarrassed to even talk to him.

"Look, Jessie," he says, "I feel terrible about what happened at Brittni's wedding. Being drunk is no excuse for mauling you like that." He clears his throat. "I hope you'll forgive me."

"It's okay."

"It's not. I don't know what got into me."

"Don't worry about it," I tell him.

"I would never do anything to hurt Holly," he says. "She's the one, Jessie."

Much as I hate it, that stings.

"I won't tell anyone," I assure him. "Water under the bridge."

"Thanks," he says.

"How's your dad?" I ask.

He talks for a few minutes more, but the cancer terminology, second nature to him by now, is foreign to me. Before he hangs up, he says something about keeping in touch, valuing my friendship, blah, blah, blah.

But I know it's not true.

He'll always be on his guard with me. It'll be awkward. We're not the same people we were when we dated. Maybe it's better we don't see each other.

**W**e win at home against Weyburn in OT, and then take a shit kicking two days later at Crescent Point Place.

"Sure wish I knew *which* team is going to show up," Bud

tells us in the dressing room after the Saturday afternoon game. "You girls are an enigma."

"Thanks, Coach," Randi says.

"It's not a compliment," Kathy says. "He means he can't figure us out, and he should be able to, right Coach?"

"That's right," Bud says. "Consistency is the key to a successful season, Ladies. If you ride the yoyo for the next two months, you don't stand a chance in the playoffs."

On the drive back to Estevan, Dad says, "You girls play much differently when Miranda's in net."

"It is that obvious?" I ask.

"You play not to give up a goal because you don't trust her to stop the soft ones. But when Amy's in net, you play with confidence because you know she'll take care of business."

I don't agree or disagree with him. It's Bud's decision to split the games between the goalies as long as we can stay in a playoff spot. Some of the older girls think Miranda should sit, and Amy should start every game. Part of me wishes this were so, and part of me wonders how fair is that to Miranda?

It's a huge commitment to go to practice and dryland and games nearly every night of the week. Should we put the best team possible on the ice?

Sometimes, I'm glad I'm not the coach.

**W**e roll through the rest of January and February, managing to win a few more games and stay ahead of the Battlefords, Swift Current and Prince Albert in the standings. Meanwhile our old pals from Weyburn are hanging out in third place.

It's looking more and more like we'll be meeting them in the first round of playoffs at the beginning of March.

Sweet.


**I**'m glad you talked Mom and Dad out of making me quit hockey," Courtney says. "I'd hate to miss playoffs."

We're in the garage, working on her shooting. She's brutal at raising the puck. Good thing ninety percent of goals slide in on the ice.

"You've improved since October. And you're having fun, right?"

She nods and strips off her hoodie, revealing her sweat-soaked tank. Even though our garage is heated, I can see her breath.

"You better not catch a cold," I warn. "Why don't you take a break while I fix the net?"

She reaches for the water bottle on the step while I wrestle the framework together where it's pulled apart again.

"Have you seen the duct tape?" I ask.

She points to Dad's tool stand, and I start rifling through

the drawers.

"I hate that Dad took my cellphone away." She takes another pull on her water bottle. "I feel like I'm living in the olden days."

I rip off a piece of duct tape and wrap it around the frame before answering. "I didn't have one when I was eleven."

"Yeah, yeah."

"So, how's Gia doing? Did she get grounded?"

Courtney fills me in. Gia has moved out of her mom's house into her dad's. I'm not sure if he's having any more luck controlling her, but at least Courtney's not spending time with her, apart from school and hockey.

"I have to shower," Courtney says at last. "Pam's mom is coming in half an hour."

"You don't want to keep her waiting," I say.

We don't have to say anything more. We know she's lucky Pam's mom still lets them hang out.

I place our sticks with the rest of the ones stacked in the corner.

Courtney pauses at the door. "Thanks for helping me. You're a decent big sister, when you're not trying to be my mom."

"You're not so bad yourself when you're not acting like a spoiled little kid," I reply.

She opens the door, and a white ball of fur streaks out.

"Jail break!" Courtney cries.

Rufus leads us on a merry chase through the garage, panting and growling, one ear flipped over so the pink shows. We finally trap him inside the hockey net.

"I'll distract him! You grab him," I say, waving at her.

She lunges, Rufus bolts, and the net collapses on top of us. We lie there on the cold cement and howl while Rufus yaps at us, a sharp, staccato sound.

When Dad comes outside to check on the commotion, his startled face is all we need to put us further over the edge.

"Look who's in jail now!" Courtney laughs.

# chapter forty-seven

**S**he covered the puck with her glove in the crease. Why isn't that a penalty shot?" I ask the referee. I try to sound objective, like I'm cupping my hands beneath her fountain of knowledge. But when it's the last three minutes of Game Five of your first playoff series, and the score is 2–2, and your team is killing a five on three, it's brutally hard.

She gives me a benevolent smile. "She realized what she did, and she took her hand away. She didn't do it intentionally."

"Okay. So if I check someone from behind, but I *realize* I did it, you won't give me a penalty?"

The smile slides like jello off her face. "Go line up," she says.

"An infraction is an infraction," I tell her, "intentional or not."

"Go line up," she repeats, her voice brittle.

When I relay this information to Bud, he glares at the referee, but he doesn't wave her over. I line up with Carla and

Kathy in Weyburn's end, where, a few moments ago, Kathy's aggressive forecheck forced Number 14 to fall on the puck. Randi and Whitney are the two players in the sin bin. I hope Randi's interference call and Whitney's unsportsmanlike don't cost us the game.

Kathy leans in, head cocked and stick poised, as the linesman snaps the puck. She wins the draw back to my side, and I fire it in deep along the boards, ready to back pedal if Number 23 beats Kathy to it.

Soon all three of us are transitioning to D as Weyburn's top line breaks out and brings the puck up the ice. I motion for Carla to take away the pass, as I focus on Number 9, who has the puck. I poke check it away, but Kathy can't get to it in time. My stomach sinks as Number 5 scoops it up, slides into the low slot, toe dragging around Carla, and pulls the trigger.

There's no possible way Amy can see the shot, not with the screen Number 18 is throwing. But her reflexes are flawless, as they have been the entire series. She snatches the puck out of the air and waits for the whistle.

"Holy, do you have x-ray vision?" I ask her, smacking her pads with my stick.

Amy tosses the puck to the linesman. "We are *so* knocking Weyburn out of the playoffs."

Kathy says, "Nothing sweeter than closing out a series in your opposition's rink."

"I sure hope this kind of talk doesn't piss off the hockey gods," I say.

Dayna, Jennifer and Larissa come out to relieve us, and I check the time on the clock as I skate to the bench. 1:15 left in Whitney's penalty, and :32 left in Randi's. The music in Crescent Point Place pounds in my ears as our fans bang on the glass. I crowd surf for Liam and Russell MacArthur, but I can't find them. I haven't seen them at a game since before Christmas.

As soon as we step inside the box, the music stops and the play resumes.

Number 3 wins the faceoff back to her right D, who rips a slapshot on net. There's a scramble for the puck, and Jennifer goes down awkwardly and stays down. The ref's whistle stops the play.

"Not good," Carla says. "I think she hurt her wrist."

We can't afford another injury, not with Miranda and one of the Rookies nursing sprains. Crystal's mom heads out onto the ice, hanging on Kathy's elbow for support.

It's a long time before Jennifer gets up, and when she does, she's cradling her right forearm.

"Good chance it's broken," I say. "We're down to three D."

Mrs. Jordan gestures at the St. John's ambulance people sitting above our box, then takes Jennifer straight to the dressing room.

"Do not pass go. Do not collect two hundred dollars," Kathy says. "Now what?"

Bud calls a timeout, and we gather around him and Sue.

His eyes roll over each of us. "Kathy, I'm moving you to D," he says at last.

"Okay," Kathy says. "Should I tell the Weyburn coach you're spotting them a couple of goals. Because that's what's going to happen."

"It's not going to happen," Sue says calmly. "I assume you've played D once or twice in your star-studded career?"

"I was a blue liner in Novice," Kathy replies. "My coach told me he'd never seen anybody with less defensive instincts."

"Your coach didn't know what he was talking about." Bud pulls out his whiteboard and uncaps the marker with his teeth.

"He was my dad," Kathy says. "Mr. Parker. I think you've met him."

Bud waves a hand in dismissal. "Today, you're Carla's new D-partner."

"Suit yourself," Kathy says.

Bud draws up the play and quickly outlines it. I've learned to pay close attention to these drills because Bud rarely repeats himself.

I skate to the faceoff dot with Dayna, who's making little burping noises.

"This is not the time to let nerves get the best of you," I tell her.

She swallows another burp. Her breath smells like vomit.

"Hey, you can do it," I say. "Deep inside, you know you can."

Despite her nerves, Dayna *does* execute – perfectly.

And so does Kathy, despite what her dad told her in Novice.

We kill the rest of the five on three, and are hanging in there for the five on four, when Number 18 takes a hooking penalty on Kathy. It's Weyburn's turn to question the call. Their assistant coach works over the referee while one of the fans threatens to trash her car.

"Correct me if I'm wrong, but weren't you hanging on to *her* stick?" I ask Kathy as I take her spot at the next faceoff.

Kathy grins and gives me a little poke before she skates away.

I take a second to soak it all in, the crowd noise, the music, the score on the jumbotron, my teammates.

Please don't let this be my last Midget game.

We need to get control of the puck in Weyburn's end, so Amy can head to the bench, and Kathy can spill back out, as a forward.

I turn my head towards Carla, my D-partner for this last crucial ninety seconds. She gives me a little nod.

The puck drops. Whitney loses the faceoff. Number 15

tries to ice it. Carla chops it down, and it falls like a gift at her feet. She slides it over to me, and I rip it in deep. Larissa and Randi pile into the corner on top of Number 14, and Randi comes up with the puck. She dodges 14, trying to create space for herself. I hear skates behind me, and I know Amy's gone to the bench. Kathy has a full head of steam as she blows by me, and she's calling for the puck as she moves into the high slot. Randi pivots and puts the puck right on Kathy's blade.

Number 27 lies down to block the shot. The Weyburn goalie is squared away, negating the corners. Kathy slides it past 27 and cuts hard to the left. When the goalie moves with her, she passes to Larissa behind the net. Larissa flips the puck behind the goalie and it rolls down her back and in.

Sick.

Howling, my teammates pile on top of Larissa while the Gold Wings move like members of a funeral procession back to their bench. There's a yard sale on Oiler equipment all over the ice.

Losers – them.

Winners – us.

"Where did you learn that move?!" I scream in Larissa's ear. It's not easy to find it under the pyramid of churning bodies.

"You're not the only one who watches the highlights on Sports Centre!" she shouts. "Ouch, you guys!"

**A**t practice on Monday Bud gives us five minutes to bask in the glory of our win.

Then it's all business. Notre Dame business. We're playing the Hounds in the next round, and they're still undefeated this year.

We have the best practice we've had all year. Even Whitney executes the drills the way she's supposed to.

After practice, I'm hauling my equipment to my car when I hear Whitney call my name.

"Can I talk to you for a sec?" she asks. "It's important."

Therapy. I should hang out a shingle.

"Sure." I hope she makes this quick. It's starting to snow.

"Will you give me a ride home?" she asks.

I want to refuse. I've got a couple of hours of homework ahead of me.

"Please?" she begs.

There's hardly room in old Sunny for one bag of equipment, much less two, but I fold down the back seats so we can stuff them in, along with our sticks.

She doesn't say anything until we're out of Estevan.

"Thanks for the ride," she says.

I adjust the setting on the windshield wipers.

She doesn't say anything else for a while. We're nearly at her turnoff before she blurts out, "I know you hate me."

"I don't hate you, Whitney," I reply.

"Well, you should. I'm the one who told Teneil you got drunk at the rookie party." She tucks her hands under her thighs. "I didn't actually tell her. I just let her draw her own conclusions. She *wanted* to believe it. She was mad at you and everyone else because she didn't make the team, and she was jealous of you for being voted captain." She pauses for a few seconds. Out of the corner of my eye, I see her looking at me expectantly.

"What about Jodi?" I ask. "Did you let her draw her own conclusions too, or did you out and out lie to her?"

Whitney starts to cry.

I don't say anything more. I'm not going to make it easy for her.

"I never thought she'd go and quit!" she says at last. "I was so jealous of you. But I didn't think Bud and Sue would find out. If I'd known all that stuff was going to happen, I never would have said anything."

I keep on driving.

"I probably should have owned up to you and the rest of the girls a long time ago."

"You got that right," I say.

She pushes her head back and stares at the ceiling. "But if you already knew, why didn't you tell everybody?"

"We got our coaches back. That's the only thing that

mattered."

Whitney sniffs loudly and swipes her fingers under her nose. "I am such a loser," she says.

We drive in silence for a few seconds.

"Start thinking like a leader," I tell her. "Next year you'll have lots of opportunities to choose between the high road and the low road. And any time you're not sure, the high road is *always* the best choice. Understand?"

"I think so," she says.

By now we're stopped in her driveway. Snow settles on the windshield in large lacey flakes, sliding and melting. I reach for my door handle.

"If I ever get to be captain, I'll try to be as good as you are," she says.

"Thanks," I say.

"I'll miss you next year," she says.

"I'll miss you too," I lie.

# chapter forty-eight

**W**hitney's dad charters a bus for Game One against the Hounds.

A real bus. With a bathroom and everything.

When we head out of the rink parking lot on Tuesday after school, we are all sure we've finally hit the Big Time.

Crystal reaches between the seats and jiggles my arm. "Remember the time we went to Davidson on the Beastie Bus, and we lay on our equipment to keep warm and squished our helmets?"

"Yeah." I lean my head against the window, trying not to get emotional.

It brings back an image of Amber Kowalski, redfaced, trying to jam on her lid. We all howled when we figured out what had happened. "Head cases," we called ourselves. I feel a little pang, thinking about Amber and how much she would've enjoyed this year. Or maybe she'd have been miserable, riding the pine and watching the Rookies take her place.

"Do you know if Amy's starting?" Crystal asks, sliding into the empty seat next to me.

"Not a clue," I lie. I plug in my ear buds and pull down the brim of my toque. "I'm going to try to get some sleep. Maybe you should too."

Crystal goes back to her own seat and leaves me to my thoughts.

Predictably, we play like scared rabbits against the Hounds. Bud starts Miranda in net, but it's clear her ankle is bothering her. She lets in four goals in the first period and limps off the ice afterward.

Amy shuts out Notre Dame for the final two periods, in spite of the fact we play most of those forty minutes in our own end. They outshoot us 41–15.

And the big goose egg on the scoreboard above Guest is a bitter reminder that many teams haven't scored a single goal against Notre Dame this year.

"If Bud had started Foxy in net, we'd have stood a chance," Randi whispers in my ear as she loosens her shoulder pads.

"We had to put the puck in the net, and we didn't," I whisper back. "We can't win if we don't score."

**W**hen we suit up against the Hounds two nights later at Spectra Place, we get our biggest crowd yet. Some football players come, but I don't see Liam.

Momentum has a lot to do with a singular act. A goal, a great save, a blocked shot, a brilliantly executed PK – all these things can get the ball rolling.

And sometimes, an old-fashioned body check can do the trick. Especially when the players are really big.

Number 15 is a monster of girl with a mean streak. Her shoulders mash our faces into the glass. Her elbows punish us in the corners. Her stick hammers our wrists and ankles.

Number 15 is coming across the ice with her head down, and Carla catches her in full stride, and they *both* soar through the air, parallel to the ice. It's a spectacular hit, and as we revisit it again and again in the dressing room after the first period, hoping Mr. Parker caught it on video.

"Betcha 15 never thought she'd be flying Air Bisson," Randi says.

**W**e're down by two goals when we head into the second. The Hounds come out flying, but Amy keeps us in the game, stonewalling them at her crease.

We play better full strength than we do on the power play. We can't generate any trash around the net when Notre Dame's PK units are on patrol.

Late in the second, Carla drives in a shot from the point, and we go crazy. It's the first goal we've scored against the Hounds since December.

We claw tooth and nail to keep the score close until midway through the third period.

Then the wheels start to fall off.

It's not Amy's fault.

We screen her on one goal and leave her high and dry, 2–0, on another.

At the end of the game, it's 4–1, and we have one more chance to keep our playoff hopes alive.

On Saturday afternoon.

A very slim chance.

On Saturday morning, Mom and I hit Highway 39 early, headed to Regina, on the hunt for my elusive grad dress.

"We'll be in the city by nine thirty." Mom slurps coffee from her travel mug. "That gives us at few hours. Do you think you can find something in that time frame?"

"I'm not fussy," I say. "If it looks good and the price is right, I'm buying the first dress off the rack. I don't want to burn myself out before the game this afternoon."

She takes another sip. "Did you remember your heels?"

I reach behind the seat and heft a shopping bag. "I can tell you one thing. This is the last time *I'm* strapping these on.

Courtney's welcome to them."

"You got yourself a grad escort yet?" Mom asks.

"I've got one in mind."

"Have you asked him yet?"

"Don't push me. I'm working on it."

Once we reach Regina, we head straight downtown and find a parking spot on Scarth Street. There're a couple of bridal stores in this part of the city, and we spend an hour in the first one. Although the store isn't that busy when we get there, more and more clientele drift in.

Competitive clientele.

As soon as I pass over a potential winner, a shark behind me snatches it off the rack.

In the second store I find a dark green, strapless, mermaid-style gown that looks fabulous in the dressing room. I pull my hair to the side, trying to imitate the look I had for Brittni's wedding. This could be it.

I push open the door and lift the dress, so I don't trip on the hem or my heels, and make my way out to the area where my mom should be waiting. But she's not there. I walk to the railing and look down and spy her by the storefront window. She's got her back to me, and she's talking on her phone, and from the position of her shoulders, I know something's wrong.

I stare at her, wondering if I should go down or wait here, like a mermaid stranded on the beach.

After a minute, she pulls the phone away and stares out the window. Finally she turns around and raises her eyes.

What is it, I think.

*Who* is it?

She tucks her phone into her purse and fords the river of girls circulating between the racks. She slowly climbs the stairs and puts her arms around me.

"I just talked to Sue," she breathes in my ear. "Your game's been canceled."

"Okay."

"It's Bud," she says. "He had a heart attack at home this morning. They took him by ambulance to the hospital." She pauses. "He died on the way. I'm so sorry, Jessie."

She squeezes me tighter, but it doesn't hurt because I already feel like all the air's been sucked out of me.

# *chapter*
## *forty-nine*

**B**ud's death hits me hard.

He's a sweet man I didn't know as well as I should have.

I didn't know he played Major Junior with the Blades back in the day. Or that he played on a senior hockey team that won the Allan Cup. Or that he taught high school math for over thirty years. No wonder he talked so much about angles. Worst of all, I didn't know he had a heart condition.

A raw March wind buffets our vehicle all the way to Holy Rosary Cathedral in Regina. The Oilers meet in an anteroom to put on our jerseys. Everybody's eyes are red and watery.

"I can't believe this is happening," Dayna says as I adjust the collar of her shirt. "How can we play Game 3 without Bud?" she asks.

"We can't talk about Game 3," I say. "Not today."

Whitney's sitting in the corner, crying her eyes out. "Why didn't I pay more attention to Bud during practice?" she sobs.

"I should have *listened* more."

Miranda sits down next to Whitney and hugs her and sings to her, just like she did for that stupid robotic doll back in September. Strangely, it soothes all of us. Amy sits on the other side and wraps her long arm around both of them. She doesn't sing, but she sways along with the song. She catches me staring, and she gives me a little smile.

I suddenly feel like crying again, but it has nothing to do with Bud.

Sue walks in. She's wearing a black silk suit, shirt and tie. Her short blonde hair is styled, and her makeup is perfect. Her eyes are dry.

We all stare at her.

Say one thing to make us feel better, I think. One little thing to help get us through.

"Tough day," she says.

She outlines how we are to behave – no sudden outbursts, no leaving the sanctuary once the funeral has started. No drawing attention to ourselves.

"We know this," I say when she's finished.

"Good," she says. "As horrible as you're feeling, imagine how it is for Bud's family. Show some respect."

When the door shuts behind Sue, Miranda says, "Did anybody else feel a chill just now?"

"She's handling it the only way she knows," Amy says.

"Let it go."

The church is packed with Bud's friends and colleagues from hockey, the Saskatchewan Hockey Association and his teaching career, with former students and players. My eyes are filmy as we walk into the sanctuary as a team, following Bud's family. I blink away the tears and curse my dripping nose. Somebody from the congregation reaches out and touches my hand, but I don't know who it is because I'm looking straight down.

Bud's daughter delivers the eulogy and manages to get through most of it before breaking down. There're some funny and tender bits in there. Bud was quite the prankster when he was with the Blades, and the story of how he met the love of his life moves us all. The priest's homily offers us comfort, and he even addresses us directly towards the end.

"Bud would want you girls to play with pride and passion," the priest says. "If he were here today, he would tell you: don't hold back. Break away from fear and doubt. Trust yourself and trust each other. Be the players and the young women you were born to be."

The internment afterwards is private, so we go back to the anteroom to take off our jerseys and pick up our jackets. We're going to the Cathedral Free House Café for a team lunch, then driving home with our families.

As soon as I walk out of the room, I see him.

Steve Brewer. My first hockey coach.

It's been two and a half years.

He's talking to some people I don't know, and he doesn't see me. It doesn't matter. I go straight to him, butting between him and the others, and I put my arms around him, burying my face against his jacket. I'm going to get snot all over it, but I know he won't care.

"Hey!" He cradles my head in his huge hands and pulls it back so he can see my face. "It's Big Mac," he says.

I can't even croak out a single word.

He lets me hold him for a couple of minutes while I sob and shudder. He leans his head on mine and strokes my hair and doesn't say anything either. He doesn't need to. When the shudders finally let go, he fishes a Kleenex out of his pocket and hands it to me.

"Better?" he asks.

I nod and blow my nose, repeatedly.

He produces another tissue and wipes his own eyes. "Bud coached me in minor hockey," he says. "He was the best I ever had. I always tried to model myself after him." He turns piercing blue eyes on me. "I hope I came close."

I finally find my voice. "Yes, you did."

"I'm glad," he says.

"Do you want to come for lunch with us?" I ask.

He shakes his head. "I have a plane to catch, and I want

to make sure I spend some time with Bud's family. It's been great seeing you, Jessie. I just wish it had been under better circumstances."

"Thanks for coming," I tell him. "It means a lot."

"We had some good times, didn't we?" he says. "I've been following the Oilers' website. You're doing great for your first year of AAA. I always knew you and Parker and Bisson would put Estevan on the map."

"We *all* put Estevan on the map," I correct him.

"Yes, you do," he says.

That's when the old Xtreme girls come over and get their share of hugs and head rubs. I drift back over to my family, who are waiting patiently.

"I have to make a phone call," I say. "Then I'll be ready to go.

Dad puts an arm around me and gives me a squeeze. "Sure, kid. We'll wait in the car."

When my family's gone, I turn on my phone and step in the anteroom. It's empty now. I scroll through my contacts until I find Liam's name. I'm not even sure what I'm going to say, but I have to say something.

He doesn't pick up, but fortunately, he has voice mail.

"Liam, it's Jessie. You told me once you were giving me your number, just in case I ever needed you again. Well, I need you now. Maybe you heard about our coach. It hurts so much, Liam. We've got one game left, and it'd mean a lot to have you and Russell there. And even if you can't make it, maybe you could give me a call, and we could get together and talk. Please."

I hang up.

# chapter *fifty*

T he Notre Dame coach calls Sue and offers to play Game 3 at Spectra Place.

"I know you'll want to honour Bud, on your home ice," she told Sue.

At least she doesn't state the obvious. We'd never beat the Hounds in Game 3, not if we played it a hundred times.

"Maybe they'll be nicer to us than they were last time," Jennifer says as we wait in the hallway beneath the stands while the zamboni finishes its flood.

"I could file down that cast so it fits inside your glove," Kathy says. "We could use you today, McQueen."

Jennifer shakes her head. "Sorry. I wish I could play."

"It won't be the same without Bud," says Amy.

"It sucks." Whitney reaches through her cage and digs a tear out of each eye.

There's hope for this girl, I think.

"Think Gia's dad will be any good?" Miranda asks.

"You've been on the bench with him."

Gia's dad is helping Sue today.

"He knows his hockey," I tell her. "Look who's here."

"Hey, guys." Teneil squeezes between Kathy and Miranda. "I'm sorry about Bud."

Nobody says anything.

"Even though I never had him for a coach, I know you all liked him," Teneil continues. "It must be hard for you to play today. And for once..." She takes a deep breath. "For once I'm glad I'm not one of you." She takes a Kleenex out of her pocket and blows her nose. "Sorry I've been such a bitch lately."

"Lately?" Kathy echoes.

I elbow her in the ribs.

"Go Oilers," Teneil says, moving back down the line, holding up her fist for knuckles.

Every one of us holds up our fist too.

Mrs. Jordan appears and opens the door for us. We place our helmets on the boards and line up on the blue line. Across from us, the Notre Dame team does the same.

Mr. Johnstone and Mr. Parker roll out a piece of carpet. Bud's daughter, son-in-law and grandchildren walk out. I can't take my eyes off Zack.

Mr. Johnstone is holding the microphone.

Don't be a phony, I think.

"This afternoon, the Estevan McGillicky Oilers would like to honour the memory of William "Bud" Prentice. Captain Jessie McIntyre will make a presentation to his family on behalf of the team."

I give my gloves to Carla and skate over to the group assembled on the carpet. Mr. Parker hands me a plaque, which is adorned with both our team picture and a close-up of Bud on the bench during a time out. There are words engraved on a gold plate at the bottom, but I can't read them because my eyes are too blurry.

I shake hands with Bud's daughter and hold out the plaque to her, but she pulls me close and hugs me.

"Thanks for everything you did," she whispers in my ear. "He loved coaching you girls."

We have three Oiler jerseys for Bud's grandkids, all with the name Prentice on the back, and Bud's number from his Allan Cup winning team. I hand out the sweaters, solemnly shaking three little hands. The kids pull them over their jackets.

"Looking good." I give them a thumbs up.

Zack gives me one too.

I hold out my fist for knuckles, as I've done so often in the past, and they all pound it.

"We will now observe a moment of silence in Bud's memory. Please rise and remove your hats," Mr. Johnstone says.

I skate back to my place between Carla and Kathy and bow my head.

Some people don't get the whole minute of silence thing. There's usually *one* loser who has to scream something asinine.

Today nobody says a word.

I turn my head a little and sneak a peek at the place where Liam and Russell and the football players usually stand. I'm expecting nothing.

But they're all here.

Liam's not painted up or decked out. But he's here.

My heart starts racing. And it has nothing to do with the hockey game.

"Please remain standing for our national anthem," Mr. Johnstone says.

Jodi takes the mic from his hand, and her throaty voice rises, pure and lovely.

I try to focus on the song and the game and Bud for the next two minutes, but my mind's on Liam.

He can only be here for one reason. He wouldn't be here unless...

"Jessie, quit gawking," Carla hisses out of the corner of her mouth.

I tear my eyes away and stare at the flag like I'm supposed to.

But my guts are tying themselves in knots. I'll talk to him after the game, I decide. I'll apologize for everything. Maybe it's not too late this time. Maybe he's not hooked up with that blonde with the cowboy hat.

"You're talking to yourself," Kathy says. "And it's not about the game."

I nod in acknowledgment and close my eyes, envisioning the power play I'm quarterbacking.

"Song's over." Carla hits me once, between the shoulder blades. "Time to go to work!"

We gather around Amy in net, shoulders, heads and blades down.

"Skate! Pass! Kick Notre Dame ass!" Kathy shouts.

"Oilers!" everyone shouts back.

**W**e're high on emotion for a while.

"For Bud," we keep telling each other.

"Make him proud."

The Hounds lead us 1–0 for the first two periods. Holding them to that one goal – never mind the shots – is a victory in itself.

Amy is playing her best hockey of the year. And so are the rest of us. We are doing all the things Bud taught us, beating them to the puck, using the boards, making our passes, driving to the net.

It's like someone – I hope it's Bud – has waved a magic wand over us.

Late in the third, Dayna's positioning herself to block a shot and deflects the puck past Amy. A defenceman's worst nightmare.

Dayna's beside herself.

"Shake it off!" I tell her. "We need a faceoff in their end. Go get it done!"

Kathy wins the faceoff back to me. I back pedal, creating room for myself, then slide it over to Dayna. Her pass catches Randi in full stride, who saucers it to Kathy. A little backdoor delivery between Kathy's skates lands right on Larissa's stick and she fires on net. The Hounds goalie' stones her, but she has to freeze the puck.

Mission accomplished.

Forty-two seconds left.

Sue calls a time out and hauls out her whiteboard.

"I want five across the line. Whitney, you're here on the boards. Kathy takes the faceoff. Jessie's here on the hash marks. Larissa and Randi are in the slot. Carla's on the point. Kathy, you win the draw back to Carla. Larissa and Randi will drive to the net while Jessie and Whitney tie up their men. Carla moves to centre and finds a shooting lane. Score on Carla's shot or on the rebound – I don't care. Just put the puck in quick." She surveys our faces for comprehension, and then quickly erases the board.

Now what?

Sue quickly draws another play. *"After* the goal, Kathy faces off. Randi and Carla line up here on the left hash marks. Whitney and Larissa are here on the right. Jessie, you're back here at centre. Kathy, you win that face off and hammer the puck into the right corner. Randi and Carla drive to the net. Larissa and Whitney go after the puck. Kathy goes to support. Jessie, you move to the high slot. From that point on you're making it up as you go along."

Good thing Bud taught us to pay attention.

Sue clutches her whiteboard against her chest. "Bud would be so proud of you girls. *I'm* proud. Go get it done."

Amy steps inside the box. We are six on five. As I skate to the left face off dot, my head is reeling. Sue thinks we're going to *tie* this up?

Then the hockey gods look into our hearts and find us worthy.

Carla fires from the point, and Randi chips our first goal in.

On the second, Larissa pulls the puck out of the corner and passes to me. I walk in uncontested and score, high glove.

Two goals in fourteen seconds.

While we scream and cry and hug each other, the Hounds are knocked back on their heels. Their bench looks like it's the one minus a coach. The Hound coach waits until both teams are lined up at centre ice.

Whistle. Notre Dame time out.

"Bring it," Sue says to us, and there are tears in her eyes. Real tears. "Bring it all. Anything can happen in OT. Anything."

But it's not easy to beat back a team that's confident.

When we line up again, the Hounds drive to our net. A perfectly executed play.

Tic.

Tac.

Toe.

Amy is sprawled on the ice, the puck behind her, while the Hounds celebrate. They haven't had many close games this year, so the victory is made sweeter.

But they don't celebrate like *we* would have.

Kathy, Miranda and I bawl like babies during the post-game routine – the final tribute to the fans, the final lap of the ice, the final group photo. Carla and Amy are stoic, but I know in their hearts they're just as miserable as we are.

"It's over," I say to Kathy. "It's all over. No more Xtreme. No more Rage. No more Oilers."

"It wish we could go back and start all over again," Kathy says.

"It just won't be the same without you next year," Randi sobs in my ear.

**Y**ou girls sure like to ride the roller coaster," Gia's dad tells us in the dressing room. "You're hard on a guy's heart."

Dead silence.

I feel for him. It just slipped out of his mouth.

"I'm sorry," he says. "That was thoughtless."

Kathy, Miranda, Carla and I take the longest to get undressed. We just sit there and exchange Bud-isms.

"Remember when he gave us the phone lecture?" Carla says.

Kathy stands up and thrusts out her belly. Her gruff tone mimics Bud's exactly. "Next time I hear a cellphone in this dressing room, it better be God or Don Cherry calling."

We laugh and cry and then laugh again.

"I'm really gonna miss this," Miranda sighs.

"Me too." Carla bends over and zips up her equipment bag. "See you suckers," she says.

We mumble goodbyes.

Kathy and I are the last ones out of the dressing room. Sue's talking to Whitney in the hallway. I can tell it's one of those private conversations, but I have things I want to say to Sue. I'm afraid if I don't say them now, there'll never be another chance.

I stop and crane my head in Sue's direction. Kathy mouths a goodbye and moves on down the hallway.

Whitney wipes her eyes and steps away from Sue. "I

better be going," she says. She gives me a tight smile and moves towards the exit.

Sue turns to me. "Great game, Jessie. No shame."

"Thanks," I reply, "and thanks for all you've done for us."

The words seem so inadequate. I've always been at a loss with her.

"No, thanks for all that *you've* done," Sue replies. "You've been a great role model to the younger girls."

I shrug and drop my gaze. "I didn't do anything."

"You did *lots*," Sue corrects me. "You listened when they needed someone to listen, and you led by example. A coach couldn't ask for more than that from a captain."

It's the biggest compliment Sue has ever paid me.

"I just feel so bad about Bud." The tears start to pool. "Whenever I think about him, there's this ache...right here." I place my hand on my chest.

She puts a hand on my shoulder and squeezes. "Don't spend too much time looking back, Jessie. You've got a great life ahead of you. Enjoy the ride. It's over way too soon."

"Well, hockey's over," I tell her.

"Not for you," she says. "Not if you want to keep playing."

"Really?" I ask.

"Really."

My next words are out of my mouth before I can stop

them. "I've never told you before, but I've learned a lot from you. You're a great coach, and I'm going to miss you next year."

"I'll miss you too," she says. "See you at the windup."

**O**ut in the lobby, my mom and dad and Courtney are waiting.

"I'm so proud of all you girls," Mom says. "You overcame a lot today."

"Thanks."

"Want to get something to eat?" Dad asks. "You pick the place."

"I'm not that hungry. I'm mostly tired. It's been a rough week."

"See you back home then." He picks up my hockey bag. "We'll order in."

"Tower Pizza!" Courtney says.

"Sure." I hand her my sticks. "Thanks for coming, Sis."

She treats me to a quick hug and a smile.

By the time they're gone, the lobby is nearly deserted. I talk to Kathy's parents for a minute, and then walk out the arena doors into the Leisure Centre.

Liam's there, leaning against the wall and checking his phone.

It's all I can do to contain myself to a walk.

"Waiting for somebody?" I ask.

He doesn't look up from his phone. "You," he says.

The word undoes me.

"Too bad about your coach," he says. "He was a great guy, huh?"

"Yes." I wipe away the tears. Will I ever be able to think about Bud without leaking?

"And I'm sorry about your playoff run. Must be tough."

I nod. "Where's Russell?"

"I took him back to the group home right after. I knew you'd be a while," Liam says. "I went through the same thing after my last football game."

"I'm sorry I missed that," I tell him. "I never watched you play, and I'm sorry about that too."

He shrugs. "Wasn't meant to be, I guess." He tucks his phone in his pocket. "I owe you an apology."

"For what?"

He stares at the floor. "For being such a jerk. I know it's no excuse, but it really hurts a guy when he likes a girl but she won't give him the time of day and then she *does* so he kisses her and he can *tell* there's a connection, and then she just *throws* another guy in his face."

"Maybe after I explain about Evan and Mark, you'll understand why I was so afraid."

"I don't need to hear it," he says. "That's your business."

"I'm too late, right? You already asked Miss Agribition to

be your grad escort, so you can't be mine. My timing is *brutal.*"

He looks at me for the first time. "Ask me."

"Say what?"

"I want to hear it from your own lips," he says.

I suck in my breath and let it out slowly. "Liam, will you be my grad escort?"

He pretends to think about it.

"Don't make me beg," I say.

"Here's the problem." He pulls off his toque and scratches his head. "We're both graduating. If I'm your grad escort, then you're *my* escort."

I sigh. "I guess I'll have to take Kathy up on the blind date with that referee."

He laughs, showing me that gorgeous gap-tooth. "In that case, I better say yes."

"Thanks."

Feels great, doesn't it, my little voice says.

Yeah, it does.

"Let's go some place and talk. We have a lot to catch up on." He pulls his toque over his ears.

"My family's expecting me at home. Will you come meet them?"

He slides an arm around my shoulders, drawing me close. "Sounds like a plan, Hockey Girl."

# chapter fifty-one

The night after my eighteenth birthday, Courtney and I are in the garage trying out my new composite stick. It's got a wicked flex.

We've hung some pie plates from the corners of the net to make targets.

The garage door is wide open, but we're sweating bullets. Courtney takes a few more slapshots, then stops, puffing, and adjusts her pony. At five foot nine, she's officially as tall as I am. She hefts her stick, bends her knees, rotates from the hip, and stares down the pie plate hanging from the right corner.

"Weight transfer," I tell her. "Follow through."

She nods, winds up, and releases.

Misses the plate entirely, and puts another dint in the gyproc.

"Not bad," I say. "You just need to work on your aim."

She shakes her head and straightens. "I can't shoot worth shit."

"You didn't even have a slapshot three months ago," I tell her. "Look how far you've come."

She smiles, obviously pleased. "Thanks." She tucks some stray hairs behind her ear. "I'll tell you a secret if you promise not to laugh."

"Deal."

"I want to play AAA one day. I know I started late, but I'll do whatever I have to. Do you think I have a chance?" The smile is gone from her face, and I know my answer will make a world of difference.

The Dream again.

"Anything's possible if you work your ass off, and nothing's possible if you don't," I tell her. "Go for it, Court."

She looks wistful. "I wish you could be here next year, to help with practice."

"I wish I could too. I had fun with the bantams, and so did Kathy."

"Are you scared about going to university?" she asks. "I would be."

"Yeah, I'm scared," I admit. "But it's the next big adventure. Sooner or later, you have to make the break."

My phone beeps. Courtney picks it up off the step, gives it a once over, and hands it to me. "It's Liam."

"Thanks." I send him a quick text.

"Are you going out with him tonight?"

"Yep."

"I like Liam," she says.

"That makes two of us."

"I hope I get to see some of your games next year," she says. "It won't be easy with my schedule."

"Speaking of that, I have something for you." I select Rambo from the other sticks and hold it out to her. "The team has a stick allowance. I won't be needing this."

"But that's your PK stick," she says.

"It's yours now."

"But I never kill penalties," she says.

"You will."

After she goes inside the house, I pull out my old Easton stick, the one I used when I played with the Xtreme. The girls all signed it at the end of the year. Looking at those names makes me feel both happy and sad.

"I hope you make as many friends as I did along the way," I say out loud, putting it back. "Go hard, Little Sis."

## about the author

**M**aureen Ulrich is a YA author and playwright who was a middle-years and high school teacher for twenty-five years. Her Jessie Mac hockey trilogy includes *Power Plays, Face Off* and *Breakaway. Power Plays* was a gold medallist, and *Face Off* a silver medallist, in the Moonbeam Awards. *Power Plays* was a finalist in three categories of the Saskatchewan Book Awards as well as two Young Readers' Choice award programs. Maureen has also written more than thirty plays for young people and adults, and has two plays published – *Sam Spud: Private Eye* and *The Banes of Darkwood.* You can connect with Maureen through her website, www.maureen-ulrich.ca, and the I Heart Jessie Mac group on Facebook.

FSC

www.fsc.org

**MIX**

Paper from
responsible sources

FSC® C016245

## ENVIRONMENTAL BENEFITS STATEMENT

**Coteau Books** saved the following resources by
printing the pages of this book on chlorine free paper
made with 100% post-consumer waste.

| TREES | WATER | ENERGY | SOLID WASTE | GREENHOUSE GASES |
|---|---|---|---|---|
| 23 | 10,449 | 9 | 662 | 2,317 |
| FULLY GROWN | GALLONS | MILLION BTUs | POUNDS | POUNDS |

Environmental impact estimates were made using the Environmental Paper Network
Paper Calculator. For more information visit www.papercalculator.org.